EMP RANCH

ROBERT WALKER

❀ Created with Vellum

1

*D*avid scrolled idly through his social media feed, the swiping action of his thumb on his phone screen almost as automatic a reflex as breathing to him. He'd only been alive for sixteen years, and there had never been a time he could remember in his life when he hadn't had a phone or tablet on him. He knew people who were his parents' age hadn't had them growing up, though, and this thought made him look up from the screen and stare around for a few moments. His mother, standing next to him, was talking to the bank teller, but most other people in the bank were standing idly in lines, staring, like he had been, at little screens in their hands to pass the time.

He looked past the throng of bored people out at the street, and that was when he saw it. David watched the motorcycle accident happen as if it were unfolding in slow motion. He had seen plenty of videos of auto wrecks on social media and had crashed his dirt bike on the ranch and in the woods more times than he cared to admit but seeing a motorcycle mishap of this magnitude play out before him on the street was an entirely different experience. With a mounting sense of horror and disbelief, his eyes followed the rider attached to the hurtling machine as if by two steel cables, as the man blasted into the intersection outside the bank…and was then T-boned by a careening F-150 truck.

"Oh shit!" David gasped, his eyes bulging in their sockets and his jaw dropping open as the motorcyclist was flung across the intersection like a ragdoll while his cartwheeling bike disintegrated in a mess of spitting metal and shattered plastic. The truck, skidding on screaming tires, spun out and slammed with a sickening crunch into a traffic light pole. David had been so captivated by the spectacle that he hadn't noticed one especially strange detail about the collision: neither the motorcycle nor the truck had made any sound other than the screeching of tires.

Alice heard the accident but only turned around in time to see the aftermath. Her eyes—sea green, like her son's—grew wide the moment she spun around. "Oh my God," Alice murmured, moving hastily toward the exit. "Davey, call 9-1-1, quick!"

"Ma'am," the teller said uncertainly, her eyes locked on her computer screen and seemingly oblivious to the tragedy unfolding just beyond the glass walls of the bank, "uh, there's been a little problem with the wire transfer. It seems um, the power's just gone out, and I don't know why the backup power isn't..."

The teller's voice faded into the general background buzz in Alice's mind; her instincts and training as a former trauma nurse were already kicking in, and she forgot about her business at the bank counter.

"Come on, Davey," she said, taking her teenage son's hand and moving with determined speed toward the door. "I asked you to call 9-1-1, have you got 'em on the line yet? That biker looks to be in a bad way," she continued, talking more to herself than David, in the manner she often did. "He's almost certainly got multiple fractures after that. The guy in the truck'll be injured, too, but not as bad as the motorcyclist. I'll do what I can to stabilize him before the paramedics—"

"It's dead, Mom, totally dead." He was surprised to see that the phone had died; a mere few seconds ago, when he'd been browsing his social media feeds, the battery had been almost full.

"Take mine," she said, fishing her cell out of her bag as she navigated her way through the crowd of people who were all milling about in disarray, all staring at their phones and tablets, their faces scrunched up with frowns of confusion and consternation.

The moment she handed David her phone, another two vehicles collided with a loud, sickening crunch in the middle of the intersection. It seemed that the drivers had no control over their cars.

"Shit!" This time it was Alice who yelled out the expletive. She glanced up at the traffic lights, wondering how two serious accidents could have occurred within seconds of each other at the same intersection. Just as she noticed that both sets of traffic lights were out, David pressed her phone back into her hands.

"Yours is dead, too, Mom."

"That's not possible. I charged it this morning, and the battery was at ninety percent when we stepped into the bank."

Another two cars rolled through the intersection, one narrowly missing the other. Inside the bank, a tide of almost palpable panic was rising, while outside, cars were rolling to a stop all over the place, bumping into each other or straddling the curb without any semblance of order or, apparently, any adherence to traffic regulations. Alice stopped in her tracks just as she and David stepped out of the bank. She slowly looked down at her dead phone and then surveyed the sudden, disorderly traffic jam, immediately noticing something unsettling; every single one of the cars caught up in the chaotic jam was silent. It was as if they'd all parked up in the middle of the street and switched their motors off. Drivers were getting out and scratching their heads. Some were popping their vehicles' hoods while others were pulling out their phones, which were all dead.

David was running his fingers of his left hand through his close-cropped, blond hair, as he always did when he was concentrating deeply on something, while determinedly pressing the power button of his phone, as if holding it tighter might somehow resurrect the dead device.

Alice touched her fingertips to her lips and chin, hearing her pulse hammering in booming thumps and bassy surges through her ears and temples. A realization had just hit her with all the force of a sledgehammer blow to the skull. "David," she said firmly, "drop the phone and come with me, quickly!" She only called him David when things were really serious.

He looked up, his long, angular face twisted into a perturbing mixture of worry and confusion. "What's happening, Mom?"

"We have to get out of the city. *Now*. Come on, move!"

Alice tossed her own phone onto the ground; it was nothing but dead weight now, and no amount of technical wizardry could breathe life into the device ever again. Alice was utterly certain of this fact. Her husband had told her that this day would come, and while she'd come around, over time, from thinking that it was a delusion to accepting that it was indeed a likely possibility, she'd never actually quite prepared herself for the reality of it happening. Was this how people felt when finally confronted with the inescapability of their own mortality? Was the look on her face right now that same look of complete disbelief and horror that she'd seen so many times on the faces of accident and heart attack victims in the emergency rooms she'd worked in?

There was no time to mull over these things,

though; she had to act, and she had to act fast. She couldn't, in good conscience, leave an injured man untreated, but at the same time, she knew that every second she wasted from this point on was an extra pound of danger and peril that she was heaping on to her chances of getting herself and her son out of the city alive, much less unscathed.

Behind them in the bank, people were already yelling and pushing, while those on the sidewalk were milling around, confused and growing increasingly afraid and agitated. The collective panic Alice had begun to sense inside the bank would soon spread like a contagious virus to those gathered outside; this was inevitable. She ran diagonally across the intersection, sure now that no more vehicles would be entering it, making a beeline for the biker, who was lying on his back on the ground, groaning and trembling. A few other people had gathered around him, but none of them knew what to do.

"Let me through, please. I'm a trauma nurse," Alice said, pulling out a pair of surgical gloves from her handbag. In her late thirties, she was a shade under five foot four and petite in build, but the tone of her voice and the calm confidence in her words added an authoritative stature to her slim figure.

The people stepped aside to let her through, and she knelt down next to the biker. He was wearing a full-face helmet, and two eyes, stark and white with pain and panic against his dark skin, stared up at Alice through the visor. His left leg was bent at an unnatural angle; it was clear that he'd suffered a major fracture there. His chest was rising and falling in a rapid, uneven rhythm.

"The light...was green," he panted raggedly, his weak voice muffled by the helmet. "But then...bike died, traffic lights died...couldn't...stop." He coughed, and a spray of red splattered against the inside of his visor. His condition was worse than Alice had hoped; she now knew that there were some severe internal injuries too.

"All right, sir, just try to stay calm," she said gently, pressing her finger against the man's neck to check his pulse. It was weak and uneven, another bad sign.

"Why aren't any of our phones working?" one of the bystanders asked. "How the hell can everyone's phones be dead?"

"Help me, please, help me, help me," the biker gasped, his weak voice raspy. He coughed again and sprayed another spattering of blood across the inside of his visor.

Alice was quickly beginning to realize that there was nothing she could do for him, especially given the fact that no ambulance would be coming, but she refused to abandon him to die alone. She took his hand in hers and gave it a reassuring squeeze, and then glanced over at David, who had squatted down across from her. He had his father's lean, lanky build, and the angle at which the late morning sun was hitting his strong-jawed face made him look even more like Phil, to the point at which the resemblance was uncanny. All that the boy had inherited from Alice was his green eyes and sandy-blond hair; the rest was all Phil. Although his face had the structure of a man's, at this moment, with the shivering accident victim convulsing and coughing between the two of them, the look on David's face was that of a terrified child. Unlike Alice, he'd never seen a man die before. David stared at his mother with a look of pleading and helplessness, wordlessly asking if the man was going to make it. She locked eyes with her son, subtly shook her head, and squeezed the biker's hand a little tighter.

"I can see…Momma," the biker wheezed. He breathed out a soft, gurgling sigh, and then his hand went limp in Alice's.

"He's gone," she whispered, setting his hand down on the sidewalk.

"Mom…" David said, his face a contorted mess of fear, disbelief, and horror.

"Come on," she said, briskly standing up and taking his hand.

"Hey, what are you doing?" one bystander demanded. "You said you were a nurse. You're just gonna leave this guy?"

"Let's go, David," Alice said, pushing past the angry man and ignoring his questions.

"I said, what are you doing, lady?" the man yelled after them as they hurried away. "You heartless fuckin' bitch, you can't just leave the man like that!"

"Mom, are you, are we, uh, can we…" David stammered, a mess of confusion and fear.

Alice led him on, her grip on his hand firm, not once looking back. "The man's dead, David, and there's nothing I, or anyone else, can do for him." Her tone was stern but not unkind.

More people were spilling out of buildings onto the streets, which were choked with stationary vehicles. People were already shouting, arguing, and pushing, and chaos was beginning to unfold. Everything felt completely surreal to Alice, as if she'd somehow fallen asleep at the bank counter and had dropped into some sort of lucid nightmare. This was no hallucination, though, no trick her mind was playing; she knew this with as much certainty as she knew that she was still breathing, and her heart still beating: this was an EMP attack. She also understood, with a chilling sense of clarity, that if she and David didn't make it out of this city by nightfall, they might not make it out of the city alive at all.

2

"Give it a try now, Fred. Remember, give her a smidgen of gas as you start her," Phil called out from the front of the tractor.

Fred, a heavyset, thirty-year-old man in mud-spattered dungarees, gave the tractor a little throttle before hitting the starter. The machine instantly roared to life, and Fred flashed his boss a gap-toothed grin as he gave the powerful diesel motor a few triumphant revs.

"Never thought you'd get the old gal started!" Fred yelled over the rumble of the engine. "Fifty years old, but now she's purring as sweet as ever! You've got that magic touch, Mr. McCabe, you sure do." He chuckled and shook his head, grinning all the while, and observed Phil as he leaned in to give the clattering motor a finetuning.

Phil was tall and lean, and as angular in his features as if his face had been hewn from stone. He had the tanned limbs and wiry muscles of a man who spent the majority of his day engaged in manual labor, but in his eyes, there was a keen and almost intimidating intelligence. His fingers worked with a quick, effortless dexterity, and he worked with a singular focus. He was almost fifty, and his short, neatly-trimmed hair, parted to the side, was more white than its former sandy blond, but he still stood with a ramrod-straight back and carried himself with the agile poise of a far younger man.

After making a few adjustments, Phil was satisfied and gave Fred a nod, indicating that he should shut off the tractor.

"I'm going to head over to the stables to see if Wyatt's finished loading the horses," Phil said. "You can take the rest of the day off, Fred. I figure you could use a little more family time, especially with the new arrival, right? If you don't mind, though, before you go, could you give the tractor a good cleaning and get her back into the barn?"

"Thanks, boss, yeah, I'll do that."

"Thank you, Fred. Say hi to Phoebe for me, and please tell her that if she needs anything for the little one, anything at all, to just let me know."

Phil left Fred to take care of the tractor and then began making his way across the ranch to the stables. He'd been waiting for Alice to call him to let him know that the buyer's money had arrived in her account before sending Wyatt out with the truck and the horse trailer to deliver the mares to their new owner.

The ranch was nestled in the foothills of the Rockies

and sprawled out over a vast area encompassing meadows, a hill or two, and some woods. A stream from the nearby mountains ran through the property, providing both the human and animal residents of the ranch with a reliable source of clean, potable water all year round. A diesel-powered purification plant made the water as clean as any spring water one could buy from a store. The stream also served as an ample source of irrigation for the many crops Phil grew on his land, from grains to vegetables and seasonal fruits in a greenhouse and crop tunnels, all cultivated on permaculture principles. It had taken over a decade of intense toil to restore the neglected sections of the ranch, of which there had been many in the wake of his late father's protracted and ultimately unsuccessful battle with cancer, but he'd done it. He'd attained his goal of complete self-sufficiency, and he was immensely proud of this achievement.

Phil paused as he rounded the back of the barn, which overlooked one of the rotational meadows on which his herd of cattle was grazing. Beyond them, some of his horses were grazing contentedly in the next field over. He hadn't stopped to admire the steers or horses, though; he veered off the path and into an addition he'd tacked onto the 19th-century bard: a small aircraft hangar.

In the hangar were a few large items, most of them hidden under tarps. Dominating the space, though, was a single prop Cessna 182, old but lovingly polished. The airplane was the last phantom of a reminder of

Phil's former career as a highly esteemed aerospace engineer. If he had stayed at the firm for just two or three more years, he could have gone on to a senior position at NASA, but as talented as he was when it came to engineering, the ranch he'd grown up on was in his blood. When his father had passed away eleven years ago, Phil—an only child and thus sole heir to the ranch—had taken it as a sign that it was time to leave the world of rockets, satellites, and space shuttles behind, and instead pursue his lifelong dream of converting the family ranch to a completely self-sustaining unit.

His success in achieving this didn't mean he didn't sometimes miss his former life, though, and he'd bought and restored the Cessna a few years ago, and had gotten his pilot's license so that once in a while he could take to the skies and be a little closer to the technology orbiting the earth that he'd once designed. Also, like all of the vehicles on his ranch, the Cessna was a simple enough vehicle that it would not be crippled by an EMP event.

While admiring the plane, Phil pulled his phone out of his jeans pocket to see if he had somehow missed a call from Alice. He was somewhat perplexed to find that the battery seemed to have died. "I could have sworn it was over sixty percent when I last looked at it," he murmured to himself.

He shoved the phone back into his pocket and left the hangar, jogging around the perimeter of the field of crop tunnels to get to the stables so he could find out if Alice had tried to call Wyatt.

When he got to the stables, the horses were already loaded up in the trailer, which was hitched up to the spare truck, and Wyatt, as laconic as ever, was leaning against the side of the stable, his heavy black eyebrows knit with consternation. Inside the trailer were two mares Alice was selling—one black, the other dun. They were beautiful animals, and while they were Alice's, Phil had always had a love for horses and was sad to be seeing these two go, even though they were elderly and long past their prime. The horses, however, were not what he was worried about at this moment. He looked past them at Wyatt.

Greeting Phil with a gesture, Wyatt tipped his white cowboy hat, which never left his head, save for dining indoors and sleeping. A sudden gust of warm wind rippled Wyatt's plaid shirt and whipped his long black ponytail out to the side.

"Hey Wyatt, have you heard from Alice?" Phil asked, noting the expression of concern on his foreman's strong-jawed face.

"Nope. You?" Wyatt, who was a few years older than Phil, was a man of few words, and when he did speak, he always cut straight to the point. He was neither rude nor brusque, though; this was just his natural manner of communicating, and it had been ever since Phil could remember. He and Wyatt had grown up on the ranch together, with Wyatt's father serving as foreman under Phil's father. This land ran thick through the blood of each man's veins, but while Phil's ancestors had owned this land for four generations, Wyatt's fore-bears had hunted and fished in this region for thou-sands of years.

"My phone died, so I don't know if she's been trying to call me or what," Phil said. "I thought she might have tried to call you. The money's surely come through by now."

The furrows on Wyatt's brow deepened. "My phone's dead too."

Alarm bells were ringing with worrying clarity in Phil's mind now. "Throw me the truck keys and go turn on the lights inside the stable," he said.

Without a word, Wyatt tossed the keys to Phil and stalked off to the front of the stable, walking with the slight limp he'd had ever since the tank he'd been driving in Operation Desert Storm had been hit by an Iraqi rocket. Phil's heart was racing as he climbed into the cab of the truck, a two-year-old Ford, one of the few new vehicles on the ranch. He slid the key into the ignition, turned it…and nothing happened at all. No dash lights, no warning lights, nothing at all. He left the keys in the switch and hopped out of the truck, feeling as if he'd just been sucker-punched by a heavyweight boxer.

Wyatt rounded the corner, and when his eyes met Phil's, he shook his head grimly. The lights were out in the stables too.

"Alice and Davey," Phil gasped, his voice hoarse. A sliver of sudden, almost crushing fear and anxiety stabbed through his guts, but he quashed the rising panic before it could overwhelm him. He drew in a deep breath and held it in his lungs for a while to compose himself, and then, feeling more confident and in control, he released the calming breath. "Wyatt, take Davey's bike and round up everyone on the ranch. Tell 'em to stop whatever they're doing and meet me in front of the main house in fifteen minutes. I have to tell everyone what's going on, and after that, I need to head into the city to rescue my wife and son."

Wyatt nodded and walked briskly around to the rear of the stables, where David's dirt bike, a simple 70s-model Yamaha, which would be unaffected by the EMP, was parked. As Phil raced up to the main house, the metallic buzz of the two-stroke motor being kicked to life rang out behind him, and he breathed out a sigh of relief; he'd been ninety-nine percent certain that the old Yamaha would be EMP-proof, but it was good to hear the proof of it.

When he got to the main house—a large, triple-story, Civil War-era farmhouse—he sped through it, dashing from room to room and checking every electronic item. When he found that each and every one of them was dead, his dark suspicions were irrefutably confirmed: there had been an EMP attack.

Around fifteen minutes later, the entire workforce of the ranch, summoned by Wyatt, who had just arrived and dismounted from the dirt bike, was gathered outside the main entrance to the house. Anxiety and worry hung in the air like a thick, choking fog, and when Phil looked out over the sea of fear-twisted faces, he knew that strong leadership skills were needed now more than ever. These people were not mere workers to him; each and every one of them had worked on this ranch for years, decades even, and Phil considered them extended family. He didn't want to cause a panic, but he wasn't about to beat around the bush about what had just happened either. He stepped out onto the porch wearing an expression of quiet determination on his face.

"My friends," he said, "I hate to be the bearer of bad news, but I have to be brutally honest with all of you."

"What's happened, Phil?" Fred called out. "Is this something to do with why all our phones are dead?"

"It has everything to do with that," Phil answered grimly. "And it's not just our phones that are dead. Literally, anything with electronics in it made in the last few decades is dead and will never work again. I'm sorry to say, my friends, that this city, this county, and maybe this state, hell, maybe even the whole country, has been the victim of an EMP attack."

3

*G*asps of shock and worry rippled through the crowd of workers, and the group started to buzz with anxious conversation. The only one who was silent was Wyatt, who stood leaning against the house with his arms folded across his broad chest and a look of stoic resilience on his face.

"EMP attack? What's that?" Fred asked.

"Electromagnetic pulse," Phil answered. "I don't know whether the weapon was detonated near us or hundreds of miles away, and there's no way of knowing whether it was done by domestic terrorists or a foreign enemy, but what I can say with complete certainty is that the entire electric grid of at least a third of the country has been fried, probably permanently."

A hush fell over the crowd as the implications of this hit home.

"You mean, all the power is out...for good?" a woman asked.

"You heard what he said," said Doc Robertson, an elderly, wispy-haired beanpole of a man, the resident veterinarian at the ranch. "The grid's gone, and it won't be coming back, not any time soon. All our gadgets and gizmos, our cars, appliances, everything, they're nothing more than dead weight now."

"What are we gonna do?" the woman shrieked, her voice cracking with rising panic.

"I know this is scary," Phil said, taking care to speak in a calm, even rhythm, "but there's no need to panic. I've made a few preparations over the years in the event of something like this happening, and you all know that this ranch can mostly run the way it did before the age of electricity. I'm sure that the whole county is down, maybe even the whole state, like I said, but we don't know if it's affected the entire nation. We need to exercise caution and act rationally, not give in to panic and assume the absolute worst has happened."

"What should we do, Phil?" Fred asked, trying to sound braver and more confident than he felt. "Tell us what to do, and we'll do it."

"Right now, you don't need to do anything but go home to your families and make sure they're safe. Those of you who live farther away are welcome to borrow our spare bicycles. Everyone else, you're gonna have to walk, I'm afraid. I don't think things are going to get too crazy just yet, but it's best to be prepared. Keep your homes locked up, and keep whatever guns you own on you at all times. Eat all your perishable food first, keep the dried and canned stuff for later. And fill up your bathtubs with water for drinking and cooking; the faucets are going to run dry soon. You're welcome to come back to the ranch with your families if you want, any time, but you *must* keep the main gates locked. You all know the combination on the padlock; don't give those numbers out to anyone, not even your family, and make sure you lock the gates up as soon as you close 'em."

"I'm pretty sure I can drive," Doc Robertson said. "If that dirt bike is still going, my old Impala'll be running. They didn't have no fancy electronics back in '67!"

"You're right, Doc," Phil said. "Many vehicles made before the early 70s should still be fine, but remember that driving in a time when almost every other vehicle is permanently dead is going to attract attention...and not the kind of attention you want to attract. You should be okay today, but after that, I'd suggest you bring your car back to the ranch or hide it somewhere where unsavory characters aren't likely to find it."

Doc Robertson nodded. "Damn straight, Phil, I don't want no target painted on my back, thank you very much. But I'm happy to give anyone who lives really far away a ride home right now before things get too crazy. After that, I'll bring my Impala back here; I can't think of a safer place for it."

"Thank you, Doc," Phil said. "Rick, Amy, Jonathan, Eddie, and Cath, you guys live farthest from the ranch. If you don't mind squeezing in, Doc can give you guys a ride home now. There are three spare bikes. Anthony, Debbie, and Zack, you guys can take those to get home.

Everyone else, it'll be a long walk, but you should be safe. Don't stop to talk to anyone; just go straight home."

"How do we get hold of you if we need you, Phil?" Fred asked. "Will regular old landlines work, since all the cellphones and computers are dead?"

"It's hard to say," Phil said, frowning. "The landline grid has always had protection against lightning strikes, so locally it might still function. You can bet, though, that outside of this state, or this county even, it'll be down. And the older your phone is, the more likely it is that it may have survived. If it's a newer handset, it'll probably have been fried, though. And if it's a powered one, you can be sure it's dead. But yeah, you might be able to ring the ranch on the landline. Other than that, though, there's no way to get hold of me unless you physically come here."

"Flare guns," Wyatt grunted, tilting his head in Phil's direction.

"Yeah, that's right, thanks for reminding me," Phil said. "I've got a bunch of flare guns in the barn, which shoot distinctive orange flares, a color I made myself by adding a few things to the flare formula. There are only enough for you all to take one flare gun per family and two flares. Only use them in the direst of emergencies, people. I'm talking about life or death situations. If you're in serious danger, use one, and we'll do our best to get to you. In the same token, if you see an orange flare in the sky, you'll all know that it's one of us signaling for help, and I hope that you'll come to the aid of that person if you can."

"Thanks, Phil," Fred said, and everyone else murmured their thanks as well.

"Go with Wyatt to the barn," Phil instructed. "He'll hand out the flare guns. After that, Doc Robertson will take some of you home, and you three can take the bikes. For those who'll be biking and walking, fill up your canteens with water and feel free to pick some fruit from the trees on your way out."

"I'll give them the flares," Wyatt, stony-faced, said to Phil, "then I'll meet you back here. I expect you're going to need some help."

"Thanks, brother," Phil said, a shadow of a warm smile on his face, his gratitude genuine. "I knew you'd stick around."

"Don't got no place else to go...and you, Alice, and Davey, are the only family I got."

"I'll see you back here in a few minutes then," Phil said. He wasn't surprised that Wyatt had chosen to stay with him; the foreman had his own house a mere mile from the ranch gates, but he was childless and lived on his own, having been divorced for over seven years, and he did little more at his house than sleep there and occasionally drown his sorrows and war memories in whiskey on the porch on his days off.

Wyatt returned after around twenty minutes, his craggy face as unreadable as ever. "They've all got flares," he said. "What's next?"

"I'm going to need your help with a few things," Phil said. "Let's go to the aircraft hangar first."

Most people would have asked what the point of heading over to the hangar was, but Wyatt Fox trusted Phillip McCabe enough to simply go along with whatever he suggested; in some ways, Phil served as a surrogate officer figure for the ex-soldier, even though Phil himself had never been in the military. Wyatt preferred to follow rather than lead, but he was no sheep. When given an order, he would fight his way to hell and back to carry it out. Phil couldn't have asked for a better comrade to have by his side in a situation like this.

When the men arrived at the hangar, Phil walked past the Cessna and made a beeline for one of the large tarp-covered objects at the rear of the space. Wyatt looked on, folding his arms across his chest, as Phil undid a few cords and then whipped the tarp off the object.

"Still runs, huh?" Wyatt grunted, staring at the spotless 50s-era Chevy truck that had been under the tarp. The truck had belonged to Phil's father, who had owned it from new.

"As sweet as the day she rolled off the factory floor," Phil said, running his fingertips lovingly across a strip of gleaming chrome. "I didn't just keep her in this condition for nostalgia's sake, though, Wyatt. I knew this day would come…I mean, I didn't expect that it would come so soon, but thank God I *did* know it was coming."

Wyatt nodded, quietly impressed. "Be a shame if

someone threw a rock at it, though," he remarked dryly. "Or took a pot shot at it, if they were real desperate."

"I won't take it out once things start to get really bad," Phil said darkly, "which may happen sooner than I'd like. But for the next few days, I think it'll be okay to use this, and Davey's bike too."

"And after that?"

A sudden grin, boyish and almost mischievous, flashed across Phil's face. "It took me a year of working in here for a couple of hours every night, three or four nights a week, to build this," he said, walking over to a much larger object beneath another tarp, "but don't worry, brother, I made sure I was prepared for the worst."

With that, he whipped the tarp off the second item, and this time, even the usually dour Wyatt couldn't suppress a toothy grin. Beneath the tarp was a massive Humvee, kitted out with ramming bars, extra lights, steel mesh across the windows, and all sorts of other hardcore modifications.

"Takes me back to my Gulf War days," Wyatt remarked, walking over to the Humvee, which was painted in a green and brown camouflage scheme, and walking slowly around it, admiring Phil's handiwork.

"EMP-proof, bulletproof, bombproof, jacked-up suspension, floodlights, even a coaxial machine gun and turret mounted on the roof," Phil said, patting the bonnet appreciatively.

"Add caterpillar tracks, a few tons of steel armor,

and a cannon out front, and it ain't too different to the tanks I was driving in Iraq," Wyatt said.

"It's as close to a tank as I could get it without making extreme sacrifices in terms of maneuverability and fuel efficiency. But as much as I'd love to take out the Humvee, it's only for emergencies. It's a fuel hog, and we have to conserve as much of that as we can now."

Wyatt nodded, but then cut straight to the point. "I know you need my help to get Alice and the kid out of the city. What's the plan?"

"We'll take my dad's truck as close to the city limits as we can get without actually driving in. We're going to have to go on foot. The whole place will be a total gridlock of dead cars blocking every street."

"How are we going to find them without phones?" Wyatt asked. "It's a big city, and locating two people in that sea of chaos will be some real needle-in-a-haystack shit."

"Alice owns a small apartment in the city, a place she's kept for just this sort of incident," Phil answered. "We said that if either of us got stuck in the city during something like this, we'd hole up in that apartment until the other person was able to get them out. She and Davey will head straight there. We just have to get to them and then get them back out."

"A simple enough mission," Wyatt muttered, "but probably nowhere near easy. Not to mention danger-ous. There are some bad folk in that city, and as soon as they figure out that law enforcement is totally crippled, things are gonna go south real fast."

"I knew that would be the case," Phil said, the expression on his face hardening into one of grim determination, "so Alice and I made sure we'd be ready for whatever—or whoever—crosses our path. Come this way."

He led Wyatt over to the opposite end of the hangar and yanked an unassuming brown rug out of the corner, revealing a locked trapdoor in the floor. He squatted down, punched the combination into the padlock, and then opened the trapdoor, revealing a steel staircase leading down into a gulf of inky darkness. He tossed Wyatt one of the gas lamps that were sitting on a nearby table and lit one up for himself, igniting the hissing jet of gas with his trusty Zippo.

Without a word, he descended the stairs, and Wyatt followed closely behind him. The light cast by the gas lamps revealed a large cellar, and when Wyatt saw what was on the walls, he let out a low whistle, both impressed and surprised. Mounted on racks on the walls were dozens of rifles, shotguns, handguns and other weapons.

"Take as many as you can safely conceal," Phil said. "I'd take a combat shotgun, but we have to be stealthy and low-key about this."

Wyatt took a modded AR-15 off one of the racks and examined it with the detailed eye of a weaponry expert. "I'd take one of these, but low-key she isn't," he said, putting the rifle back. "As many as I can carry, huh?"

"Safely and stealthily, yes," Phil answered. He'd taken off his plaid shirt and was strapping a shoulder holster onto his left side.

With a nod, Wyatt picked up a .45 pistol, a 9mm pistol, a diminutive .32 ACP pocket pistol, and a .357 revolver.

"Ammo's in those drawers to your left," Phil said.

Wyatt loaded all of the firearms, while Phil did the same with the two .45 pistols he'd taken.

"Locked and loaded," Wyatt said, after tucking the final firearm and the .32 into one of his cowboy boots, which had a fair amount of room around the outer calf area.

"Thank you for doing this," Phil said, taking a moment to look Wyatt in the eye and convey his gratitude. "There's nobody I'd rather have by my side in a situation like this."

"You're as much a brother to me as Al," Wyatt said, referring to his older brother, who now lived in Texas. "Let's do this…and pray that we don't have to use these things today."

"I hope we don't have to take the guns out," Phil said, "but I have a bad feeling that we're going to have to do more than just take 'em out. Come on, let's move."

4

"*W*hy are we going back to the car?" David asked. "You said every vehicle is dead; surely ours will be too?"

"It's as dead as every other car, yes," Alice answered, "but there's something important I need to get out of it."

"Man, this is crazy," David murmured, trailing behind his mother and staring around him in awe at the surreal sight, "it's like *The Walking Dead* or something, but uh, without the zombies." He kept fidgeting with his phone, more out of habit than anything else. He'd resigned himself to the fact that the device would never work again, but he couldn't bring himself to throw it away.

Alice and David were now walking on one of the main streets, heading for the multi-story parking garage where her sedan, a late model Ford, was parked.

The long, straight street, lined with high-rise office buildings and businesses, was eerily silent. Usually, this street would resound with the racket of thousands of running motors, horns blaring, and people yelling over the noise. Rows of cars extended as far as the eye could see, packed in haphazard jumbles as if some gigantic toddler had tired of playing with them and had simply dumped them in a mess. Crowds of people were milling around in confusion. Many of them had collided, but aside from the motorcycle accident near the bank, Alice and David hadn't seen any bad wrecks or serious injuries.

Almost all of the stores along the strip had shut and locked their doors. People knew that this was more than just a power outage, but Alice suspected that very few of them knew that it was an EMP attack. Most people, she guessed, wouldn't even know what that was even if she told them.

Thus far, she hadn't seen any signs of police. She wondered what the government response would be and how soon it would be before the national guard or even the army would be called in…if they were called in. Nobody was rioting or looting stores just yet. It was too soon for such behavior, but Alice knew that it wouldn't take desperate people—who already had little food and other supplies—very long to figure out that the police had little power to stop them from simply taking what they wanted. With starvation imminent, law and order and the rules of a civilized society would quickly go out the window, and she didn't want to be anywhere near this city when that happened.

"Mom, I think that guy's hurt pretty bad."

David's words snapped Alice out of the trance of thoughts she'd been in, and she stopped to follow her son's pointing forefinger. Across the street, a group of people, all looking concerned, were gathered around an elderly man who was lying on the ground, groaning. A few feet away from him were two crumpled cars, which appeared to have smashed into each other at speed.

Alice was focused on getting to her car as quickly as possible, but she couldn't ignore an old man in pain. She took David's hand. "Come on. I'll see if there's anything I can do for him." She hoped she sounded more confident than she felt.

They hurried across the street and made her way through the group of people gathered around the injured man, a thin, white-haired fellow in his seventies.

"Everyone, I'm a trauma nurse, and I need you all to stand back and give me some space, please," she said.

The crowd, uncertain of how to help the man, did as she said and moved back. With a sinking heart, Alice realized that the old man was actually one of the lucky ones. Many more people would be injured on these streets in the days and weeks to come, but there would be nobody to help them. The thought that innocent people may well die in protracted agony on the streets made her want to break down into a fit of uncontrollable weeping, but she fought back the tears and let her nurse's instincts and training take over.

"Where's the pain, sir?" she asked the old man as she knelt down next to him and checked his pulse, which was strong and even, a good sign. "Davey, fish that little flashlight out my bag, please."

"My, my sh-shoulder and r-ribs," he groaned.

Alice quickly checked over the old man's limbs to make sure there were no fractures. David handed her the flashlight, and she used it to check the man's pupils. He was mostly fine; she was relieved to find. His shoulder, however, was dislocated, and his ribs on his left side possibly cracked. He would live, though…although for how long if he couldn't get out of this city, she couldn't say.

"Sir," she said gently, "you're going to be okay. You don't have any major fractures, but your ribs might be cracked from the seatbelt and the impact. Your shoulder is dislocated too. I'll pop it back into place for you, but I must warn you, it's going to hurt. Once it's done, though, you'll feel a lot better. Davey, can you help me here a second? Just press down on his chest here, hold him in place." She looked up at the crowd. "Does anyone have something he can bite down on for a second?"

A young businessman took off his tie and handed it to her. "Will this do?"

"Thank you," she said, folding up the tie. "Sir, you're

going to need to bite down on this while I pop your shoulder back in. My son's going to hold you down too. Like I said, it'll hurt bad for a second or two, but it'll be over fast, and you'll soon feel better. Are you ready?"

"Thank you, ma'am," he groaned and nodded, opening his mouth so she could stick the folded-up tie into it. He bit down on it and closed his eyes.

"Davey, hold him here and here," Alice said, pointing to two spots on the man's chest, "push down hard so he can't move."

David knelt down and put his weight on the man's chest, while Alice positioned the man's arm, gripping it tightly.

"Okay, sir, on three. One, two, three!" She jerked the man's arm swiftly, and his eyes bulged with agony as he screamed into the tie, biting down on it with all his force.

As quickly as the searing pain had blasted through his shoulder, though, it began to fade, and he let out a long, slow sigh of relief. Alice took the tie out of his mouth, and then she and David helped him to his feet, and then assisted him over to his car, where they helped him get onto the back seat.

"Th-thank you, ma'am," he stammered. "My shoulder's already starting to feel a little better."

"Get some rest here for a while," she said. "Then go straight home, you hear? Things are going to get... pretty crazy."

"I'll do that, thank you again."

Alice gave him one more nod and a sad smile; she'd done what she could for him, but she had no idea if he would be okay, and if he'd be able to get home—wherever that was—before the madness began. He wouldn't stand a chance if he got caught up in all of it. She prayed that it wouldn't erupt for at least another few hours, and hopefully, the old man would be able to get out of the city before nightfall. She knew there would be a full moon tonight, but even so, the city would be a terrifying place without any lights, and the darkness that would engulf the place would only aid and abet any criminal elements in whatever nefarious activities they would no doubt get up to.

"Come on, Davey," she said, taking her son's hand, "we gotta move."

They were almost at the parking garage, but another three or four miles lay between the car and the dubious safety of Alice's apartment where she and David would await rescue from Phil. They hurried across the street and rounded the corner, and Alice sucked in a sharp breath of relief when she saw the parking garage a hundred yards ahead of them. "Okay, in and out, then straight to the apartment," she said, more to herself than David.

Just as they got into the garage, though, a thunderous boom crashed through the streets, the earsplitting echoes of it ricocheting off the skyscrapers.

"What the hell was that?" David gasped.

Before Alice could answer, sharp cracks and chattering crackles of gunfire rang out, and they saw an ominous plume of black smoke rising into the sky, coming from a mere few blocks away. From a distance came screams and shouts from what sounded like hundreds of people.

"It's starting," Alice murmured. "Quickly, Davey, let's go, hurry!"

5

*P*hil and Wyatt saw the towers of black smoke rising from the city before they'd even driven through the two small towns that were en route.

"Shit, things are getting bad sooner than I'd hoped," Phil muttered.

Wyatt, who was driving, stomped on the gas pedal, and the truck surged forward. Grim-faced, he swerved around a sedan abandoned in the middle of the road, and then, when they came across a minor car pileup on the outskirts of the first town, he veered off the blacktop, plowing through the long grass on the side of the road. Phil had raised and upgraded the vintage vehicle's suspension and put some off-road tires on it so detours off the beaten track could be undertaken with ease.

People in the town had seen the pillars of smoke rising from the distant city, and they were gathered in groups on the streets, staring with fear and confusion at the black plumes on the horizon. The sound of a functioning vehicle immediately drew their attention away from distant smoke, though, and they stared at the truck as it hurtled past them. A few of them tried to wave down the truck, but Wyatt kept the accelerator floored and his eyes on the road.

"That's it, brother, keep on going," Phil said grimly. Pangs of guilt shot through him as he averted his eyes from the people trying to flag him down. He longed to help them but knew there was nothing he could do for them. And now, with the city on fire, he knew he couldn't afford even a second's delay if he wanted to make sure his wife and son got out of there alive.

Coming back through these towns would be a lot more dangerous, especially if darkness had fallen. People would be more desperate, and therefore, more aggressive by that stage, and Phil was certain that they would do more than simply attempt to wave down his truck. He would cross that bridge when he got to it, though. His hand slid down to the .45 holstered at his side, and his fingers curled around the pistol's grip. He prayed that he wouldn't have to use it, but he realized that the odds of getting in and out of the city without firing a shot in anger were growing slimmer by the minute.

They roared out of the first town and raced on toward the next. Wyatt hurled the truck through the mountain road curves, his jaw set and his hands white-knuckled on the wheel. He dealt with every obstacle with grim determination and razor-sharp focus; he was an expert driver who, after his stint in the military, had dabbled in rally racing for a while. The skills he'd learned there were paying off in this madcap race to get to the city.

They passed a few more abandoned cars and a motorcycle or two on the winding road, but when they got within sight of the next town, coming over a rise that looked over it, Phil caught a worrying glimpse of an obstacle up ahead. A makeshift roadblock had been thrown up, with abandoned vehicles, garbage dumpsters, and other large items completely blocking the road through town.

"Pull over, quick, pull over," Phil said to Wyatt, who grunted out a wordless reply and pulled the truck to the side of the road but kept the motor running. They'd gone down a dip in the road, and they wouldn't be visible to anyone manning the barrier—if anyone were manning the roadblock—unless they carried on driving for a few dozen yards. "Wait here, and keep her in gear," Phil instructed, jumping out of the car. "I'll be back in a sec."

He jogged up the road, moving between the trees to stay concealed from any unfriendly eyes that might be watching, and headed back up the rise to get a closer look at the roadblock. Once he was high enough to get a view of it again, he took a pair of binoculars out of his backpack and peered in closely.

Two men with rifles were manning the roadblock. From the way they were dressed, it looked like they were civilians rather than police or military. Phil didn't know whether they'd set the roadblock up to keep looters out or whether it was for a more sinister purpose, but he wasn't about to take any chances. He put away the binoculars, jogged back to the truck, and climbed in.

"There are guys with rifles at that roadblock ahead," he said. "We can't go this way. There's the old forestry track a mile back that'll allow us to skirt this town and get within a half-mile of one of the main arteries leading into the city."

"Will the old girl be able to handle the river crossing?" Wyatt asked, raising a skeptical eyebrow.

"She's no tank, but she'll handle a couple of feet of water without complaint."

"The current will be stronger than usual after last week's heavy rains," Wyatt said, still sounding a little uncertain.

"I'd rather take my chances with the river than with men with guns," Phil said. "And even with the stronger current, I'm confident we'll get across."

"Forest track it is then." Wyatt turned the truck around, raced back up the road, and then veered off the blacktop onto the old dirt track that wound through the woods. The track was beyond merely bumpy and rough; it was heavily rutted, with rocks and boulders up to a foot in height jutting out of it in places. A regular sedan would have had its undercarriage smashed up and possibly an axel broken after a few hundred yards, and even trucks and 4x4s would have had a difficult time on the track. Thanks to both Wyatt's skills behind the wheel and to the work Phil had done on his dad's truck, preparing it for just this sort of terrain, the old vehicle handled the rutted track well enough.

When the track disappeared into the river, Wyatt pulled the truck up to a stop. While he was impressed at the vehicle's off-road capabilities, he still wasn't entirely certain it could handle a deep river crossing, especially with the exceptionally current. "You sure about this?" he asked.

"I know what this truck is capable of," Phil said, determined and resolute. "I factored a possible river crossing into my calculations. Let's do this."

Knowing that Phil had factored a situation like this into his truck's design gave Wyatt the confidence boost he needed to shift into first and edge the vehicle cautiously into the river. Both of them had crossed the river at this ford on horseback a number of times, so they knew it well enough…but that was when the river was lower and the current weaker, and even then, the water covered the horses' legs completely, coming up to their bellies.

"Easy does it," Wyatt muttered under his breath, creeping forward and already feeling the force of the current pushing with relentless urgency against the vehicle before the water was even two feet in depth.

All four wheels were in the water now, and Wyatt kept his pace slow and steady. After a few more tentative yards, the water was up against the lower sections of the doors. Nothing was coming in, though. Phil had made sure every square inch of the vehicle was completely watertight. The unrelenting force of the current was nonetheless unsettling, though; it felt as if the truck were being battered by hurricane winds. Phil glanced across at his friend. While Wyatt's face was as stony as it always was, he could see how tightly he was gripping the wheel, and he noticed that beads of perspiration were glistening on his forehead. He was clearly nervous about this. Speed didn't worry Wyatt in the least, but water made him nervous; it always had, ever since a near-drowning incident as a young boy.

"You're doing well, brother, just keep her steady. You're doing well. Twenty more yards and we'll be out," Phil said, doing his best to bolster his friend's confidence.

Wyatt plunged the truck into the deepest part of the river, and for a heart-stopping moment a surge of the current lifted two of the wheels, with the truck tilting dangerously and almost flipping over. Wyatt gave it steady throttle, though, and one of the tires found some grip against a boulder on the riverbed, and the truck lurched forward and slammed back down onto four wheels. Wyatt released a long, slow sigh and whispered a silent prayer of thanks.

Phil, who had been something of an adrenalin junkie in his younger years, whooped with glee and laughed. "This was the fun route, right?" he said, grinning.

In response, Wyatt scowled and shook his head; he

wasn't ready to chuckle about almost being swept away just yet. He pushed the truck onward and gunned the throttle when the front wheels finally emerged from the water onto the opposite bank. "Thank God," he muttered.

Now that they were back on the forest track, the brief moment of levity that had come from successfully fording the river crumbled, and a sense of dire urgency settled upon both men. While racing along the winding forest track, lurching and skidding through mud and obstacles, they caught sight of the open sky through a gap in the trees and saw that the plumes of black smoke from the city had grown taller and thicker.

"I hope we get there in time," Phil murmured, staring ahead, half in a daze, his thoughts now on his wife and son. "I really hope we get there in time…"

6

---

*D*avid and Alice jogged up to the fourth floor of the parking garage, and before they headed over to Alice's car, they took a look out over what they could see of the city. At least one of the skyscrapers nearby was on fire, and the city was belching out towers of black smoke from all over.

"This is not looking good, not at all," Alice said. She and David would have to cross some of the burning areas to get to her apartment. Thankfully, the block on which her apartment building was located did not seem to have been affected by the explosions and fires...at least not yet.

"Who's setting off these bombs and starting these fires?" David asked. He was trying to put on a brave face, but Alice could clearly see the worry and fear in his eyes.

"I don't know, but we have to get to the apartment right away."

"How long are we gonna have to stay there? Is Dad coming to help us? I- I wanna go home, I wanna get out of here, Can't we just, like, walk home?" David pleaded.

"David, listen to me," Alice said, holding her son by his shoulders and staring straight into his eyes. At over six feet in height, he towered over her, but with every syllable his mother uttered, he felt as if he shrank a few inches. "I know you're scared, and it's okay to be scared. Look, I've got everything we need to survive for a while in that apartment, and your dad knows that he'll find us there. We can't just walk out of the city right now; we'll barely make it to the outskirts by dark. Then we'd have to try to get through the suburbs into the woods in the dark, and then what? Sleep on the ground in the woods? I've got a flashlight and a compass in my bag, but even so, we might get lost. And I'm willing to bet that the woods are going to be more dangerous than ever tonight…"

"There won't be any mountain lions or anything this close to the city," David said weakly. "C'mon, even I know that."

"It's not wild animals I'm worried about, Davey."

"You've, you've got a gun in your purse…"

"Yeah, and there's another for you in the car, but I'm praying that we don't have to use them," Alice said, shaking her head. She was still reeling from the surreality and craziness of it all, and trying to maintain a brave front for her frightened son was exacting a mental and emotional toll on her. "David, please, for your sake and mine, just do what I tell you, okay? I know it's scary. I know everything is uncertain and the world's been flipped on its head, but you have to trust me, okay? I know what I'm doing."

David breathed in deeply, doing his best to calm himself. He bit his lower lip and nodded.

"Okay, Mom. Okay, I trust you."

She gave him a quick, tight hug, and then led him over to her car, a late model Toyota SUV.

"How are we gonna open it?" David asked. "Surely, the remote won't be working?"

"I'm not going to use the remote," she said, taking out the tactical survival knife and the pair of leather gloves she always carried in her handbag. "Stand back." She put the gloves on and used the glass-breaker attached to the knife to smash a hole into the rear passenger window. Then she used the blade to knock any remaining glass fragments from the window before leaning in, lowering one of the passenger seats and pulling out a black backpack from the trunk. She tossed the backpack to David. "Take the gun out and slip it into your belt. The knife, too," she instructed.

While David was doing this, she got a pair of sneakers out of the car and discarded the pumps she was wearing to put on the more practical shoes.

Inside the bag were a 9mm pistol and extra ammo, a survival knife, headlamps, a large medical kit, space blankets, water purification tablets and a water purifying bottle, a portable gas stove, some dehydrated meals, duct tape, face masks with dust and smoke filters, some bandannas, lightweight, stab-proof vests, and hand sanitizer.

"Whoa, you really are prepared for anything, Mom," David remarked.

"Did you think your dad and I were messing around when we taught you all that survival stuff?" Alice asked, a hint of annoyance coloring her voice. "And I've shown you this bag before, but your nose was too buried in that damn phone of yours to pay attention." She stopped here, realizing that now was not the time to be giving her son a lecture. "Anyway, tuck the pistol somewhere where it isn't too conspicuous, then put the stab vest on under your shirt. Hand me one too, please. We don't wanna draw attention to ourselves, but we need to have things where we can get to them quickly."

"Okay, Mom." David took off his T-shirt and slipped a stab-proof vest on, while Alice took off her blouse, stripping down to her bra, and put hers on too. After that, they got dressed again, and Alice gave a satisfied nod when she saw that the vests weren't really visible beneath their clothes unless one looked very closely.

"Put the backpack on and let's go," she said. Before heading down to the ground level, Alice took a few moments to survey the city, taking note of where the fires and smoke plumes were, and mapping out a route in her head that would allow her to bypass these locations without taking too much of a detour.

When they got out of the garage, they saw more people wandering around; the crowds were growing larger and denser, as Alice had suspected they would. People were also beginning to move with more of a sense of direction and urgency now, rather than aimlessly milling around in confusion. The confusion and worry were still there en-masse, of course, and in addition, there was real fear in people's eyes after the sounds of explosions, gunfire, and screaming. Alice guessed those people who didn't live in the city would now be trying to get out of it, while those who had apartments within its confines would be trying to get home where they could hole up against the unknown terror.

She wondered who was responsible for the fires, gunshots, and explosions. Were they mere looters and opportunistic criminals pouncing on the opportunity, or was there something more sinister going on? Given that an EMP had been used, she had to assume it was the latter, and that this was all part of a coordinated attack. By whom she had no idea, but if they were vicious enough to deploy such a device, they had to be extremely dangerous. One thing she was sure of was the fact that she'd need to stick to alleys and side streets. If there were any more explosions—and there almost certainly would be—it was most likely that they would happen on main streets. Terrorists like those who had attacked the city would want to cause maximum damages and exact maximum casualties from their bombs and missiles.

She led David across the main street, half walking, half jogging, wanting to move fast but not draw attention to herself, and then hastily swerved into an alley to cut across the block. The alley was deserted, but Alice wasn't about to let down her guard. She kept her handbag positioned across her midriff and kept her right hand in the bag, with her hand curled around the grip of her pistol in there. If necessary, she could whip the weapon out in the blink of an eye. She hoped it wouldn't come to that, though.

"Quickly, Davey," she urged, breaking into a fast jog now that there weren't other people around. She intended to move through the city in this exact manner, zigzagging toward their destination, running when she could, and walking as briskly as possible when there were other people around.

Another explosion boomed like a clap of thunder in the distance, followed by more bursts of gunfire and screams. Alice looked back at David, who had stopped in his tracks. The fear in his eyes was unmistakable.

"Come on, Davey," she said, doing her best to sound calm. "We'll be okay as long as we keep moving."

He swallowed slowly and nodded, trying to force down the fear. They jogged through the alley and got to another main street, which they crossed as quickly as possible, weaving their way through a throng of confused and frightened people. David stopped for a few seconds, watching wide-eyed as two men got into a violent scuffle a few yards from them. Alice strode on a few yards before she realized David was no longer next to her. She spun around, with a sense of rising panic swelling rapidly within her and saw him staring at the brawl.

"David!" she snapped. "Ignore them, get your ass over here and—"

There was a flash of blinding light followed immediately by the loudest, most skull-splitting boom Alice had ever heard, and for a brief and terrifying moment, she felt a sickening, lurching sensation and the horrifying feeling that she was airborne and spinning. Then everything went black.

7

"This is as close as the forest track will take us," Phil said as they approached a fork in the bumpy dirt track. "Right will take us deeper into the woods, away from the city, left, to the edge of the northern suburbs."

"How close do we get before ditching the truck?" Wyatt asked as he veered left.

"Keep going another mile or so," Phil said. "From what I remember, there's a lookout point around a five-minute hike off the track. It'll give us a view of the northern suburbs and the city itself. I'll take a good look with the binoculars from there and then decide how close to take the truck."

They drove onward, and Wyatt dropped the pace somewhat so they could keep an eye out for the land-mark that marked the start of the trail: a huge, moss-covered boulder. After around a mile of driving, they swung around a bend in the road, and Phil caught sight of the boulder, half-hidden by thick summer undergrowth.

"That's it. Pull over," he said.

Wyatt pulled off the road and killed the engine. "You go on ahead, Phil. I'll keep an eye on the truck and the road." He took out the .357 revolver; with its 6.5-inch barrel, it was the most accurate of the handguns for ranged shots, and he didn't intend to let anyone get even remotely close to the truck.

"I'll be back in a few minutes," Phil said, hopping out and racing down the overgrown trail.

It only took him around two minutes to reach the lookout point, and when he did, he drew in a sharp gasp of shock. For the last twenty minutes of driving, their view of the sky had been obscured by the tall trees of the forest. Now that he had a clear view of the city and the sky above it, though, he was able to see just how much had happened in the last half hour. A number of new plumes of dense, black smoke had appeared in different locations throughout the city, and when he looked through his binoculars, he could see that a few of the skyscrapers were actually on fire. A distant boom echoed across the valley. Powerful blasts of some sort were exploding through the city. An equally ominous sound accompanied these thunder-clap bangs, the muted rattle and chatter of faraway gunfire.

"Shit! Son of a bitch, shit!" Phil cursed himself for not acting sooner. All he could think of was the fact that his wife and son were somewhere down there, stuck in the middle of whatever anarchic violence and chaos were erupting. "Breathe Phil, breathe." He forced himself to take a few deep breaths and calm himself. Panicking wouldn't allow him to help Alice and David. He had to think rationally and act logically, despite the situation of extreme stress and pressure—something that, thankfully, he'd developed a talent for in his years as an aerospace engineer.

He pulled the binoculars back up to his eyes and forced himself to look away from the burning city, focusing instead on what he could see of the northern suburbs. While the roads weren't clogged with dead cars like those of the city were, there were certainly enough abandoned and crashed vehicles littering the streets of the suburbs to make a passage through them more difficult.

Of course, he could easily just drive over sidewalks and people's lawns, but any working vehicle, especially one driving like a maniac, would draw all sorts of attention. And, considering that violence and gun battles had already broken out in the city, attention was the last thing he needed. People would be getting desperate, and he wouldn't want to get into any sort of situation in which he and Wyatt might be targeted by carjackers or other criminals who wanted the truck... and who'd be prepared to kill to get it.

"I can't take the truck through the suburbs," he muttered to himself, scrutinizing the suburban streets through his binoculars. "It's too risky."

Having to walk through the suburbs to get to the

city, however, would take hours, and expend a lot of energy. Phil wished for a moment that he hadn't loaned out his spare bicycles, but the brief regret quickly passed; his workers had needed them to get home, and he didn't regret helping them at all.

"There's gotta be another way in, a quicker way," he murmured, "an inconspicuous way." He surveyed the suburbs and the outskirts of the city, rapidly running a number of ideas through his head. Then, as his gaze fell on the sparkling ribbon of water that wound its way through the suburbs and into the city—the same river they'd crossed in the truck earlier—he had his eureka moment and knew exactly what to do. Without another moment of hesitation, he raced back to Wyatt and the truck.

"See anything?" Wyatt asked when Phil came crashing through the undergrowth.

"Enough to know that we can't waste a single moment," Phil said. "You get driving, I'm gonna get busy in the back of the truck to save time," he continued, jumping into the bed of the truck. A large locked trunk was bolted to the front of the bed, closest to the cab.

"What are you doing?" Wyatt asked.

"Preparing to get us into the city quickly and quietly, without having to walk for hours through the suburbs," Phil answered. "Look, there's no time to talk," he said. He had unlocked the trunk and was taking out a hand pump. "Hop back in, drive another two miles, and then take the right fork when you get to it, that'll take us down to the river again."

"It'll be deeper there," Wyatt said, looking doubtful. "We barely made the last crossing, and I can tell you right now, Phil, that as tough as the old girl is, if the water is even an inch deeper, we'll be swept away,"

"We're not going to be crossing the river there," Phil said, rummaging in the trunk. "Just trust me, okay? Drive to the river, and my plan will be ready by the time we get there."

"All right," Wyatt said uncertainly. He climbed back into the truck, started it up, and took off down the dirt track, while Phil began putting his plan together in the back.

8

"Good thing you had it back there," Wyatt said when he hopped out of the truck.

"My dad rammed home the whole 'be prepared for any possibility' thing when I was a kid, and it's stuck with me ever since," Phil replied. His arms and shoulders were burning from the intense exertion of the last ten minutes, but he'd succeeded in what he'd needed to do: with a hand pump, he had inflated the small rubber dinghy, one of a number of very useful items he'd long since packed it into the bug-out box in the back of the truck.

Wyatt had parked the truck up in a clump of trees close to the riverbank. Across the river were the last houses of the suburbs, which were eerily silent. No sign of life could be seen from any of the houses. Either the occupants had left, or they were hiding in their basements in fear. On the horizon, the air over the city was thick with black smoke, and they heard more explosions and scattered gunfire every couple of minutes.

"Here, put these together," Phil said, tossing pieces of oars to Wyatt. "I'm gonna get some branches." While Wyatt started screwing the oar pieces together, Phil took a machete out of the bug-out box and went off to cut some branches off the nearby trees and shrubs. "There's an ax in there, too," he said to Wyatt as he started chopping. "When you're done with the oars, you can help me cut."

"Will do," Wyatt grunted. He wasn't too happy about having to travel in a rubber dinghy on the rushing river, especially one as tiny as this—it could barely seat two adults—but he knew that the boat would save them many hours, as well as the effort of trudging on foot through the suburbs. Once he'd put the oars together, he dragged the dinghy down to the water's edge and leaned them against it, and then he jogged back up the bank to grab the ax and help gather some branches.

A couple of minutes later, Phil and Wyatt had gathered enough branches and foliage to cover the truck. As urgently as Phil wanted to get into the city, he knew he had to hide the truck; this was their lifeline to get them all safely back to the ranch once he'd rescued Alice and David. The two of them made sure the truck was properly concealed, and then they packed some backpacks full of useful items from the bug-out box, locked up everything, and then hurried down to the river.

Phil could see that Wyatt was nervous about getting into the dinghy, so he clapped his hand onto his friend's shoulder and gave it a firm, reassuring squeeze. "I've done white water rafting in far crazier rivers than this one, Wyatt. It'll be a bumpy ride, but don't worry, this little rubber duck is tougher and a lot more seaworthy—river worthy, I guess you could say—than she looks."

Wyatt swallowed slowly, his eyes still glistening with traces of fear, but he nodded stoically and climbed into the dinghy. Phil pushed the dinghy out until he was knee-deep in the water and then jumped in. The dinghy wobbled and lurched, but stayed stable enough, and once the two of them began paddling the boat smoothed out.

"We just have to get into the meat of the current," Phil said, "and once we're into, it's a matter of just keeping the nose facing forward. By the way, brother, keep a gun on your lap where you can reach it easily. I don't think we'll see anyone on the banks while we're moving through the suburbs, but that'll definitely change once we get into the city. You keep your eyes on the right bank. I'll keep my eyes on the left."

Wyatt nodded, his hands white-knuckled on the oar as they traveled over a series of minor rapids. Once they were through them, he took out the .357 and laid it across his lap. Phil kept one of his .45s on his lap as he rowed.

As Phil had said, once they steered the vessel into the current, progress became swift and easy. While it took some effort and skill with the oars to keep the nose of the dinghy pointing forward, Wyatt quickly got the hang of it, and despite his fear of water, he was soon paddling and changing direction like an experienced boatman.

They didn't come across anyone for the first few minutes, but when they got closer to the city, they saw a group of people standing on a jetty on the riverbank. The people didn't seem to be armed and appeared to be more bewildered and scared than anything else. They stared with frightened eyes at Phil and Wyatt as they passed. Nobody waved; they just stared, their faces full of fear and uncertainty. The protracted silence of the moment was eerie and unsettling, and Wyatt and Phil, while keeping a wary eye on the people as they passed, were happy to be away from them. It was an ominous sign of things to come. Phil's heart went out to the people who were caught up in this disaster, but he knew that there was nothing he could do for them. Large clouds of smoke frequently hovered at the river's edge, obscuring the sight of what lay beyond the banks.

They continued on along the river, traveling under a bridge that was jam-packed with abandoned cars. A few people were standing on the bridge, and they stared with confusion and worry at the two men in the dinghy as they passed underneath on the rushing river. Again, the silence and forlorn stares of the people on the bridge were deeply unsettling. Neither of the men said anything to each other, but each knew that the other was thinking about this.

There was one more bridge up ahead, around a mile downstream, but this was a huge bridge that funneled freeway traffic into the city and served as one of its main arteries. Phil knew they were entering dangerous territory now, and they'd gone as far as was safely possible on the dinghy. The scattered gunfire they kept hearing every few minutes was louder and closer now, as were screams and shouts of panic.

"Let's pull up to the bank over there," Phil said, pointing to the left bank of the river. Further down, the banks became vertical concrete canal sides, so this was one of the last places they could land the craft anyway.

Wyatt offered no protest; he was happy to be getting out of the water. They steered the dinghy over to the bank and beached it, and then climbed out, surveyed the immediate area for any sign of danger, and then holstered their firearms.

"What do we do with the boat?" Wyatt asked.

"Drag it out of the water and leave it and the oars here," Phil said. "It's served its purpose for us, but someone else might find some use for it. There are going to be tens of thousands, even hundreds of thousands of people who'll be desperate for any way out of this city in the next few days. If I can give even two or three of 'em a little helping hand, I'm happy to do so."

Wyatt nodded and helped drag the dinghy across the muddy bank as far out of the water as they could before they reached the concrete canal wall, a couple of yards from the water's edge. Drifts of smoke from a nearby burning building were spilling over the wall and partially obscuring visibility here. A few dozen yards down, some stairs led up the wall onto the promenade that followed the course of the river. Once they were up those stairs, they'd be in the city.

"Get ready," Phil said to Wyatt, his expression one of grim determination and gritty resolve. "Things are about to get a lot more dangerous."

Wyatt laconically patted the grips of the .357 holstered on his hip. "I'm ready," was all he said. Then the two of them jogged up the steps and disappeared into the smoke.

9

*W*hen Alice came to, all she could see was billowing clouds of smoke, and the only thing she could hear was a shrill, monotonous whining, screaming deep inside her eardrums and feeling like a dentist's drill boring into her brain. A sharp pain burned in her midriff, but all she could think about was her son. Despite feeling dizzy and disoriented, she struggled groggily to her feet and screamed. "David! David, where are you?! David!" She dropped to her knees, coughing from the acrid smoke and a burning in her lungs and throat. When she raised her hand to her mouth, she saw that her forearm was covered with blood. Despite her injuries, all she cared about was finding David.

The shrill whining persisted in her ears, and her own voice sounded as if it were coming from a million miles away. Alice staggered through the smoke, coughing and gasping and calling out her son's name.

The ground was strewn with debris and broken glass, and over the ringing in her ears, she could hear someone screaming in pain. It was a woman, though, not David...but whether this was a good sign or a bad one, she did not yet know.

Her foot struck something soft and heavy, and she almost crashed to the ground, regaining her balance at the last second. She looked down and saw a blood-spattered corpse, and she screamed with fright. She'd seen plenty of dead and dying people in the emergency room, of course, but that was different. She expected to see them there and had been mentally and emotionally prepared for it every time she'd gone to work. Seeing bodies here, on the street of this usually safe, friendly city was something entirely different, though. It almost seemed like it couldn't be real.

Alice knelt down and examined the body with shaking hands. There was no pulse; the victim—a middle-aged man—was certainly dead.

"Mom..." David's voice was barely louder than a croak, but Alice knew it the second she heard it, even with the terrible ringing in her ears.

She sprang to her feet, relief and joy rushing through her like floodwater from a broken dam, and she forgot temporarily about the burning pain in her midriff.

David was standing there, still as a statue, in a thick, swirling cloud of smoke. Alice ran over to him, desperate to see if he was okay.

"Davey, are you okay, are you hurt, talk to me, talk

to me," she said.

David stared wide-eyed at her midriff and pointed with a trembling hand. "Mom," he gasped. "Your...you..."

"I'm okay, dammit," she insisted. "Are you hurt, David? Are you okay? Turn around, let me see your back!"

David gulped, and his eyes looked like they were about to pop out of their sockets, but he did as Alice and said turned around. He was grubby, and bits of debris and small pebbles of broken glass were all over his hair and clothing, but he was uninjured aside from a few minor cuts and scrapes on his arms. Now that Alice knew this, she finally felt okay about looking down at her own injuries...and when she did, she almost passed out. Sticking out of her lower right side was a twisted shard of metal, and around it, her blouse was dark and sticky with blood.

"Mom, you're, you're hurt bad," David murmured, finally managing to utter a complete sentence.

"I'm okay, honey. I'm all right. It looks worse than it is," she answered. Alice knew she'd have to pull the shrapnel out, but she couldn't do that just yet. The wound would have to be stitched up right away, and she only had the tools to do that at the apartment. If she pulled it out now, she might lose too much blood to even make it to the apartment. She had no doubt that the stab-proof vest had saved her life. Even though the shrapnel had pierced it, it hadn't gone deep enough into her flesh to do any serious damage. If she hadn't been wearing it, though, she had no doubt the twisted metal would have ripped through her stomach and intestines, and she would have died a slow, agonizing death.

"Are you, are you *sure*, Mom?" David asked, his eyes locked on the blood-covered metal shard.

"Trust me. I'll be okay. Come on. We have to get—"

A piercing scream from nearby cut Alice off. It was the same woman who'd been screaming before. This time, though, it was quickly followed by a man's voice, hoarse and desperate.

"Oh my God, Stacey, oh God, oh my God! Help! Someone help us, oh God, Stacey! Someone help us, please!"

Even though she was injured herself, Alice knew she couldn't just leave an innocent person laying wounded on the sidewalk to fend for themselves. "Come on, Davey," she said, barely able to hear her own voice over the ringing in her ears. "Let's see if we can help."

She and David moved through the billowing smoke, debris, and broken glass crunching under their every step until they came across a young couple. The man was kneeling down next to the woman and holding her hand, his face contorted with anguish. Her face was a mask of pure agony. Both of them had been injured by the blast, but the woman's injuries were far worse. One of her legs was badly broken, with the bone sticking through the skin. The wound was bleeding heavily.

Alice hurried over to them. "Excuse me, sir, I'm a

nurse. I can help."

"I, oh God, please help, yes, thank you," the man stammered.

Alice knelt down, put a pair of nitrile gloves on, and quickly checked the woman over for any other fractures. Thankfully, it seemed it was just her leg that was broken.

"Davey, you need to help him move her, we have to get her off the street."

"Where to, Mom?" David asked. As crazy as the situation was, he was beginning to regain his composure.

"Can you see anywhere that might be safe?"

David looked up and down the street, narrowing his eyes as he tried to peer through the billowing clouds of smoke. "There! Just a couple yards farther down, the convenience store, it looks like the door got blown off by the blast. We should take her in there."

"Yeah, good thinking," Alice said. "I can't help you carry because of my own injury, but come here, David, hold her under her left armpit. Sir, if you could hold her under her right armpit? Yeah, that's right. We don't need to lift her totally off the ground, just hold as much of her weight up as you can," she instructed. "All right, let's move people, let's move."

David and the man dragged the woman across the glass-littered sidewalk and pulled her into the convenience store. While they were doing that, Alice quickly scoped out the inside of the store, which seemed to be deserted. It was as safe a place as any, for the moment.

Once everyone was inside, Alice got to work on the woman and told the guys to move some heavy objects around to barricade the door.

"Take one of these, sweetie," Alice said to the woman. She handed her a morphine pill—she had a few of them in her bug-out bag—and a bottle of soda from the convenience store fridge. "It'll help with the pain."

There was little she could do for the woman with the minimal first-aid equipment she had on her. Still, she knew that she could at least stabilize her condition.

"I'm gonna have to clean up this wound, sweetie, and I won't lie, it's going to hurt. It's going to hurt real bad, but I have to do it, okay? You gotta be brave, just for a few seconds."

The woman looked terrified, but she could see the compassion in Alice's eyes and could feel it in her gentle touch, and she trusted her.

"Boys, I'm gonna need you to hold her down while I do this. And give her something to bite down on."

David hastily scanned the nearby shelves until his eyes alighted on something that would be useful for this purpose. "Will this do, Mom?" He pulled a rubber chew-toy for dogs off a shelf.

"Perfect," Alice said. She took the label off the chew-toy and got the woman to bite down on it. She then took a bottle of water and an unopened cleaning cloth off a nearby shelf and got some surgical alcohol out of her bag. "You ready, sweetie?" she asked.

With tears in her eyes, the woman nodded and bit

harder into the chew-toy.

"Sir, you need to hold her down tight, you, too, Davey."

The two of them did as Alice said, and she got busy cleaning up the wound where the broken bone was sticking out. First, she used the water to gently wash the area and get any grit and dirt off it.

Then came the part that would cause the woman immense pain: cleaning the wound with surgical alcohol. "I'm sorry, sweetie, but this is gonna hurt. Bite down hard." Alice did the job as swiftly as she could, and the woman writhed and kicked like a wild bull, screaming horrifically, her cries muted by the chew-toy in her mouth.

David and the man had to use all their strength to hold the woman still.

Finally, Alice finished, and she gave the woman's hand a quick squeeze. "You did well, sweetie. You're very brave. I just have to tie a tourniquet now to stem the bleeding, and then we're done, okay?"

There were tears in the woman's eyes, but the morphine was starting to kick in, so the ferocious pain was at least beginning to fade a little. She spat the chew-toy out of her mouth. "Thank you, ma'am," she said hoarsely.

Alice used a T-shirt from a nearby rack to tie a tourniquet around the woman's thigh and then stood up, as did David and the man.

"Thank you. Thank you so much," the man said with tears in his eyes. "I don't know what we would have done without you. Do you, um, do you know what's happened? What is this, some sort of terrorist attack?"

"Somebody has attacked us, yes," Alice answered. "Beyond that fact, I don't know much. I can tell you— as you've no doubt already noticed—that nothing electronic is working, and it won't for some time. Y'all need to get to a hospital as soon as possible; even without much of their equipment working, a surgeon should be able to operate and take care of that leg. Check in the stock room at the back; there should be a hand truck or something like that you can push her in."

"The nearest hospital is five miles away," the man said, looking despondent. "You mean to tell me no ambulances are coming?"

Alice grimly shook her head. "No ambulances, no police cars, nothing. You're going to have to use your muscles to get her to a hospital."

"I'll...I'll do whatever I have to," he said resolutely. "What are you going to do?"

"My son and I have to get home," was all Alice said. "And that's exactly where we're going now. I wish you two the best of luck. Get moving soon, keep away from crowds, and stay off the main streets. That's the only advice I can give you."

"Thank you again, and good luck."

Alice took David's hand, and they took one last look at the couple, and then hurried through the store, exiting via the rear entrance into a smoke-choked back alley.

*A*lice and David moved speedily but cautiously through the city, sticking to back alleys where they could, and hurrying across whatever larger streets they came across. Alice made sure to avoid crowds, and whenever she saw groups of people, she would make wide detours to veer around them. She'd already caught sight of a few masked looters, smashing storefront windows and running out with whatever they could carry. On another occasion, the masked men she saw seemed to simply want to destroy things and cause more chaos; they were throwing Molotov cocktails into stores and setting buildings alight. She made sure she made extra wide detours any time she caught sight of such people.

The pain in her midriff from the jagged piece of shrapnel was growing worse, and walking was becoming increasingly difficult and agonizing. She could have taken a morphine pill for the pain, but she refused to do this; it would dull her senses and slow her down, and she needed to be fully mentally alert.

Finally, she and David got to the building where her studio apartment was. She breathed out a sigh of relief; it had taken over two hours of walking to get there, and the whole time she'd been worried that she might find the building on fire or being ransacked by looters. The stores on the ground floor were locked up, but there was no sign that anyone had tried breaking in, nor were there any fires near the building.

"We're here," she said to David, and when she turned and looked at him, she could plainly see the relief on his face.

Everything about the apartment had been chosen with disaster survival in mind, specifically that of an EMP attack. There was a mechanical lock on the front door, which was a simple but extremely sturdy steel door set in a small alley to the side of the building. The five-story building was one of the older buildings in the city, and as such, was solidly constructed. There was no elevator, only stairs. There was a water reservoir tank on the roof and a fire escape on the side of the building, which wasn't accessible from the ground.

Alice took the front door key out of her bag, entered the building, and then quickly locked the door behind her. She and David trudged up the four flights of stairs to get to her apartment, one of six apartments on the floor.

She unlocked the door, let David in, and then locked the place up, deadbolting the door shut behind her. While the interior of the apartment had a few standard items of furniture, like a sofa, chairs, a dining table, and all the rest, it was immediately clear to David that this was no regular apartment. A set of water drums had been set up, along with an electronically controlled pump and drain system that flushed them out and refilled them every few days. There were gas canisters for the cooker, gas lamps for illumination, and rifle safes bolted to the wall. While there was a double bed, there were also camping cots in case more people needed to sleep in here. The cupboards were filled with canned, dehydrated, and long-life foods, as well as protein powders and meal replacements that could be mixed with water. Bulletproof vests and gas masks hung from a rack at the back of the room. There was also a cupboard full of clean clothes, and Alice took a T-shirt, a jacket, and some jeans for herself.

"David, could you get some beans or something cooking on the gas stove?" Alice said. "I need to go to the bathroom and take care of my wound."

"You don't need any help with that, Mom?" David asked, staring at the bloody shrapnel sticking out of his mother's midriff doubtfully.

"I can take care of it on my own," she said. "We both need a good hot meal to keep our energy levels up. You take care of that, please."

"If you're sure…"

"I'm sure, David."

Alice opened one of the cupboards, took out a large medical kit, hobbled into the bathroom, and shut the door behind her. The pain in her midriff was beyond excruciating now. She stripped down to her underwear, cleaned her hands with surgical alcohol, and folded up a clean washcloth to bite down on. She knew that this was going to hurt, but she had to do it without painkillers dulling her senses.

She gripped the jagged metal with a pair of forceps and bit down hard on the washcloth. Then she ripped the shrapnel out of her body. Sharp pain blasted through her midsection, and she shrieked into the rag, her cry muffled. As she'd predicted, a wash of blood gushed out of the now-open wound.

With trembling hands, she held open the wound, inspecting for internal damage. Thankfully, as bloody as it was, it was a flesh wound. The metal hadn't pierced her deeply, and the stab-proof vest had saved her from catastrophic damage.

Washing the open wound out with surgical alcohol was an experience beyond excruciating; it burned so horrendously she thought her teeth were going to crack from how hard she was biting down on the rag. It had to be done, though. Gasping and shaking from the pain, she forced herself to steady her hands, and then she got busy with stitching the wound closed, which sent more blasts of pain through her midriff.

Finally, however, she got it done and closed the wound. After this, she put a sterile dressing on it and simply lay on the floor, panting and trembling.

"Are you, uh, are you okay in there, Mom?" David asked, his voice muffled through the door.

"I'm…fine," Alice managed to reply. "Don't…worry." After resting for a few moments, she got up, washed her hands and face, and then got changed into clean clothes.

By the time she left the bathroom, David had finished heating up some beans and sausages on the gas stove. "It's nothing fancy, Mom, but it's something, at least, right?"

"Thanks, Davey," she said, easing herself down on the sofa.

"Are you sure you're okay now?" David asked, still concerned.

"I'm fine now, don't worry. Dish me up some beans and a couple of sausages, thanks."

Just as David began ladling beans onto a plate, however, the silence was shattered by thunderous gunfire from right outside in the street. This was followed by the sounds of men shouting, and then the crash of glass shattering.

"Oh no," Alice groaned.

David ran over to the balcony door to go check what was happening, but Alice yelled at him before he could open it.

"No! Don't open it! Whoever's doing that shooting outside might be looking for signs of life in here. Just keep quiet and stay away from the windows."

Alice got up, got her pistol out of her purse, and tiptoed over to the door, signaling to David that he should draw his weapon too. Before she got to the door, she heard the muffled thumps of someone kicking the downstairs door; people were trying to get in. She pressed her ear against the door to listen more closely. The thumping continued, then stopped. Alice waited with bated breath for a few seconds and then exhaled a long sigh of relief; the thugs had probably given up and moved on to another building.

Suddenly a sharp, booming blast echoed up the stairwell, accompanied by aggressive shouts of triumph from below. The invaders had breached the building, and soon the sounds of their stamping boots could be heard coming up the stairs.

"*L*et me do the shooting if any shooting needs to be done," Wyatt growled, his eyes darting from side to side as he and Phil moved through the first alley, which they'd entered after crossing a main street near the river. "I know you've never killed a man before, Phil. Trust me, it's something you'd do well to keep off your conscience."

Phil knew that Wyatt was no stranger to killing; he'd seen his fair share of battle during his service in the Gulf War, and he had the physical, mental, and emotional wounds to show for it. It was true, Phil had never shot a man or even pointed a firearm at anyone in anger, but even so, the thought of anyone attempting to harm his wife and son put enough righteous fire in his blood that he knew that if it came down to it, he wouldn't hesitate even a second to pull the trigger if it meant saving their lives.

"I appreciate you saying that, Wyatt," he said, "but if

a situation arises in which I need to use my guns, you'll bet I'm gonna be using 'em. There won't be any time to argue about who's doing the shooting."

"I'm just warning you that it changes you. It's not like you see in the movies. Once you've put a bullet in a man, you can never go back."

"And that's a price I'm willing to pay if it means saving my wife and son…or you, Wyatt."

Wyatt grunted and nodded, his eagle eyes scanning the urban landscape for dangers, which were abundant. They hadn't heard any more explosions since getting into the city, but bursts of distant gunfire and the sounds of shouts and screams were still frequent.

Because it had become plainly evident that the streets were rapidly descending into deeper chaos and anarchy, the men carried their guns openly now. Wyatt had his .357 in his right hand, a .45 ready on his hip, and a 9mm tucked into the back of his belt as another backup. Then, in case of a dire emergency, the tiny .32 ACP tucked into his boot. Phil carried one of his .45s in his hand, and the other he kept holstered on his belt. He had spare ammunition for all the firearms in his backpack.

As Phil and Wyatt approached the end of the alley, which opened out onto another main street, a group of masked looters, carrying crowbars and baseball bats and bulging bags full of stolen items, turned into the alley. There were six or seven of them, all with black balaclavas over their faces. They stood and stared menacingly at the two men, but Wyatt didn't give the looters a moment to even think of trying anything.

He coolly aimed his revolver at the closest man's chest. "Turn around and keep walking, assholes," he growled.

The looters didn't take long to decide that it wasn't worth messing with two armed men. They turned and took off, flipping off Wyatt and Phil and spitting some curses their way, but not looking back.

"The sight of guns will put them off trying anything with us for now," Phil said darkly, watching the masked looters as they walked down the street, looking for easier prey. "but as things get more desperate, it's going to take more than just threats to scare 'em off."

"All the more reason to get out of this shithole ASAP," Wyatt said. He had always hated cities, and the present situation made him loathe them even more.

Phil looked up at the sun. It was edging closer to the western horizon. "We've still got two, maybe three hours of daylight left," he said. "We'd best use it wisely. Things are going to get a lot crazier once darkness falls."

"It's going to be the darkest night this hellhole has ever seen," Wyatt muttered, "in more ways than one."

"The coast's clear," Phil said, now that the looters had moved a suitable distance away. "Let's move."

They hurried across the main street, weaving through the jumble of abandoned cars that were completely blocking the entire street as far as the eye could see in both directions, and then they moved swiftly along the sidewalk on the other side for a while, heading to the next alley. The sidewalk was littered with broken glass and other debris from what looked like a bomb that had gone off in one of the stores they passed. Phil paused for a moment and peered inside the wrecked store, from which clouds of smoke were belching. Blood was sprayed across the nearest inner wall, and he saw the gruesome sight of a disembodied human leg lying among the rubble of the half-collapsed interior. He shuddered and moved on.

The looters weren't the only people they saw. Many more people were drifting aimlessly around, some looking almost like they were in trances. Others were sitting alone on the sidewalk or on the street, in the midst of the jumble of crashed and abandoned vehicles.

Nobody said anything to Phil and Wyatt as they passed, but what was universal among all of them was the expression on every person's face, in every individual's eyes: a look of complete and utter fear, blended with deep confusion and immense worry. It had been hours now since the EMP attack and the subsequent terrorist attacks, and people had realized now that rescue was not, as they'd earlier believed, on its way. Most of them, the city dwellers, especially, who rarely if ever left the comfortable bubble of their urban lives, didn't have the mental or emotional resources to deal with a catastrophe of this magnitude. The rug had been yanked with extreme violence from under their feet, and their lives had, in a mere few seconds, been hurled into complete turmoil. They were, understandably, at a complete loss as to what to do or where to go.

Phil's heart went out to them. He wished there was something he could do for these lost souls, but he knew that bringing even one of these confused, terrified people along with them would completely jeopardize his mission and would put his wife and son at risk.

"Down here, right?" Wyatt's words jolted Phil from this trance of contemplation.

Phil looked up and saw Wyatt pointing down an alley to their left. "Yeah, that way."

Thick, black smoke with a pungent chemical stench was pouring out of the alley. Phil took two industrial masks out of his backpack, putting one on himself and handing the other to Wyatt. Once they were protected against the smoke, they headed up the alley.

It was a relief to head into the smoke-choked alley and get away from the despair, hopelessness, and destruction of the larger city streets. Any respite the two men felt, however, was to be short-lived. When they were about halfway up the alley, a piercing scream of terror resounded through it. It was a young woman's scream, and it was coming from close by. Phil and Wyatt shot each other a glance in the murky gloom, and each gave the other a nod. They raced through the smoke, their firearms pointed ahead of them.

They passed a smashed-open door, which was where the black smoke was belching from, and after a second or two of running cleared the cloud of smoke. They saw that two looters had dragged a young woman into the alley and had pinned her down behind a dumpster and were pawing viciously at her clothes.

"Hey!" Wyatt yelled aggressively, sprinting toward them with his .357 aimed at the closest man's chest.

They stopped what they were doing and looked up. Phil caught sight of the second man's hand moving for what could be a gun at his side. He dropped down onto one knee, gripping his .45 with both hands and taking careful aim, and when the man did indeed pull out a gun, he fired.

The bang of the shot crashed through the alley, and the thug yelped in pain, dropping his gun and staggering back. Phil had always been a crack shot, and his perfectly placed bullet had shot the gun out of the looters' hand and smashed his hand into a mess of ripped-up flesh and shattered bones. The injured man, howling with pain, gripped his wrist and ran away, and the other one, wide-eyed with fear, released the woman and fled after his friend.

The young woman, who was almost delirious with panic and fear, scrambled to her feet, pulled her blouse closed and sprinted down the alley past Phil and Wyatt, screaming and weeping, before they could talk to her or offer any assistance.

Wyatt kicked the gun under the dumpster and then turned to face Phil, giving him an impressed nod.

"Good shooting there, brother," he said. "I didn't know whether you had it in you."

"I said if I came across a situation where I'd have to use a gun in anger, I would," Phil said, feeling a bit shaken up by the rush of adrenalin that had surged through him. "And I did. And I'll do it again if I have to."

Wyatt clapped his hand onto Phil's shoulder. "I've got your back if you do," he said.

"Come on," Phil said, not wanting to linger. "We need to keep moving."

They exited the alley, scanned the street—which, like most, was clogged with abandoned vehicles—for danger, and then moved quickly along the sidewalk. A buzzing crowd of people was gathered up ahead, and a man was standing on top of a car in front of them, yelling something about the government and conspiracies, but Wyatt and Phil hastily crossed the street and gave the crowd and the agitator a wide berth.

It took them around an hour to get to the last alley before Alice's apartment. During that time, they saw more looting and chaos, more crowds of people gathering and listening to angry rants, and heard more distant explosions and bursts of gunfire coming from all directions.

Phil paused in the alley to talk to Wyatt. "We're almost there. There's plenty of food in the apartment, so we'll sit down and rest and have a good, hearty meal. We need to keep our energy reserves up because we're gonna be walking until the early hours of the morning to get back to the truck."

Phil was doing his best to disguise the worry in his eyes, but his old friend could see it clearly. Wyatt knew that anxiety about Alice and David had to be eating

Phil up inside at this moment. "I'm sure Alice already has something hot and tasty waiting for us, just like her Sunday roasts on the ranch," he said, smiling reassuringly at Phil.

"I'm sure she does," Phil said. "Come on, let's go."

Before he could take a step, though, a sudden barrage of nearby gunfire blasted its thunder down the alley. It sounded as if it had come from right outside Alice's building. Raising their firearms, Wyatt and Phil moved with cautious haste out of the alley, their hearts pounding in their chests and adrenalin stirring in their veins.

When they emerged from the alley, they saw the huge fire billowing out of the smashed-open storefront at the bottom of the apartment building, and they saw a group of armed men by the door in the side alley. They didn't look like the many opportunistic looters they'd seen up to this point. They were all holding guns, and they had other weaponry on them as well. One of the men blasted the door lock open with his shotgun, and then the rest cheered in triumph. Then the armed men raced into the building.

"Oh no," Phil murmured, the color draining from his face. "Oh no…"

"What's going on out there, Mom?" David asked, looking worried.

"Shh, quiet," Alice whispered, pressing her ear up against the door. She couldn't hear exactly how many men there were, but she was fairly certain that there were four or five of them. She'd heard at least three distinct voices, although what they were saying wasn't quite discernable yet. They seemed to have stopped on the floor below hers.

"Mom, who is it?" The fear in David's voice was growing more discernable.

"Get behind the sofa there, and keep your gun aimed at the door. Do it!" Alice's voice was firm, and this was no request; it was a command.

David was too frightened and worried to argue with her, so he did as she said and knelt down, using the sofa as cover, and aimed his pistol at the side of the door closest to the handle.

From downstairs, they heard two of the men shouting. This was quickly followed by a woman shrieking with terror, but her screaming was cut abruptly and ominously short by the blast of a gunshot. Alice jumped with fright, and David's already-wide eyes protruded from their sockets even more, and his jaw dropped open with shock.

Harsh laughter echoed up the stairwell, along with the sounds of items being smashed; it seemed that they had forced their way into one of the apartments and murdered whoever was in there.

Alice swallowed slowly. Her mouth was dry with fear, and her pulse was pounding in her temples and ears. She prayed that the invaders would turn around and move on to another building before coming up to her floor. An almost irresistible instinct within her was urging her to run and hide, but she knew that she had to stay strong for David's sake. She didn't want to panic and then get him in a panic as well.

She waited, listening through the door, her palms clammy on the pistol. The men kicked open another door, but this time there was no shooting; the place they'd just invaded was unoccupied, she guessed.

"Uh, Mom…"

"Not now, David!" Alice snapped, her nerves on edge. "Keep your damn mouth shut!"

"Mom! Look out the window!"

David's insistence that she listen to him did not come from any sense of rebelliousness or argumentativeness. Alice could hear the urgency in his tone. She looked behind her at the window looking out onto the balcony and let out a gasp of shock, for she saw thick, black smoke blotting out the sight of the city. She didn't need to look at the smoke for longer than a few seconds to ascertain that it was coming from their building. The only question was whether it was the store on the street level that was on fire or one of the apartments below hers.

"Oh shit," she muttered, torn by a sudden and urgent sense of indecision. To go out into the hallway now, with armed killers roaming through the building, would be suicidal, but if the entire building was on its way to burning down, then it would be just as dangerous to stay put. Would there be enough time to wait for the killers to leave and then escape without being trapped by the growing flames? Or should she risk trying to get out of the building via the fire escapes, and then possibly be spotted by the killers anyway? And then, if the entire building did burn down and they had to flee, how would they find Phil?

"What do we do, Mom? What do we do?!" David asked. His heart was jumping like an out-of-control jackhammer in his chest, and his mouth was dry.

"Just hold on, I'm trying to think. I'm trying to think!"

David got up and scrambled over to the balcony.

"Hey!" Alice yelled. "I told you not to—"

It was too late, though. David had already opened the door and dashed out onto the balcony. He leaned out over the edge and looked down, and through the clouds of dense smoke, he saw that huge flames were devouring the store at the bottom of the building. None of the other apartments were on fire—at least not yet. Coughing and gasping, he staggered back into the apartment and shut the door.

"It's the store downstairs that's burning," he said to Alice, his voice hoarse. "None of the other apartments are burning, but the fire looks bad. I think it'll spread."

Alice bit her lower lip and nodded. She didn't want to do any unnecessary climbing if she could help it. Any strenuous activity would rip open the stitches in her midriff and get the wound bleeding again. If the fire was, at this stage, only on the street level, it would probably take a while to spread through the building.

"We'll stay put until these men outside leave the building," she said to David. "After that, we get the hell out of here."

"Okay, Mom," David said, getting back into position behind the sofa. He was still racked with fear and anxiety but was doing his best to put on a brave face.

"Shh, they're coming up the stairs!" Alice whispered. Her heart was pounding so violently now she thought it was going to burst through her ribcage, and she was finding it difficult to breathe. Her apartment was the one closest to the stairs, and she was certain that they would try her door first. She'd installed a solid oak door in this apartment when she'd renovated it a few years back. The solid locks and the oak would withstand a lot of kicking and shoulder barging, but if the men were determined to get in, they could shoot their way through it. One of them almost certainly had a shotgun, and judging from the fact that he had blown open the downstairs door, she figured he was using some potent ammunition. Now the men's voices were more discernible, and Alice could hear exactly what they were saying.

"That fat bitch had plenty of gold jewelry," one of them said as they marched up the stairs.

"No diamonds, though," another muttered. "Maybe we'll strike it lucky on this floor."

"That slut and her kid we seen going into the building earlier, they had bags with 'em, I bet they got cash."

"That lil' milf got somethin' else I wouldn't mind takin'," one of them growled. "Mm, yeah, she had a tight lil' ass." The others all laughed harshly.

Alice was sure they were talking about her and David, and the things they were saying were making her heart race even faster. Fear-chilled blood oozed like ice-water through her veins. She'd been trying to mentally and emotionally prepare herself for a life-or-death encounter like this ever since they had left the bank, but now that one was almost upon her, she didn't know if she had it in her to pull the trigger. She tried to focus on David. Regardless of what these brutes wanted to do to her, she knew that if she thought about them trying to harm David, her motherly instincts would kick in and she'd be able to fight.

"Where are they, Mom?"

"Shh!" she hissed. "They're almost up the stairs!

Don't breathe another word, and if they break in here, you shoot, do you understand?!"

"Okay, okay, I'll...I'll do it if I have to."

"Quiet now!"

Alice's hands were shaking madly, and she could barely keep a grip on the gun. Just on the other side of the door, she heard the men stop outside her apartment. Her heart almost jumped out of her mouth when one of them bashed on the door.

"Yo, whoever the fuck is in here!" one of them roared through the door. "Open this fucking door now, or we're blowing it down! Open up and we'll let you live...but if you don't, we'll make sure you fucking die...slowly!"

13

"Now I'm wishing we brought those AR-15s with us," Wyatt said as he watched the last of the armed men run into the building.

"Me too," Phil murmured.

Wyatt looked at Phil. "Don't get too mad at yourself. You couldn't have known that things would descend into anarchy this fast."

"I should have known that it would go downhill fast, though," Phil said, shaking his head and curling his left hand into a fist. "Dammit! Why didn't I see that?"

"It's no use beating yourself up about it now. I'm as much to blame as you are but forget about that. It's not like we're unarmed anyway or walking into a gunfight with knives in our hands." Wyatt drew his .45 pistol and gripped it in his left hand, dual-wielding his firearms. "If we go in after 'em, we're going to be in a tight, enclosed space. Handguns are a lot more maneuverable in spaces like that anyway. We *are* going in after those thugs, right?"

"You bet," Phil said determinedly. The thought that his wife and son might be in there and at the mercy of these armed, dangerous predators had injected liquid fire into his veins. Now that he'd had his first taste of shooting a man, he knew that he could line up a human being in his sights and pull the trigger if he had to.

Before they could say anything else, a woman's scream rang out from inside the building, and it was cut off a loud gunshot blast. Each man saw the sudden alarm on the other's face.

"That wasn't Alice," Phil said, although it was not relief that he was feeling.

"We better move. We can approach the building head-on," Wyatt said. "They'll be in the stairwell, which I'm guessing doesn't have windows or look out onto this street?"

"No," Phil answered. "The stairwell only looks out onto the alley."

"Hmm. You know, they'll probably have left a lookout by the door," Wyatt said. "And since there are more of them then there are of us, we don't want him alerting his buddies that we're coming in."

"If we shoot him, his friends inside will hear the gunshot and know something's up."

"That's why we have to take care of him another way," Wyatt said. "Silently. If I go around the block, can I come up that side alley from the rear?"

"Yeah, it exits onto the street parallel to this one. If

you go around that sporting goods store on the corner, you can get onto that street. You'll see the exit of the alley next to a Chinese takeout place."

Wyatt holstered his guns. "Go to the corner by the building entrance," he said. "Give me a minute or so to get around the block. When you see me coming up the alley, make a noise, say something, get the lookout in the doorway to come out. Keep your gun behind your back, don't let him see you're armed and a threat. Just get him to pop his head out of the door if you can. I'll take him out, quick and quiet."

Phil nodded. He extended a gloved hand to Wyatt, who gripped it, and they gave each other a quick, tight hug. "Good luck, brother," Phil said.

Wyatt raced off toward the sporting goods store, weaving through the abandoned cars on the street. Phil, his heart thumping in his chest, crept across the street, keeping an eye both on the alley where the entrance to Alice's building was, and the fire raging in the storefront at the bottom of the building. He could see that the fire was growing fiercer, and it would only be a matter of time before it started to consume the entire building. He could only hope that they were able to deal with the armed invaders before that happened and get Alice and David out of the building...if they even were in the building. There was so much uncertainty in the air at this moment; Phil just wanted to see his wife and son and know that they were okay. The thought that those predators were in there and could be going after them was driving him crazy, and he could hardly bear to hold himself back from simply charging in with guns blazing. He knew, however, that Wyatt was right. If the lookout alerted the others, they would have a major battle on their hands. They were outnumbered and had to use the elements of stealth and surprise to their advantage.

He crept up to the front of the building on the other side of the alley; he couldn't go near the burning store at the bottom of the building because the flames billowing out of it were too fierce. Even by this building, he could feel the intense heat. From here, he could see a little inside the entrance to Alice's building, and he could see the partial figure of a man holding a shotgun there—so there was indeed a lookout by the door.

He peeked his head around the corner to glance down the alley, and he saw Wyatt coming up it from the far end. He had a baseball bat in his hand, taken, presumably, from the sporting goods store. The men gave each other a quick nod of acknowledgment, and then Phil ducked back around the corner before the lookout caught sight of him. He guessed it would take Wyatt another fifteen or twenty seconds to creep right up to the door, so he pressed himself up against the wall and took a few deep, evenly spaced breaths while counting down from twenty. When the countdown was over, he knew it was time to act. He drew in one last deep breath, and then stepped into the alley, keeping his .45 in his hand with his finger on the trigger, but tucking it behind his back, so it was hidden.

A surge of relief rushed through him when he saw Wyatt pressed up against the wall just behind the open door, ready to act.

"Hello?" Phil said, stepping up to the door. "Is anyone in there?"

"Get the fuck outta here, jerk-off," the man in the door growled. "Go on, move it."

"But I'm coming to see my friends who live here," Phil protested, doing his best to sound calm even though his heart was racing.

The man stepped out of the doorway and pointed his shotgun at Phil's chest. He was a tall, heavily-built man in his thirties or early forties. While his face was hidden by a balaclava, it was plain to see that his eyes were full of malice and cruelty. "Are you deaf or stupid or both, shithead?" he growled. "Get the fuck out of here before I put a hole in your chest. This is my building now, you stupid fuck. Move, now!"

That was when Wyatt moved. He darted out from behind the door and brought the baseball bat down in a woodchopping blow like an ax on the back of the man's skull. The man grunted and staggered forward, but he wasn't out yet. Phil lunged forward and yanked the shotgun out of the thug's hands, and before the stunned goon could react, Wyatt smashed the baseball bat into his head a second time. This time the man's body went limp, and he flopped to the ground like a clubbed fish.

"Nice work," Phil said.

Wyatt nodded and tossed the baseball bat aside and

then drew his .357 and .45 again. Phil quickly checked the shotgun over; it was a combat shotgun, and it was fully loaded, except for the one round that had been fired to blow open the door lock.

"I'd use that in the building if I were you," Wyatt said.

"I'm going to." Phil tucked his .45 into his belt and gripped the combat shotgun in both hands. "Let's do this."

Wyatt nodded. "These assholes aren't playing games. Shoot first, ask questions later."

"Roger that," Phil said. "Let's go."

They moved into the building, and they could hear the men talking in loud, harsh voices in the stairwell. They jogged up the stairs, moving as quickly as they could. But keeping their footfalls light and silent. Each man had his gun aimed out ahead of him; everything he saw was through the sights of his scope.

From upstairs came the sound of one of the men bashing on a door. They heard him viciously threatening whoever was inside the apartment, who clearly didn't want to let them in.

Driven on by a sense of urgency, both men hurried up the stairs at a faster pace, their hearts hammering. If these criminals were at Alice's door, Phil thought he'd open fire without a second thought and keep squeezing the trigger until every last one of them was dead.

When they got to the last set of stairs before Alice's floor, one of them yelled out, "That's it bitch, you're fucking dead!" A booming blast from a shotgun firing echoed down the stairs.

This spurred fresh urgency through Phil's veins. He raced up the last few stairs and burst out of the stairwell into the hallway. He saw that the men had just shot open Alice's door. There were four of them, all waiting to charge into her apartment.

"Hey!" he roared, possessed by righteous fury.

The men spun around, and the one who'd just shot open the door swung his shotgun in Phil's direction, but it was Phil's gun that thundered first. He fired two shots into the man's chest, and the force of the shots flung the man off his feet. As the others raised their firearms, Wyatt charged out from behind Phil, both guns blazing. With his left hand, he pumped a couple .45 bullets into the closest man's torso, while one well-aimed shot from the .357 blew another's skull wide open.

The farthest man, a tall, powerfully built man with tattoos covering his muscular arms and neck, opened fire wildly with his 9mm pistol, and Wyatt grabbed the back of Phil's shirt and yanked him down the stairs while the criminal sprayed the hallway with bullets. The thug emptied his whole magazine, and when Phil and Wyatt heard the empty clicking of the trigger, they raced out into the hallway again, only to see the back of the man as he dived down the staircase at the far end of the hallway.

Phil started to dash after him, his blood on fire with battle fury, but Wyatt lunged forward and grabbed his shirt again. "Let him go, man. It's over," he said, breathing hard.

Phil was panting, and his hands were shaking. He looked down at the three dead men in the hallway. Their blood was sprayed against the walls, and their bodies were limp. He'd killed them, and the whole thing felt like some surreal, terrible nightmare. He could hardly believe any of this was real and almost knelt down to touch one of the corpses to make sure that this was actually happening.

Before he could do that, though, he heard a voice that sent intense emotion surging through him.

"Phil," Alice gasped. "Oh my God, it is you, Phil. It really is you!" She threw down her gun, and with tears streaming down her cheeks, she rushed out of the apartment, the door of which had been blasted open, and flung her arms around her husband. Phil pulled his smoke mask off and embraced her tightly, with tears welling up in his own eyes and a lump rising in his throat.

"I've got you, Alice. You're safe now," he said hoarsely as they embraced. "Where's David? Is he okay?"

"I'm right here, Dad," David said, emerging cautiously from the apartment, his eyes wide and his pistol still in his hand. He stared down at the bodies on the floor and the blood sprayed across the walls, and his eyes grew even wider.

"Thank God you're both okay," Phil said. "Thank the Lord that you're both all right."

"I hate to break up the party," Wyatt said, "but the fire's spreading. We need to move." He pointed at the stairwell. Thick clouds of smoke were now billowing up it.

"I'll grab some food," Alice said, stepping away from her husband. "Give me ten seconds to throw as much as I can in a bag. We still have a long night to get through."

"I'll help," David said, eager to get away from the nightmarish sight of the bodies in the hallway.

"Hurry," Phil said. "We have to move fast."

Alice and David scrambled to shove as much food from the cupboards as they could into some spare gym bags. They also tossed in some water bottles, a portable gas stove, and some camping plates and cutlery.

"The smoke's getting thicker!" Wyatt yelled. "And I can see flames at the bottom of the stairwell! There's no more time. Go, go, go!"

Alice and David grabbed the gym bags and the large medical kit and raced out of the apartment. Wyatt, his pistols in his hands, keeping an eye out for the last thug, led the way down the stairs while Phil brought up the rear, also watching for the criminal in case he tried to ambush them from behind.

They got down to the second floor, but they had to stop there, for the entire ground floor was now a wall of flame.

"We're trapped," Alice gasped. "Oh God, we're trapped!"

14

"The fire escape!" Phil said. "Hurry, back up the stairs! And if that doesn't work, there's a lot of rope in the apartment."

They turned around and began to race back up the steps, but then, at the top of the stairwell, a masked face appeared. "You can all fucking burn!" he howled. It was the surviving invader, the one who'd gotten away. He tossed a Molotov cocktail into the stairwell, and it exploded into a billowing ball of flame. He tossed two more down the stairs and then fled.

Now the group was trapped between a wall of flames above and the raging inferno below. Acrid black smoke was quickly filling the entirety of the stairwell. Phil grabbed two more masks out of his backpack and shoved them into Alice and David's hands. "Hurry, put these on!"

"Onto this floor," Wyatt said, running up the stairs

to get off the stairwell and into the closest hallway. "We can break down the door of one of the empty apartments and use their fire escape."

As he stepped out into the hallway, though, he was greeted by a hail of bullets from the far end of the hallway. He jumped back into the stairwell and lost his footing and was only saved from tumbling back down the stairs by Phil, who caught him and helped him stay upright.

"Who's shooting?!" Phil demanded.

"I don't know. I couldn't see 'em. The hallway was filled with smoke. I don't know if it's a frightened resident or the same asshole who's trying to kill us," Wyatt growled.

"Hey!" Phil yelled, hoping that it was a resident who had been shooting. "We're not looters. We're just trying to get out of this building! The fire is spreading, and this whole place will be up in flames in minutes! Please just let us through!"

"Yeah, and you motherfuckers can all burn with it!" came the vicious reply. They now knew that it was the invader who had shot at them. To add emphasis to his vehement hate, he fired a few more bullets in their direction. He flung another Molotov cocktail at them, which exploded with a deep whoosh near the stairwell, blocking them from entering the hallway.

"That son of a bitch," Wyatt growled, his jaw clenched with rage. "I don't care if I burn. I'm gonna rip his damn head off!"

He moved to charge out into the flames consuming

the hallway, but Phil grabbed his arm and held him back. "Don't throw your life away on account of that scumbag," he said. He was as furious as Wyatt was, of course, but he forced himself to think rationally about their situation.

"Phil, what are we gonna do?" Alice demanded, almost overcome by hysteria. The flames were creeping up the stairway and seemed to have completely consumed the ground floor. The smoke in the stairwell was so thick now it was difficult to see, let alone breathe.

"We're stuck on the stairs, but there is a way out," Phil said, his mind racing at a million miles an hour. He'd always been able to thrive in situations of extreme pressure. "The stairwell windows, smash 'em!"

"We can't jump from this height!" Alice protested. "We'll break our legs at best, and likely die!"

"We're not going to jump," Phil said. "Remember, nothing electrical is live anymore." He pointed at the dead lights above them in the stairwell. "We're going to climb down."

"We can't. I left the rope in the apartment!" Alice said.

"Don't worry, I've got an idea," Phil said. "Wyatt, get me up on your shoulders, quick!"

Wyatt dropped down to his knees so Phil could get up onto them. When Wyatt stood, Phil was easily able to reach the ceiling. He pulled his knife out of his belt, pried the light fitting out and then ripped it out of the ceiling. "Lift me up a little higher," Phil said. Wyatt extended himself to his full height, and Phil was able to get his head inside the hole where the light fitting had been.

He was barely able to see anything, but it didn't take too much groping around to find a relatively thick electrical cable. He grabbed it and yanked it, ripping it out of its fittings, and he kept pulling until he encountered resistance. Then he pulled some more, until eventually, he couldn't pull any more of it out. "Let me back down!" he yelled to Wyatt, gripping the cable.

While Wyatt lowered him down to the ground, Phil kept a grip on the cable. "Help me pull all of this out!" he said once he was back on the ground.

Both men gripped the cable as if it were a rope in a tug-of-war, and they pulled as much of it out of the ceiling as they could. When they had a good length of it, Phil sawed through it with his knife, since there was no danger of being electrocuted. "Wyatt, tie one end around the banister," he instructed.

While Wyatt was tying one end of the cable into a sturdy knot around the steel banister, Phil smashed out the window with the butt of the shotgun and knocked out any remaining shards of glass until it was clear.

"Get your gloves on!" he said to David and Alice.

Alice had leather gloves in her bug-out bag, and she took these out and put them on.

"Davey, you go first. Remember how we do it when we abseil? Just like that son, just like that."

David nodded, trying to look confident in front of his father.

"Is the cable ready, Wyatt?" Phil asked.

Wyatt gave a quick, hard tug on the cable to test his knot. He was satisfied that it would hold, so he tossed the rest of the cable out of the window. It easily reached the ground and was more than thick enough to support the weight of even a very heavy man. "All ready," Wyatt said.

"Come on, Davey, time to go," Phil said. He and Wyatt helped David out of the window, and then David began lowering himself down the side of the building, gripping the cable and rappelling down to the ground, which was a good couple of yards down. The family had been abseiling for fun a number of times before, so everyone was familiar with the technique.

"Alice, you're next," Wyatt said, keeping an eye on David's progress. "All right, he's almost down. Come on, let's get you out the window."

Phil and Wyatt assisted Alice out the window, and then she too began to make her way down. Phil turned to Wyatt when Alice was near the ground. "You're next, buddy," he said. "I'll help you out the window."

"You should go," Wyatt said. "Your family needs you."

"The captain should always be last off the sinking ship, brother. No more arguing, you need to go."

Wyatt realized it was pointless to fight, so once Alice was almost on the ground, he climbed out of the window and started scrambling down the side of the building. The flames had engulfed the second floor now, and Phil was finding it hard to breathe, even with the mask on. Also, the steel banister was heating up from the nearby flames, and Phil was worried that if it got too hot, the cable housing would melt, weakening it significantly. "Come on, buddy, come on," he muttered, watching Wyatt descend and feeling his own anxiety rise as the flames and smoke grew in intensity and proximity.

Finally, just as the flames began gushing up the stairs alarmingly close to Phil, Wyatt got close enough to the ground to jump. Phil didn't waste another second, and he slung the shotgun over his shoulder with its strap and scrambled out of the window and scampered down the side of the building as fast as he could. The descent was hair-raising because halfway down, the flames started billowing out of the window Phil had climbed out of, and he knew it wouldn't be long before the cable melted and snapped. When he got close enough to the ground to jump, he did. He landed heavily and rolled to cushion the impact.

"You good, Phil?" Wyatt asked, helping him up.

"I'm good," he said. "Any sign of the bastard who tried to kill us?"

"That maniac probably ended up trapping himself in there with all those bombs he was tossing around," Wyatt muttered. "He couldn't have gotten out. He's probably burning to death as we speak. Anyway, he's not out here."

"We need to go," Alice said. She was very shaken-up but doing her best to be level-headed.

The whole building was aflame now, consumed by a massive inferno.

"Agreed," Phil said, dusting himself off. He got the shotgun back in his hands, and then led them out of the alley into the burning city, over which darkness was beginning to fall.

15

The group moved quickly through the streets, stopping only when they were a few blocks away from the burning buildings. They took shelter in the back room of an empty laundromat, rested and ate some of the food that Alice and David had taken from the apartment and rehydrated themselves with sports drinks. Wyatt and Phil took turns standing guard at the front of the laundromat while the others rested and ate. Aside from the glowing reds and oranges of the buildings on fire, there was almost no light in the city. Gas lamps could be seen burning in a number of windows, but the streets themselves were pitch black. The sounds of distant—and not-so-distant—gunfire continued to echo through the streets, as well as the odd explosion or two. No aircraft, military or civilian, was seen in the skies, and the group had still not seen any sign of law enforcement or the army.

"Where do we go from here?" Alice asked as she,

Phil, and David sat around the candlelit table, eating beans and sausages they'd heated up on the portable gas stove.

"My dad's truck is across the river, near the edge of the northern suburbs," Phil answered. "It'll be a long walk to get to it, four and a half, maybe five hours, depending on how quickly we can move through the streets, and how many obstacles are in our path."

"I can't do anything too strenuous," Alice said. She lifted up her blouse to show Phil the dressing on her abdomen.

"What happened?" he gasped, shocked. "Are you okay?"

"I'm all right," she said. "An explosion went off near me, and a piece of metal hit me. It was real close, and my ears are still ringing from it. I was wearing a stab-proof vest under my top, though. It saved my life. I managed to stitch up the wound myself, and I'll be okay as long as I don't do anything too difficult that'll bust the stitches open. I almost thought they'd break while I was scaling down the building, but thankfully they've held."

"I'm so glad you and Davey are okay," Phil said, putting his fork down and reaching across the table to hold Alice's hand with his right, and David's with his left. "I don't know what I would have done if either of you two had been hurt bad…or worse."

"We're all okay, and that's what counts," Alice said, squeezing Phil's hand tightly.

"Thanks for coming to get us, Dad," David said.

"When those guys blew open the door, I thought it was all over."

"I'm just thankful I got to you guys in time," Phil said. Everyone sat in emotion-drenched silence for a few moments, each of them feeling immensely grateful that they were safe and together, even if there were still a great amount of peril they still had to get through.

"What's our next move?" Alice said. "Are you sure we should move through the city in darkness? Maybe we should just wait out the night in here and move at first light."

Phil chewed on a spoonful of beans and shook his head. "No, we can't wait. Things have gotten way worse, way faster than I imagined they would just over the course of a day. People have already realized that no help will be coming from the government, the cops, or the army—at least not any time soon. It's going to make them even more desperate than they already are. After a night without food or water—which will be the reality of this situation for a lot of people—they'll turn this place into an even worse warzone than it already is. And as scary as it'll be moving around out there in the dark, it'll be a lot safer for us; nobody is going to be able to see us like they would in daylight. There'll be some dangerous people out; I know that for sure. But there'll be way more dangerous people prowling around, looking for victims in the light tomorrow."

"I guess you're right," Alice said. "I really don't like the thought of heading out there into the pitch black, but I know that as scary as it is, yeah, it'll be safer than moving around tomorrow during the day."

"I'm gonna go swap places with Wyatt so he can sit down and eat," Phil said. "After that, we need to get moving."

"You sure you've had enough, honey?" Alice said. "You need to have your energy levels up if you're gonna lead us safely out of here."

Phil took two bananas out of his bag. "I'm good, Alice. Don't worry about me. I've got plenty of energy for the trip ahead. Make sure Wyatt eats his fill when he sits down; I'll feel better knowing that he's working at his best too."

"I'll do that," Alice said.

Phil got up, picked up his shotgun, and walked over to the door to speak to Wyatt. "Hey brother, I'll take over the watch from here. You go sit down and eat."

"I'll do that." Wyatt's voice dropped in volume as he continued, and he glanced over his shoulder at David and Alice to check if they were listening in. "Hey, listen, I'm a little worried about something."

"Go on."

"Getting back across the river might be a challenge," Wyatt said. "I don't know who these sons of bitches are who are sowing all this chaos, but I think a lot of 'em are a lot more organized than we think. Something about this whole thing smells like a coordinated attack. Yeah, there are plenty of opportunistic looters, like those punks who tried to rape that girl earlier, but the ones we shot outside your wife's apartment, they looked like they were prepared and ready to attack people."

"I hear what you're saying, and a lot of this does feel like a terrorist attack," Phil said. "But how does that tie in with being worried about crossing the river?"

"If this is some sort of large-scale terrorist attack and they're doing their best to slaughter people and take over this city, they'll have blocked off all the bridges. They won't want people coming in, and they sure as hell won't be letting people out. Look, it's just a theory, and I don't know if it's the case; maybe those assholes were just opportunistic criminal scum, but we should consider the possibility that they're a lot more organized."

"I agree. Look, you go fill yourself up with some good, hot food. I'll have a think about an alternative means of getting across the river."

"You do that," Wyatt said, and he headed into the room to go eat with the others.

The most obvious means of getting across the river and out of the city was the rubber dinghy but going to where they'd left it would be a far less direct route than heading straight toward the northern suburbs, adding extra miles of walking and more hours to their journey. Plus, it was a gamble; chances were high that someone else had taken the dinghy by now. If they got there and found it gone, they would have made a long and dangerous journey for nothing.

"There has to be a better, more direct way," Phil murmured to himself, staring out at the firelit city skyline and the patches of impenetrable darkness between the areas lit by burning buildings. "A raft," he said after a while. "Yes…a raft, that'll do. But what materials?"

He thought about this for a while and then chuckled. The answer was simple and nearby. It wouldn't be a rugged or glamorous raft, but it would be enough to get them from one side of the river to the other quietly and away from any bridges.

The others got up from their meal after some time and made preparations to leave.

"What's the plan, Phil?" Wyatt asked. "You figured out how to get us across the river?"

"I have, yeah," Phil answered. "We need to make a quick stop at that sporting goods store where you picked up that baseball bat."

"All right," Wyatt said. "That ain't too far away. Let's go."

"You guys okay to go?" Phil said to David and Alice.

Alice drew in a deep breath. "We're ready," she said.

David simply nodded, trying to look more confident than he felt.

"Okay, let's do this," Phil said. He led them out into the pitch-black street.

Behind them, the flames from Alice's building, which was completely engulfed by fire now, lit up the whole block. She stared sadly at it, and Phil reached over to her and gently gripped her hand. "The ranch will be okay, and that's our home," he said softly. "I know we've lost a lot today, but we've still got each other and our home. We just have to get back there."

"Tread carefully," Wyatt said. "There's debris and broken stuff all over the place, and the last thing we need is someone with a sprained ankle or broken wrist from a fall that could have been prevented."

"Yeah," Phil added. "Keep your eyes open for danger but pay close attention to what's on the ground in front of you too."

They had to go back a block to get back to the sporting goods store, but getting there was easy enough because of the illumination from the burning building. Everyone kept their eyes peeled for danger, but the streets around here seemed completely deserted. Phil guessed that people had probably fled from the nearby buildings, fearing that the inferno would spread—which it likely would, soon enough.

"You guys wait outside," Phil said. "I'll just head in, grab what I need and come straight back out."

"You don't need any help in there?" Wyatt asked.

"I'll be two minutes," Phil said. "You guys keep an eye on the street and holler if you see any dangerous-looking people nearby."

"Will do," Wyatt said, his trusty .357 in his hand.

Phil, with his shotgun slung over his shoulder, headed into the store, which was easy enough; looters had long since smashed out the glass storefront. It was dark inside the store, but Phil took an emergency glow stick out of his backpack and activated it. He didn't want to use the gas lamps outside in the street for fear of attracting unwanted attention, but he figured it would be okay to use them in here. The eerie green glow from the glow stick lit up the inside of the store enough for Phil to see what he was doing and where he was going.

He made a beeline for the camping section, which was near the back of the store. He got there and started hurriedly browsing the shelves for what he needed… and that was when he heard the click of a pistol hammer being cocked close behind him. Before he could whip his shotgun up, a raspy voice spoke behind him.

"Drop the gun and get down on your knees, asshole. Do exactly what I say, right now, or I'll spray your goddamn brains all over those shelves."

16

---

*P*hil knew he had to act fast. The man
behind him, whoever he was, didn't have
any source of light himself and had presumably only
been able to sneak up on him after he'd lit up the glow
stick. With his heart pounding in his chest, he acted. In
one movement, he flung the glow stick across the store
to his left while diving to the ground to his right. He hit
the ground and rolled as darkness swallowed him, and
he scrambled to get behind a shelf.

The man behind him cursed with rage but didn't
shoot. "Fuckin' asshole!" he roared. "You think you can
come in here and just steal my stuff, you dirty thief!
Yeah, go ahead, you crawl around like the worm you
are. I'll find you! I can hear you over there, and I'm
gonna start shootin' in five seconds unless you throw
your gun over this way!"

"I'm no thief!" Phil called out. He now had his

shotgun in his hands and was crouched behind a shelf, aiming the firearm in the direction of the man, who seemed to be the owner of the store.

"What the hell are you doing in here if you ain't a thief?!" the man demanded. "It ain't like you were dropping in to say hi, you scumbag!"

"Okay, you're right, I need some stuff. But I'll pay for it, all right?" Phil answered, hoping he could negotiate his way out of this situation rather than having to shoot his way out.

"Phil, what's going on in there?!" Wyatt yelled from outside. He'd heard the commotion and had seen the glow stick being flung across the store.

"It's okay, Wyatt!" Phil called out. "Nothing's wrong. There's no problem here!" He then lowered his voice and spoke to the store owner. "We don't have a problem here, do we? My friend outside has a .357 in one hand and a .45 in the other, and my wife and son are also armed. We don't have to do this the hard way. I'm happy to pay for what I need."

"If anyone inside has a gun to my friend's head, I'm gonna make you seriously regret it!" Wyatt roared from outside.

The store owner knew he was outgunned and was no fighter anyway. "Okay, okay," he muttered. "No guns. I won't shoot."

"Throw your gun down," Phil said. "I swear I won't rob you. I'll pay for what I need."

"You throw yours down, and I'll throw mine down."

Phil sucked in a deep breath and chewed on his lip for a few moments. He didn't want to relinquish his firearm, but he decided that it would be a worthwhile show of goodwill to the store owner to do so. He tossed the shotgun in the man's direction. When the store owner heard the gun hit the ground, he threw his own gun down.

"All right," the man said, somewhat nervously. "There's it's done, I'm unarmed. What do you want?"

"I just need a few inflatable camping mattresses and a pump," Phil said. "That's all. I've got two hundred dollars on me, which you can take as payment. I'm sorry for coming in here like that, but…as you must have noticed, these are desperate times."

"I wouldn't recommend sleeping on the street tonight," the man said gruffly. "Why don't you go break into a hotel room or something, at least sleep on a real bed?"

"We don't need them for sleeping," Phil answered. "We're from out of town, and we need to get across the river. I don't want to try to cross any bridges because whoever has attacked us is probably guarding them. I'm planning to raft across a quiet spot on the mattresses."

The store owner sighed, and when he spoke again, he sounded like a broken man. "The whole world's gone to hell, just in the space of one day," he said, his voice cracking. "None of this feels real. It's like, it's like some insane nightmare I can't wake up from. My wife and kid are in the upstairs apartment, scared out of their goddamn minds. So many looters have come in here and stolen things, mostly baseball bats and shit they can use as weapons, but also plenty of camping goods and stuff. I'm just scared that once they've cleaned out my shelves, they'll come for my home upstairs."

Phil stood up; it was clear now that the danger had passed, and that there would, thankfully, be no fighting. "Do you have any light up there?" he asked. "Food, water, the essentials?"

"I've taken all the camping supplies, snacks, sports drinks, and stuff from the store and kept 'em upstairs. We've got gas stoves and everything up there, so I ain't worried about that. It's people coming to take that stuff by force I'm worried about, when they figure out we're up there."

"You'll need to make sure you barricade the entrance to your apartment well," Phil said. "But the best thing to do is not let anyone know you're up there. Don't use lights at night, or if you do, make sure they can't be seen from outside. I don't know how long this is going to go on for, but I suspect it'll be a long time. Weeks, months, possibly longer. I'd offer you some of our food, but it sounds like you've got enough of that."

"Thanks," the man said. "All right, well, go get your light, figure out what you want, and then you'd best be on your way. Moving around in here with a light is gonna attract attention."

"I'll do that," Phil said. He got up and groped his way through the darkness until he got to an area illuminated by his discarded glow stick. He picked it up, headed back to the camping section, and there he finally saw the man he'd been talking to. The store owner was a middle-aged, balding man with a worry-worn face, and Phil felt quite sorry for him. He wished there was more he could do to help the man and his family but realized he was powerless to assist him in any meaningful way.

He took three double-sized inflatable camping mattresses off the shelf, as well as a hand pump, and then took two hundred-dollar bills out of his wallet and handed them to the man.

"Again, I'm sorry for coming in like this," Phil said. "And I hope you and your family are able to stay safe during these difficult times."

The man nodded, quietly taking the money from Phil and stuffing it into his pocket. The look of fear and worry in his eyes was immense and haunting. "Thanks," the store owner murmured. "Good luck to you and your family. I hope y'all get home safely."

He and Phil picked up their respective firearms, and then looked at each other for a few more moments before Phil gave him a nod and then turned and walked out. He stuffed the glow stick into his backpack and turned around to look one final time at the store owner before he stepped out into the street...but the man had already been swallowed up by the darkness.

"What the hell happened in there?" Wyatt asked. "Who were you talking to?"

"Doesn't matter," Phil said sadly, the haunting look

on the man's face burned into his mind. "He's stuck in this place. I hope he and his family will be okay…but I don't think they will be. I don't think anyone in this city will be. Come on," he said, as emotion welled up inside him. "We'd better move."

he group kept to the shadows, moving fast, talking as little as they could, and avoiding any signs of life, or any areas where fires and burning buildings lit up the streets. The darkness was almost impenetrable, but their eyes soon grew accustomed to it. While visibility was by no means clear, each of them was at least able to see far enough ahead that they wouldn't trip over obstacles or debris.

Phil led them through the deserted streets, going on as direct a route as he could toward the main bridge that led out of the city into the northern suburbs. For the most part, the city was eerily silent, but this silence was often broken by the sound of gunfire, the odd explosion, glass and other items being smashed, as well as screams of terror and yells of aggression and violence. From somewhere on the south side of the city was the distant roar, like faraway ocean waves, of what sounded like a large crowd rioting. There certainly appeared to be a lot more fires on the south side of the city, and things seemed to grow quieter and darker the farther north they traveled, but Phil did not allow himself to slip into any sort of complacency. He knew danger could spring out from anywhere, especially when least expected, and he made sure his senses were on full alert for the entirety of the journey.

The four of them stopped after around an hour of walking, stepping into an inky-black alley to have some snacks and water and take a quick break before moving on. After Phil and Wyatt had done a quick sweep of the alley and made sure that nobody was hiding in it, Phil finally gave the go-ahead to the others to sit down and speak. They gathered some discarded crates from the alley and sat down to rest their weary legs.

"How much longer, Dad?" David asked. "I don't recognize this part of the city…not that I can see much in this darkness anyway." He reached into his pocket, almost subconsciously, and fingered his phone. Even though he knew the device would never work again, he hadn't been able to bring himself to throw it away, and old habits were hard to break.

"We've got about another forty minutes of walking before we're at the river," Phil said. "This is the industrial section of the city we're heading into. Warehouses, packing plants, manufacturing workshops, auto mechanics, and other such places. I don't expect we'll run into too many people around here, but don't let your guard down—that goes for all of you."

"Here," Alice said, handing out snacks and sports drinks from her backpack to everyone. "We have to keep up our energy. Eat up."

"Thanks, honey," Phil said, taking a chocolate bar and a pack of nuts from her. "How's your wound feeling?"

"The dressing's still in place, and the stitches are holding up, so I'm good, as long as I don't have to do anything too strenuous."

"Touch wood, it'll just be a very long walk," Phil said. "The only mildly strenuous thing we'll have to do is raft across the river, but you and Davey can go on one mattress, and he can do the hard work, right son?"

"Sure, Dad," David said, trying his best to sound confident.

"How are we gonna get these mattresses across the water?" Wyatt asked. "You didn't pick up any paddles to go with 'em."

"I didn't want to have to lug paddles across the city," Phil said, "seeing as we're already carrying enough stuff. We can pick up some two by fours or discarded poles nearer the river. There are plenty of broader sections where the current isn't particularly strong, and we don't have to get across in a perfectly straight line anyway. As long as we can get from one side of the river to the other, that's all we need to accomplish, and some makeshift paddles will allow us to do that."

Before anyone else could ask any questions, a distant but very recognizable sound cut through the night—a sound that none of them had expected to hear

—dirt bikes. In the gloom, all four of them stared at each other with wide eyes and expressions of surprise on their faces.

"I thought all the cars and bikes and stuff were dead, Dad!" David exclaimed.

"They are, son, I promise you that," Phil said, "except for one important exception: cars and motorcycles made prior to the mid-seventies, especially those with simpler electrical mechanisms and motors, like two-stroke dirt bikes. Like your old Yamaha on the ranch."

"It's still going strong," Wyatt said to David. "I took it for a ride earlier."

"Is that why you insisted on keeping that old bike around instead of getting me a new one?" David asked, an expression of understanding and realization coming across his face.

"That's it, son," Phil said. "And aren't you glad you still have a working Yamaha, old seventies model that it is, instead of a new KTM or something that's dead and will never work again?"

"I guess I am. I won't ever complain about the old bike again, Dad."

"Never mind all that," Alice said, cutting in. She had a look of worry drawn across her face. "Who's riding dirt bikes through this city now, in the middle of the night? And why are there so many of them? I don't like this. I don't like it at all."

Now that the sound was becoming louder and clearer, they could hear that there were indeed a number of dirt bikes. It sounded as if there were a whole pack of them, a dozen or even more. Worryingly, accompanying the buzzing and whining chorus of two-stroke motors was the sound of automatic gunfire, coming from approximately the same direction as the moving bikes.

"If it were one man on a single vintage bike," Phil said, looking grave, "I could pass it off as someone desperate looking for supplies or lost family members, but a whole gang of guys who all happen to have early seventies or sixties model bikes? Hell no. There's something really worrying about this whole thing."

"Terrorists," Wyatt grunted. "They've gotta be. Whoever launched this whole attack was well prepared for the aftermath. Only reason a large group of guys would have the kind of bikes that would survive an EMP attack is that they were prepared for it and planning something. And the sound of automatic weapons firing tells me that whatever they were planning sure as hell ain't good."

"Come on," Phil said, standing up. "We'd better move. Those bikers are still far away, but whatever they're doing, we don't want to give 'em any opportunity to get close to us. We need to get the hell out of here as fast as possible and get across that river."

Everyone got up, packed their things, and got moving. Phil led them swiftly but carefully through the darkness, his senses on full alert. David and Alice followed closely behind him while Wyatt brought up the rear, watching their backs.

They came across one or two burning warehouses and saw signs that others had been broken into and looted, but for the most part, they saw no other people, at least not close up. The gang of bikers seemed to be getting steadily closer, and the increasingly loud and clear sounds of their motors put speed into the group's steps and got their hearts pounding with rising anxiety.

"We're almost there," Phil said, doing his best to reassure everyone. "Just a few more blocks and we'll be at the river."

They emerged from an alley onto a large, broad street. There were a number of abandoned vehicles on the street—like there were on all of the other city streets—but there were by no means so many that the entire street was clogged, as was the case in most of the city. These streets around the warehouse and packing districts were very wide and open to allow heavy-goods vehicles to move around. This worried Phil; if the bikers got to this section, they would be able to ride around with a lot more speed and ease than in the rest of the city, where they were no doubt having to weave between abandoned cars and ride on the sidewalks.

Also worrying was the fact that there were a number of big-box stores in this area, which would no doubt be prime targets for raiders. Unfortunately for the group, there were no more alleys here, and to get to the river, they would have to travel along some of the larger streets for a few blocks.

"Everyone, keep your eyes wide open," Phil said to the others before they all stepped out onto the street.

"We're going to have to be moving around in the open here. It's dark, yeah, but it's still a risk. We're going to stick to the middle of the street while we move."

"The middle?" Wyatt asked. "What for?"

"Cover," Phil answered. "We moved from car to car; they're the only cover we've got here. If those bikers come along, we hide under the nearest car until they're gone. Judging by what I can hear, there are a lot more of them than there are of us. We're outnumbered and outgunned, if most of 'em have automatic weapons, which it sure sounds like."

"Got it," Wyatt said.

They stepped out onto the street, wary and ready for whatever may come their way. At least two of the warehouses along the long, straight road were on fire. This was bad news for the group, not only because it indicated the presence of raiders and looters, but also because of the light the raging blazes threw onto the street. When they passed the burning warehouses, they would be fully visible to unfriendly eyes, and there was nothing they could do about it.

"Move fast, everyone," Phil said, setting off at a jog. "Alice, if this is too strenuous, let me know."

"Keep it to a slow jog, and I'll be okay," she said.

They jogged along the empty street, passing empty cars as well as large eighteen-wheelers, left abandoned along with their full loads. Outside one big-box store, a group of six or seven armed men was keeping watch, and they had set up fires burning in steel oil drums all around the perimeter of their warehouse. Phil kept the abandoned vehicles between them and the armed men, who watched them pass in grim, terse silence.

"Don't look at 'em, just keep moving," Phil said in a low voice to his group. "They're just protecting their property."

They hurried past the big-box store, and finally, they saw a most welcome vista, illuminated by a burning building on its edge: the river, the broad swathe of water glistening with thousands of sparkles of orange, yell and red from the nearby inferno.

"Almost there," Phil said. "A few hundred yards, guys. Quickly."

Then, however, terror flooded through their veins, driving out the surge of hope that the sight of the water had provided. Blasting out of a side street onto the street they were on, and driving a wedge between them and the river, came the biker gang.

---

*P*hil acted immediately. "Wyatt, under the truck ahead of us, David and Alice, under this SUV just behind us, move it!"

The bikers had bright LED headlamps on their helmets. This was another indication to Phil that, whoever they were, they had been prepared for this situation—they had to have protected these headlamps in Faraday cages during the EMP strike. He briefly wondered what other technology they had protected, but he didn't have too much time to ponder this, for the blazing white beams from their headlamps seared through the darkness, flooding the long, dark street in front of them with light.

Phil and his group were in a patch of darkness, having gone past the oil drum fires of the big-box store, but this darkness wouldn't remain in place for very long, for the bikers were already accelerating down the street.

"Go, go, move, quickly!" Phil urged, helping Alice get under the large SUV they'd just passed.

David was already under the vehicle, his heart pounding and his eyes wide.

As soon as Alice was under the truck, Phil dashed a few yards ahead to the truck where Wyatt was hiding, keeping his body crouched and his head low. He discarded his backpack and dived to the ground and scrambled under the truck just as the white glow of the first of the bikers' headlamps swept across the vehicle.

With his heart hammering in his chest and his shotgun gripped tight in his hands, Phil lay on the street under the truck. The first of the motorcycles raced past to the right of the truck, followed quickly by the next, this one racing past the left of the vehicle. The other bikes zipped past, too, all speeding past in rapid succession. Phil and Wyatt held their breath, as did Alice and David, nobody daring to make the slightest move. All of them were praying that none of the bikers had seen them scurrying under the vehicles. As the final few bikes sped past the truck and the SUV, hope swelled within each member of the group; it seemed that they hadn't been spotted.

Phil heard the first of the bikes gearing down and coming to a stop near what seemed to be the big-box store and guessed that the bikers had come here to raid it. As bad as he felt for the men guarding their store, he knew that the conflict that was no doubt about to erupt would provide enough of a distraction for him and his family to slip away unnoticed by the bikers and escape.

Whatever hope he had of remaining undiscovered, though, was dashed when the final two motorcycles skidded to a stop alongside the truck, one on each side of it.

The bikers left the motors running and kicked out their bikes' kickstands and dismounted. Phil stared at the closest biker's boots, mere inches away from him, and slipped his finger onto the trigger of the shotgun, slowly and silently aiming at the man's ankles. To Phil's side, Wyatt was doing the same with his revolver.

"We saw someone go under this truck," the one biker said. "Whoever you are under there, come out, c'mon, we just wanna talk."

Wyatt glanced across at Phil, who met his gaze and quietly shook his head. The men remained silent.

"Listen, assholes," the other said, his voice gruff and harsh, "we know you're under there. Come out now or we toss a fucking grenade under the truck."

"I'm not gonna say it again, you chicken-shit little motherfuckers," the first biker said, his voice a lot more aggressive now. "This is your last chance to come out from under there in one piece. I've got a grenade in my hand, and I'm about to pull the fucking pin."

Up ahead, Phil could hear a heated yelling exchange going on between the bikers and the men guarding the store. He had no doubt that these bikers were at best opportunistic raiders and, at worst, terrorists who were part of the group that had orchestrated the whole attack. There was no time to think or to hesitate. If they wanted to escape, they would have to act immediately.

Phil turned to shoot an intense gaze at Wyatt, and the army veteran knew exactly what this look meant: start shooting. Just as both of them were about to squeeze their respective triggers, though, a firefight broke out outside the big-box store. The crackling gunfire behind them provided the perfect impetus for Phil and Wyatt to act. Each of them fired their weapons simultaneously, and at point-blank range like this, there was no chance of missing. Phil's blast from his shotgun took both of the man's feet off, blowing his flesh and bone to shreds, while Wyatt's .357 round smashed a destructive passage through both of his adversary's ankles. Both bikers fell, screaming to the ground, but they didn't scream for very long. The moment their torsos hit the ground, Phil and Wyatt pumped them full of bullets. The men were dead in the blink of an eye, and Phil knew that now was the time to move.

"Out, out, hurry, move it, damn it!" he roared at Alice and David. His heart was pounding, and his blood was charged with the energy of combat. He scurried out from under the truck and jumped to his feet, his shotgun at the ready.

The rest of the bikers were engaged in a fierce battle with the store defenders down the road and were so focused on their own fight that they hadn't noticed the gunshots from Phil and Wyatt—or, at least, Phil was praying that was the case.

"Take his headlamp!" Phil instructed, looking over the hood of the truck at Wyatt, who had just scrambled out from under the truck. He snatched the headlamp off the helmet of the dead biker at his feet. He looked down and saw an AK-47 on the ground, the firearm the dead biker had dropped. His combat shotgun was almost out of ammo now, and he had no more shotgun ammunition on him, so he discarded it and picked up the AK instead. He also took a spare ammunition clip for the AK from the dead man and tucked it under his belt. "Davey, get over here, move it!" he yelled.

They could now see the firefight happening a hundred or so yards behind them. The bikers had parked their dirt bikes around the rear of an abandoned eighteen-wheeler, and they were using it and some other abandoned vehicles for cover. Most of the defenders had been killed, and only two men were still returning fire at the bikers from behind some bags of cement they were using as makeshift sandbags. Phil watched, both fascinated and horrified, as one of the bikers unclipped a grenade from his belt, pulled the pin and threw it. His aim was true. It cleared the cement bag barrier and exploded with a devastating bang a half-second later before the defenders could even think of reacting. Their fire fell silent; they were all dead now. The bikers stopped shooting and whooped out harsh cheers and shouts of triumph. It was only a matter of seconds before they realized that two of their number were missing, and since the bikes were still standing with their motors running next to the truck, they'd know exactly where they were.

"Davey, take this and get on the bike," Phil said, his tone urgent as he shoved the headlamp into David's hands. "You're gonna drive your mother, and Wyatt's gonna drive me. We're not going to the river down that way; we have to outrun the bikers first. Take a right at the end of this street, okay, go one block and then turn left. Go into the park and take a right onto the cycling path that runs along the river. Keep going as fast as you safely can until you pass a footbridge on your left. If there are people guarding the bridge, keep going, do you understand? If not, stop there, but if there are guards, keep going until you get to the statue of a man on horseback, and wait for us there. If we don't get there in ten minutes, you and your mom need to get across the river yourselves."

"Dad, I—"

"There's no time, Davey!" Phil yelled. "Get on the bike and go! Now!"

David was too overwhelmed to do anything but what his father told him, so he slipped the headlamp on and hopped onto the bike.

Phil gave Alice a quick, tight hug and a kiss. "Go on, honey, get on the back of the bike. You know Davey's a great rider. You'll be safe with him."

With tears in her eyes, she nodded and hurried over to the motorcycle and climbed onto the back.

"Tony, Jake! What the fuck are you clowns doing down there?" one of the bikers yelled from up the street. They still hadn't noticed that their friends were dead. "Y'all ain't gettin' shit from this store, mother-fuckers! We did the shootin', so we do the lootin'. You assholes can keep watch! Get over here. What the fuck are y'all doing down there?"

"Wyatt, you're driving!" Phil said.

Alice, meanwhile, had gotten onto the back of David's bike. In the gloom, the bikers couldn't see what was going on, but they'd know something was up as soon as the group took off in the opposite direction. Phil knew they had to get as much of a head start on them as possible if they wanted to have any hope of escape.

"I'm ready," Wyatt said. He was seated on the bike, his guns holstered.

Phil climbed onto the back of Wyatt's bike but sat back-to-back with him, facing backward, with the AK-47 in his hands so he could shoot at the bikers if they started pursuing them. It was now or never; they had to flee while the window of opportunity for escape was still open.

"Davey, go!" Phil yelled. "And don't stop until you get to the bridge or the statue! Go, go, go!"

David clicked the bike into gear and took off at speed, spinning the rear wheel as he launched.

"Stay close behind him, brother," Phil said to Wyatt. "You go, too. Go, go!"

Wyatt grunted wordlessly, and then took off, racing into the darkness with his headlamp lighting the way. Behind them, the bikers yelled out shouts of confusion, and a few of them hopped onto their bikes and raced over to the truck, where they saw the dead bodies of their comrades and realized what had happened.

"Some sons of bitches killed Tony and Jake and took their rides!" one biker yelled. "There they go, get those motherfuckers!"

The other bikers roared out howls of fury and jumped on their bikes, racing down the street in pursuit of Phil and his group. The chase was on.

*P*hil watched grimly as a dozen bright headlamps came charging down the street behind him. He and his group had gotten a good head start on the bikers, but because they were two to a bike, the extra weight would slow them down and the bikers wouldn't take long to catch up. Phil's only hope was that he could shoot enough of his pursuers off their bikes to deter the rest from continuing the chase.

While the extremely bright headlamps made it easy for the bikers to navigate the pitch-black streets, it also meant that they became easy targets. All Phil had to do was aim for the piercing lights and fire. Of course, seeing as he was being bounced around on the back of the bike and squeezing his thighs to the point of burning pain just to hang on, this was a lot easier said than done. Digging his knees into the tail end of the bike to try to stabilize himself, he raised the AK to his shoulder and tried to take aim at the closest of the headlamps as the bikers gained on them.

The combination of moving like this and being shrouded in thick darkness made zeroing in on the bikers nigh on impossible, but Phil could at least get a vague sense of aim in, and when he thought he was as on target as he could be, he squeezed off a few rounds at the leading biker. The AK chattered in his hands, the muzzle flare bright against the gloom, but his shots missed, and the bikers kept coming.

"Shit," Phil muttered, clenching his jaw and squeezing his thighs and knees tight as he tried to better stabilize himself.

Before he could unleash another burst of fire, though, some of the bikers started shooting, firing pistols with their left hands while keeping their right on their throttles. Their view of Phil and his group was a lot murkier than the view Phil had of them, so they were mostly just firing into the dark and hoping they got a lucky shot in. Even so, the danger of one of those bullets hitting home was there, and Phil and Alice—on the backs of the bikes—were in most danger of being hit.

Driven by the urgency of being shot at, Phil did his best to up his concentration and fired off another few rounds at the bikers. This time one of his shots hit home, and he saw one of the leading bikers' headlamps jerk up and back and then tumble wildly into the darkness as the man ragdolled across the street, while his bike went down and skidded along the road in a spectacular shower of orange sparks.

Seeing their comrade go down like this didn't stop the other bikers, though; instead, it simply made them madder, and they fired off angry bursts of shots from their pistols, while steadily getting closer to their quarry.

Up ahead of Phil, David reached the end of the street and veered around the corner in a fast turn that had Alice shrieking with fright and got the right foot peg of the bike dragging along the street in a spray of bright sparks.

"Hang on, Phil!" Wyatt yelled over his shoulder as he entered the turn, sweeping through it at speed, leaning the bike over low.

As Wyatt straightened up the bike, the first couple of bikers swooped through the curve as well. They were illuminated by the blazing inferno of a nearby building on fire, and Phil took this opportunity, seeing the men in bright light like this, to fire at them again, unleashing a long, hammering burst of fire in a deathly arc. He was getting more accustomed to shooting from the back of the bike like this, and this time his aim was better. Two more of them went down, their bikes sliding and cartwheeling in eruptions of sparks, their bodies tumbling and bouncing across the unyielding surface of the street.

As more of them sped through the corner, Phil fired off another burst of rounds at them and took out another one. Even then, though, the bikers didn't halt their pursuit; they only became more enraged.

Before Phil could shoot again, Wyatt grunted a warning from behind him. "Hold on, another corner coming up!" This time the speeding motorcycle tipped over to the other side, and then they were into the park.

Ahead of them, David veered around a dead body—someone who had been shot and robbed of their bicycle during the earlier chaos of the day—lying across the bicycle path, but Wyatt didn't see the corpse until too late, and he ran right over it. He managed to keep the bike upright, but the cadaver served as a ramp, launching the bike into the air, and it came down with such a violent jolt that Phil was almost hurled off the back. The AK flew out of his hands and clattered off the path into the bushes, but Phil couldn't draw his pistol because he was flailing too desperately with his arms, trying to find a secure part of the bike he could grab onto to stabilize himself before he fell off.

He managed to get his fingers around a section of the subframe, and for a few terrifying seconds, it was all he could do to hold on for dear life, as Wyatt sped along the winding bicycle path, weaving and zooming around obstacles in the dark. Finally, however, Phil managed to stabilize himself enough that he was able to sit upright again, and he saw the ominous lights of his pursuers coming after them through the park.

Cursing himself for dropping the AK-47, he drew his .45 and squeezed off a few shots in the direction of the bikers, but none hit home. He had extra ammo clips for the .45, but they were all in the backpack, and there would be no way of getting them out without stopping and getting off the bike—and stopping now would mean certain death. Phil prayed that the footbridge would be open; it might be their only way out.

He fired off a couple more shots at the bikers, who were getting steadily closer. Again his shots hit nothing but air, and he was desperately aware of the fact that he now only had two or three bullets left in the gun.

"The bridge is open!" David yelled from up ahead, his voice only barely audible over the rushing wind. "It's open, Dad. It's open!"

"Go over it and wait on the other side!" Phil yelled. Now that he knew the bridge was open, a plan began to come together in his mind, but it would have to be speedily enacted if it were to work.

The footbridge was a strongly curved, elegant structure of iron and wood, and it was very narrow so that only two people walking abreast could cross it at a time. David rode the motorcycle up the steps and onto the bridge and then navigated it as quickly as he could.

"Stop the bike halfway across the bridge, then get off and run!" Phil yelled at Wyatt.

"What? *Why?*"

"Just do it. It's our only chance!"

Wyatt rode up the stairs and then got onto the bridge, and when he got halfway across—the highest point of the arch of the bridge—he slammed on the brakes, getting the bike's tires squealing as he brought it to a sudden stop. As Phil had instructed, he kicked out the kickstand, hopped off the bike and sprinted the rest of the way, leaving the bike running in the middle of the footbridge.

Phil scrambled off the bike just as his pursuers got to the foot of the bridge. He took aim with the .45…but not at the bikers. He shot a hole clean through the bike's fuel tank, and gasoline started pouring out of both the entry and exit holes. He jogged a short distance away as the first of the bikers rode up onto the bridge in pursuit, dropping down onto his hands and knees and fumbling in his pocket, until finally, his fingers curled triumphantly around what they'd been seeking: his Zippo.

The trail of gasoline reached him, and he lit it up with the Zippo. With a whoosh, the gasoline caught fire, and the flame raced back along the gas trail toward its source, the bike's leaking fuel tank. The biker reached the bike just as the flame got into the tank. The motorcycle exploded into a fireball, and the biker was engulfed by flames. The screaming man ran around on fire for a few moments before leaping off the bridge into the black water twenty feet below to douse the flames, while his companions gathered on the city side of the bridge, shooting blindly into the darkness and screaming insults at Phil and the group, who were now hiding behind the large concrete pillars on the suburban side of the river, with the headlamps turned off.

The bikers wouldn't be able to cross the bridge until

the flaming motorcycle had burned out, and Phil guessed that that would be at least another fifteen or twenty minutes, enough time to get away from the bikers.

They waited in silence for the bikers to stop shooting, which they did after a while.

"Come on, everybody," Phil whispered to them. "Let's go, nice and quiet now, nice and quiet."

They tiptoed away and melted into the inky shadows of the trees. They had finally made it out of the city, but they were nowhere near safety just yet.

2 0

*P*hil didn't know whether the bikers would come after them, or whether they'd give up and return to the city to continue raiding, but he had to assume that they'd continue their pursuit.

"Come on, everyone. We have to move fast," he said, jogging along the path through the trees. He kept the headlamps off, for the lights would act as beacons to their enemies. It was difficult and somewhat dangerous to jog along the path in almost complete darkness, and he hoped he wouldn't trip over anything and hurt himself. As risky as moving with speed through the dense darkness was, though, the consequences of not moving fast enough and getting caught by the bikers were far worse. "Let's go, come on, move, move!" he urged.

The others didn't need to be told twice. Adrenalin was racing through their veins after the drama of the bike chase, and their hearts were pounding. Alice's wound was hurting, and she suspected that some of the stitches might have broken during the chaos of the motorcycle chase, but she couldn't stop now. She bit her lip and forced herself to stay silent, despite the stabbing pains in her midriff.

After ten minutes of hasty blundering through the shadows, they emerged from the park onto one of the main streets of the northern suburbs.

"Which way from here?" Wyatt asked.

"The truck's at least a two, two-and-a-half-hour walk from here if we take the shortest route," Phil answered, "but that route will put us on some of the main streets, which we obviously want to stay off. In fact, we want to keep off anything even resembling a street if we can help it."

"Don't you think the bikers will expect us to keep off the main streets, though, Dad?" David asked. "Maybe by taking the shortest and most obvious route, we can use, like, what's it called, reverse psychology on them. They wouldn't imagine we'd do something that obvious, so they'll be looking for us on the backroads."

"You might be right, but if they catch us on a main street, we're gonna be in a world of trouble. And there are other dangers besides those bikers that we might run into on a main street. I don't think it's worth taking that kind of risk, even if it might fool the bikers for a while."

"Who do you think they were?" Alice asked. "I couldn't believe it when I heard the sound of working motors and saw those LED headlamps. Do you think they were the ones who orchestrated the attack?"

Phil shook his head. "I doubt it. They seemed too stupid and thuggish to have masterminded anything like that. They may have been part of a cell connected to a far larger and more sinister terrorist group, though. They seemed like grunts, on the ground, doing the dirty work of their masters. Or they may have just been preppers with an inclination toward evil. Not all of us who prepared for the downfall of organized society are good people. Some people have been waiting for this day like hungry wolves, and those scumbags may have just been some people like that. It doesn't matter, though. The fact is that such people are out there, and they're extremely dangerous. We have to be hyper-alert and prepared."

"I've got all the preparation I need right here," Wyatt growled, holding his .357 up in front of his face. "Let 'em try mess with us again. Just let the bastards try..."

"Everyone needs to have their guns in their hands from this point on," Phil said. "Get 'em out, and let's keep moving. We've wasted enough time standing around talking."

"But, uh, Dad, you haven't said which way we're going from here," David said.

"We're going to stick to the river as far as we can," Phil said. "As long as we stay under the cover of the trees, we've got some protection from the bikers and any other enemies we may encounter. In here, we've got cover we can fire behind, and because of the trees and bushes, they can't swarm us."

"But that'll take us well over four hours, closer to five by my reckoning, to get to the truck," Wyatt said. "Going around the big bend in the river will add a couple of difficult miles to this trip."

"We're not going to follow the course when it gets to the bend," Phil said. "River's Edge High is there, and if we cut through the school, it'll take a few miles off our trip. By cutting through the school, I'm hoping we can get to the truck in just under three hours."

"You don't think it might be dangerous to cut through the school?" Alice asked.

"It'd be about as dangerous as walking along any of these suburban streets," Phil said. "I don't think that anyone will be in the school, though. Besides looting the cafeteria and kitchens for food, there isn't much there that raiders would be after."

"They might want computers and TVs and stuff," David said.

"I doubt the kind of people we're worried about would be going after computers, son. The most dangerous ones will know that all electronic items are nothing but dead weight now. There might be some low-level idiots stealing computers and TVs there, but a few warning shots should be enough to keep morons like them away from us. Come on, enough arguing now; let's go." Phil's tone was firm and authoritative, and everyone knew that it was pointless to continue arguing. Without another word, Phil set off, heading back into the pitch-black darkness of the trees at a brisk pace, and the others followed wordlessly behind him.

After fifteen minutes of fast walking through the darkness, they heard the sound of the motorcycles again—but this time, the sound was clearly coming from across the river. The bikers, it seemed, had stayed inside the city. While this realization brought a measure of relief to the group, they were careful not to let down their guard, for there could well be many more dangers in store for them here in the suburbs.

It didn't take too long for their eyes to become accustomed to the darkness, and while they certainly couldn't see like cats, they were at least able to make out obstacles in the path and perceive their surroundings with a degree of clarity. Even so, everyone tripped over bumps and other small obstacles in the path regularly, although none of these stumbles were bad enough to send anyone crashing to the ground.

They half-ran, half-walked in silence, their eyes and ears peeled for any hint of danger. Across the broad river, the city was burning. There were more fires now than ever, and it appeared that at least a quarter of the city, perhaps even more, had been engulfed in the spreading inferno. The sluggish river sparkled and gleamed in tones of orange, red, and yellow, quietly reflecting the terrible chaos the group had managed to escape from. Distant sounds of gunfire and screams and shouts resounded across the water like eerie echoes of a nightmare. There was also a deep and frightening roar, like the faraway sound of ocean waves crashing against a shore—the sound of a huge crowd rioting.

From the suburbs just beyond the narrow strip of trees that lined the side of the river, there were also scattered echoes of gunfire and the occasional shout or scream, although, for the most part, the suburbs were shrouded in complete darkness and silence, with the odd building on fire here or there in the distance. Phil suspected that most people here were hiding out in their houses with all the doors and windows locked, and those who owned guns were no doubt gripping them in their hands. In a few windows, they saw gas lamps burning, but most of the houses were completely dark.

After around an hour and a half of steady walking, they reached the big bend in the river. From that point on, they would need to head out of the cover of the trees and cut through the large high school.

"Let's stop and have a quick drink and a snack," Alice suggested. She also wanted to take a look at her wound, which she felt had gotten worse. She was light-headed and woozy and suspected she was losing blood. She didn't want to alarm Phil, though, and knew that they needed to keep going until they reached the truck.

Phil was also of the mind that it would be a good idea to stop and have a quick snack to replenish their energy. After cutting through the school, they'd have to hike through the woods in darkness for half an hour before they got to the truck. He was feeling weary, even though he was very fit, and he knew that everyone else would be feeling quite worn-out too. "Good idea," he said to his wife. "We need to keep our energy up, especially for this last push."

While the rest of them ate, Alice excused herself from the group, saying she needed to use the bathroom in the bushes. She went behind a large tree, then took out her Zippo and flicked it on. Her eyes were so accustomed to the darkness that even the weak glow of the flame seemed almost blinding, and she had to keep her eyes half-closed until she got used to the light.

When she was able to open her eyes fully, she looked down and was alarmed to see that the lower front half of her blouse was soaked with blood, as was the top part of her jeans. The stitches had definitely burst, probably during the motorcycle chase, and the wound had been bleeding since then. She now understood why she was feeling so weak. She lifted up her blood-soaked blouse and saw that the dressing was dark and wet, soaked with blood. "Shit," she muttered. In her haste to escape the apartment, she had left her main medical kit there, and wouldn't be able to stitch up the wound again, at least not until they got to the truck, which had another large first aid kit in it.

Alice didn't know what she was going to do. She doubted she could make it all the way to the truck without passing out, but she couldn't rest here. They had to get to the truck, but how, if she was growing ever weaker? She couldn't very well ask any of the others to carry her; they were all exhausted enough

147

already. She thought briefly about cauterizing the wound with a hot knife, but quickly realized that this would likely cause more damage than it would solve; it didn't work in real life the way it did in movies.

Then the answer came to her: the school. If they could get into the school buildings, she could find the nurse's room, where there would almost certainly be the equipment she needed to stitch the wound up again. The only question was, however, whether Phil would be willing to take the risk of breaking into the school building when his plan had only been to go around the buildings and across the sports grounds. Either way, Alice knew she had to tell the others about the seriousness of her wound.

She kept the Zippo burning and walked back to the others. "Guys," she said, "there's something I have to show you. Let your eyes get used to the light again and tell me when you're ready."

The others squinted against the brightness of the flame, which felt as piercingly bright to them as it had to Alice a few minutes ago. After a while, though, their eyes became accustomed to it. Alice lifted up the bottom of her blouse, and everyone gasped when they saw how much blood she'd lost.

"Oh my God," Phil murmured. "Why didn't you say anything sooner? You can't go on. You're going to have to make camp here tonight, and Wyatt and I will head into the suburbs to try to find a medical kit somewhere."

"No, we can't do that," Alice said. "There's a better

option anyway, although there's some risk involved."

"Go on," Phil said, a grimace of deep concern on his face.

"The nurse's room in the school will have what I need to stitch this cut up again. I know there's some danger involved, but if we can get into the school, I can fix myself up well enough that I'll be able to get to the truck, at least."

"Are you sure? You've lost a lot of blood, honey," Phil said.

"All the more reason to do this," Alice said. "If it gets to the point where I need a transfusion, we've got the equipment to do that on the ranch, and if I'm unconscious by then, Doc Robertson will be able to do that. But for any of that to happen, I need to get to the truck so I can get to the ranch."

Phil nodded grimly; he understood now just how important it was to break into the school and get Alice to the nurse's room.

"All right," he said. "It's going to be risky, but I don't see what else we can do at this point. Come on, everyone; we're going to have to break into the school."

Alice put out the light, and everyone put their backpacks on again. Then they headed out of the cover of the trees, crossed the street, and hopped over the school fence, then they headed into the dark, ominous-looking grounds of the sprawling institution, praying that they would be able to navigate its shadowy corridors without running into any more predators of the night.

21

*L*ike everywhere else, the school was shrouded in darkness. The parking lot was full of abandoned vehicles, adding to the dreamlike surreality of the place, given how dead and utterly silent and deserted everything felt here. The windows of the school buildings were little more than inky-black squares on charcoal-colored canvases, hinting at intense and impenetrable darkness within. Phil knew that they'd have to at least use Zippos inside the school buildings to see where they were going, and he hoped this wouldn't attract the attention of any prowlers who might see the lights from outside.

Phil's sense of unease grew as they approached the first of the buildings. "Davey, that friend of yours, what's his name again, Zack, right? He goes to this high school, doesn't he? You ever been in here?"

"Yeah, Zack goes to River's Edge," David answered.

"I've been here once or twice, but I just waited for him outside, so I don't know much about the layout of the building."

"Do you at least know what this building is?"

"I'm pretty sure this is the main entrance, and inside to the right are a bunch of classrooms. I'm not sure what else."

"It's as good an entry point as any, I'd guess," Wyatt suggested.

Phil sighed, his reluctance obvious, but then he looked across at Alice. Even through the gloom, he could see that her face was pale, and he could see the pain and suffering she was silently suffering through writ plain across her pretty features. He knew that they had to do this and get her to the nurse's room as quickly as possible. "Come on then," he said, shoving aside his reluctance and replacing it with grim determination. "Let's head inside."

They walked up the concrete stairs to the large twin wooden doors. Phil tested one of the handles, and, as expected, it was locked. While the EMP had hit during the middle of a school day, the kids had presumably been sent home and the place locked up instead of merely being abandoned.

"Locked," Phil said. "We could try to batter the door down or smash the locks, but that'd make a bunch of noise, and we don't want to attract unwanted attention. I think we'd best look for another way in."

"Agreed," Wyatt said. "Let's look around the back

and side of this building. There's gotta be other doors, or maybe some big windows we can get in through."

They walked around the side of the building, looking closely at all the windows to check if any might provide a viable point of entry. Nothing on the front of the huge building seemed suitable, though. All the ground-floor windows were almost six feet up, which would mean Alice would have to climb up through them, which would likely tear her wound open farther.

Around the side of the building, it was the same story. They walked along, keeping their eyes peeled for any possible point of access but found nothing suitable. Around the back, though, Davey noticed that a third-floor balcony door had been left ajar. A large tree stood next to the building, and some of its boughs hung over the balcony.

"There!" he said, pointing up. "It's open, and that balcony has a fire escape ladder. If I can get up there, I can lower the ladder, and we can all get in that way."

"Let me guess," Phil said warily, "you think you can climb up the tree to get onto that balcony?"

"I don't see why not," David said. "It's not that high."

"Son, if you fall out of that tree, which you probably will, given how dark it is, I'm pretty sure you're gonna break a few bones, and the last thing we need is another person with life-threatening injuries. No, forget about it. We'll keep looking and find another way in."

"Come on, Dad, we've got those headlamps, with a bit of light it'll be an easy climb."

"Have you forgotten how bright those headlamps are? And what about if—no, *when*—someone sees a headlamp flashing around in the tree?" Phil said. "It'll be like a bonfire on a hilltop, calling out to all the wrong sorta people. Just forget about it, Davey. That's the last I'm gonna say about this. Now come on, we need to keep looking. We'll find a way in that doesn't involve risking breaking anyone's neck and sending up the equivalent of a signal flare to every prowling scumbag for miles around."

"All right," David said with a disappointed sigh. "We'll keep looking."

They moved on and headed around the back of the building but found nowhere there whereby they could gain access to the school.

"Dammit," Phil muttered. "This place is locked-up tight."

"Except for the door on the balcony…" David said cautiously.

"Your boy's right," Wyatt said before Phil could respond. "Short of breaking down a door or smashing out some windows and climbing through 'em—which might mean we cut up on broken glass—there isn't gonna be an easy way to get in."

"But the headlamp is gonna be seen for miles around," Phil protested. "I'd rather just make some noise by breaking down a door; it'll attract less attention from afar."

"You've got some extra clothes in your bags, don't you?" Wyatt asked. "All you need is a T-shirt, really."

"What for?" Phil asked.

"To dim the headlamp. Davey can put the headlamp on, then wrap a t-shirt or something around his head over it. It should dim the light enough that it won't be seen by anyone outside, especially given how thick the tree's foliage is, but it should also give off just enough light that Davey can see what he's doing."

Phil had to admit that Wyatt's idea was a good one. "Okay," he said. "I've got a spare shirt in my backpack. But Davey, you have to be real careful up there in the tree, okay? Don't try any Spiderman crap. I seriously do *not* want to have to deal with any more serious injuries."

Davey grinned, his teeth bright in the murky gloom of the night. "I'll be fine, Dad, don't worry." He put on the headlamp, and Phil handed him a spare shirt from his backpack, which Davey tied around his head like a bandanna.

Since they were around the rear of the building and couldn't be seen from the street, this was as good a place as any to test Wyatt's theory. David turned the headlamp on, and its usually bright glare was greatly dimmed by the shirt wrapped around his head. The light that now came from the headlamp was a gentle, almost candle-like glow.

"Perfect," David said. "Just enough to see by."

"Turn it off until you're in the tree," Phil said

sternly. "It might not be bright, but it's still a light, and it can be seen in this darkness from a long way off."

David turned it off, and they headed back to the tree. Phil and Wyatt gave David a boost so he could reach the lowest of the boughs, which was quite high off the ground, but once he was on it, he was fine. He turned the headlight on and scampered up the tree, moving with simian-like agility through the branches.

"He always was a great climber," Alice said, watching from the ground.

Phil noticed her voice was sounding softer and weaker, but he didn't say anything. Instead, he just reached over to her and squeezed her hand gently in his.

David got onto the long bough that hung over the balcony. He had to straddle it and shimmy his way along for a while, but after some time, he found himself directly over the balcony. He lowered himself off the branch until he was hanging fully from it, with both arms straight up above his head, and then he let go. It was only a three or four-foot drop from the bottom of his feet to the balcony, and he landed with acrobatic grace.

"Nice going!" Phil yelled from below, "but turn off that light now! Anyone could see it!"

David hurried to turn off the light, and then he got busy with setting up the fire escape ladder, which, after a few minutes, he lowered to the ground.

"You good to go up the ladder?" Phil asked Alice,

and she nodded. "Okay, honey," he said. "Just take it real easy. And I'll come right up behind you."

Alice went up the ladder first, and Phil followed closely behind her. Wyatt brought up the rear. Alice ascended the ladder slowly and carefully. Each step she went up caused a shot of sharp pain to rip through her midsection, but she gritted her teeth and bore the pain in silence because she didn't want to make anyone else worried. It took quite an effort for her to get up because she was dizzy and light-headed, but she eventually got to the top, and David helped her up onto the balcony.

Phil and Wyatt came up quickly behind her.

"Best pull the ladder back up," Phil said. "Just in case anyone else is out there. We don't want to make it easy for any of the wrong kinda people to come in here after us."

David and Wyatt pulled the fire escape ladder back up, while Alice sat down for a while to rest. She was praying that they would find the right supplies in the nurse's room; if they didn't, she didn't know what she would do.

"All right, the ladder's all up," Wyatt said.

"Let's go inside," Phil said. "Davey, head in and turn that headlamp back on. We'll follow."

David opened the door and headed inside, and when he turned the headlamp on the pitch-black darkness, like that of the inside of a deep mine, was banished for a few yards by the soft glow. Phil helped Alice up and onto her feet, and then she, Wyatt, and

Phil headed in through the door, which Phil quietly closed behind them.

And deep inside the school, figures waited in the shadows, listening to the unexpected sound of footsteps echoing through the hallways, and they curled their fingers around their weapons.

22

"Stay close," Phil said to the others as they moved cautiously through the darkness. He didn't want to use the LED headlamps unobstructed, because while they would flood the hallways with light, that light would certainly be seen from outside. With David's headlamp dimmed by the shirt wrapped around his head, the soft glow it emitted only enabled the group to see a couple of feet in front of them.

The others didn't need to be told this. If they lagged too far behind, they would be swallowed up entirely by the darkness, which was so dense in here it felt like a physical presence, as if it were fog or mist. One could not see one's hand even an inch in front of one's eyes in this blackness.

All of them were on edge. It didn't seem likely that anyone else could be in the school, but the fact that they were in a huge and unfamiliar building, moving through almost impenetrable darkness meant that they couldn't help imagining danger lurking around every corner.

"The nurse's room is likely to be on the ground level," Phil said. "There's gotta be some stairs around here somewhere."

This floor seemed to be all classrooms, with the only other rooms being bathrooms. David stared forlornly at the rows of lockers as he passed them and wondered not only when he would go back to school again, but if he ever would. Considering everything they'd seen and experienced thus far, a return to normality anytime soon didn't seem likely.

They rounded a corner, and at last came to a stairwell. They headed down the first flight of stairs and were about to go down the second when Wyatt held up his hand. "Hold on," he said, his voice low and urgent. "Does anyone else smell that?"

"Smell what?" David asked.

"Kerosene," Wyatt answered. "I swear I caught a whiff of it. Very faint, but it was there." He sniffed at the air again, as did everyone else.

"I don't know. I can't smell anything," Phil said after a while.

"I can't either," Alice said.

"Neither can I," David added.

"It might be the edginess of this situation making you pick up phantom smells," Phil said. "This place is spooky as hell, and your mind might be playing tricks on you."

Wyatt shook his head. "No, Phil, I didn't imagine

that. I promise you. I smelled a hint of kerosene in the air."

"All right, well, let's be extra cautious then," Phil said, doing his best to sound confident and assured. "Guns at the ready, everyone…just in case." The truth was, he was feeling very jittery and on edge, and the creepiness of this ultra-dark labyrinth was getting to him. He didn't want to look nervous or worried in front of the others, though. He knew they needed strong leadership, and he had to provide that to get them through this situation.

They headed down another flight of stairs, and again, Wyatt stopped them, sniffing at the air again. "Dammit," he muttered. "Didn't anybody else smell that? I swear I caught another whiff of it."

"Don't worry about it. Let's keep going," Phil suggested. Actually, he too thought he'd caught a hint of kerosene in the air, but he didn't want to stop moving. The more often they stopped and obsessed over these phantom smells, the more their minds would start screwing with them. He just wanted to get Alice to the nurse's room, get her wound stitched back up, and then get the hell out.

They headed down the final flight of stairs, the one that took them to the first level, but just as they were about to exit the stairwell, they heard a sound that was definitely not a phantom conjuration of their troubled minds. Echoing through the hallways was the sound of footsteps, somehow sprinting through the darkness. It only lasted a few seconds, but they all heard it and froze in their tracks.

"Oh my God," Alice gasped, her heart hammering in her chest. "You all heard that, right?"

"Shit," Wyatt grunted, raising his revolver and aiming at the impenetrable darkness in front of him. "I told you I didn't imagine those smells. Someone's down here."

"What do we do?" David asked, the shakiness of his voice betraying his fear. His heart was thumping in his chest, and his hands were shaking.

"We go on," Phil said grimly. "There's no other option. Your mother has to get to the nurse's room. And if whoever's out there has a gun, we'll see them if they want to try anything with us. You can't see your hand in front of your face in this darkness, so if they want to take aim at us, they'll have to use a light source of their own."

With everyone feeling jittery and nervous, they pushed on through the pitch-black hallways. In the distance, perhaps a few hallways down, they heard the frightening sound of someone sprinting through the darkness again. They all froze, aiming their guns into the shadows, but as quickly as the sound had appeared, it was gone, evaporating into silence.

"Dammit," Wyatt muttered. "Who the hell is out there, and why the hell are they sprinting around in complete darkness? I don't like this. I don't like it one bit."

"Come on," Phil said, trying to bolster the group's

courage. "We've just passed a couple of offices, so the nurse's room has to be around here somewhere. As soon as we find it, we can get out of here and leave whoever this freak in the darkness is behind."

They rounded one more corner, and David let out a sigh of relief when, in the weak glow from his head-lamp, he spotted a welcome sign above a nearby door. "There it is!" he said. "The nurse's room!"

Phil made a beeline for it; he couldn't wait to get out of the school. When he tried the door handle, though, he found the office was locked. "Shit," he muttered.

"Man, let's just shoulder-barge the damn door open," Wyatt said. "Whoever's in here already knows we're in the building, so making some noise won't matter."

"I wouldn't do that," Alice said. "There are a lot of addicts in the city, and plenty of the schools around here have beefed up the security around their nurse's rooms in recent months. The door might be a lot stronger and better reinforced than it looks, and you might just end up hurting your shoulder. The last thing we need is more injuries to deal with; I'm already feeling so weak that I hardly know if I can stitch myself up properly."

"Well, we have to get into this damn room some-how," Wyatt said.

"Dad, you were an engineer, what do you think?" David asked. "What's the best way to get in?"

Phil, who'd been examining the door up close

while the others had been talking, simply chuckled in response. "Well, ramming or kicking it would be a real bad idea," he said, "because this door opens outwards. It wasn't designed to be a secure door back when they built this school, and I don't think they took that into account when they put new locks on it. I've got some screwdrivers and hand tools in my backpack. We can take the hinges off and get in like that."

"I think...I'd better sit down while you guys do that," Alice said. She was feeling even woozier than before, and her energy was draining out of her like water from a leak.

Phil could hear that she was in a bad way, and he helped her to sit down on the floor against the wall next to the door. "Is there anything we can do to help you get some energy back?"

"Sugar and caffeine...will give me enough of a temporary boost...to get me through the task of... stitching myself up again." Alice sounded very haggard and weary.

"I saw a vending machine with sodas and candies and stuff in it on the third floor," David said. "They've probably got Red Bulls or stuff in there. I could go get some for you, Mom."

"You're not going up there on your own," Phil said sternly.

"I'll go with him to make sure he's safe. You stand guard here," Wyatt said. "We've got the other headlamp you guys can use."

"Let them go, honey," Alice said weakly. "I need an energy boost to get through this."

Phil didn't like this, but he knew that it would have to be done. "All right," he said. "But just go straight to that machine, grab what you need, and come straight back."

"Believe me, I don't want to be wandering around in this darkness any longer than necessary," Wyatt said. "We'll make sure we haul ass." He handed Phil the headlamp he'd used on the bike, and Phil put it on and wrapped a spare shirt around his head to dim the light.

"Okay," Phil said. "You'd better get going. I'll work on the door in the meantime."

Wyatt nodded, and he and David moved off into the darkness while Phil got busy working on the door hinges. Being alone now, with his weakening wife, made him feel a lot more vulnerable, and when he heard someone suddenly sprinting along the hallways —this time quite close to them—he almost jumped out of his skin. "Dammit!" he roared into the darkness, almost cracking. "Who the hell is out there?!"

"Just get the door open, honey," Alice said, feeling almost too weak to be freaked out by the creepy stranger who was running through the hallways in complete darkness.

Feeling rather shaken and very much on edge, Phil got busy with the door. They didn't hear the running stranger again, and Phil managed to get the hinges off the door. He helped Alice inside, and to their relief, there was an extensive range of medicines and medical supplies in the room. Phil helped Alice up onto the bed in the nurse's room, and she instructed him on how to remove the dressing and clean the wound so she could sew it up again.

Upstairs, meanwhile, Wyatt and David had reached the vending machine. Inside it were plenty of high-caffeine energy drinks, candy bars, and other items that would likely give Alice enough of a boost to make the final trek to the truck in her weakened state. Of course, like everything else electronic, the vending machine was dead and would never work again.

"How are we gonna get the stuff out?" David asked. "I guess we could just use a chair or something to smash out the front glass, right?"

"There might be an easier way," Wyatt said. "Come here, use your light to have a look around the side of the machine."

David took a look around the side and saw that the front glass was a door locked by a simple padlock. "All we have to do is break this lock, and we can get in," he said.

"I've got a hatchet in my backpack," Wyatt said. "A few good whacks with the back of it should break this lock. Then we don't have to risk getting shards of broken glass all over the food and drinks."

Wyatt dropped down to his knees, set his revolver on the floor and started to look around in it for the hatchet—and that was when someone veered around the corner and sprinted right past them. The figure was visible only as a dim blur on the periphery of the circle of weak light emitted by David's headlamp, but it was enough to scare the hell out of both of them. Wyatt grabbed his gun and jumped to his feet, growling wordlessly and aiming at the impenetrable darkness the figure had run into, and David pointed his gun in that direction too.

"Shit!" David yelped, his hands shaking.

"Whoever you are, I'm gonna kill you, you son of a bitch, if you come near us again!" Wyatt roared. "You hear me, you crazy psycho? I'm gonna—"

A dull thud cut Wyatt's shout short, and David swung around in terrified surprise as he saw Wyatt's limp form crumple to the floor. He barely had enough time to swing his gun around before a percussive blow thumped through his skull. There was a flash of bright light behind his eyes from the impact, and then everything went black as he slipped into unconsciousness.

23

"*D*id you hear that?" Phil asked, looking out at the pitch-black door while Alice stitched herself up.

Her hands were moving with painstaking slowness, and it seemed to her that every stitch took a monumental effort to complete. "I don't know," she murmured. "I'm just…trying to concentrate…on this."

"I swear I heard Wyatt yelling something," Phil said, looking concerned. "And he didn't sound too happy. I don't like the sound of this…at all."

"If you want to…check it out…I'm okay here…by myself," Alice said, breathing hard.

"I'd have to leave you here and use the Zippo for light, and I don't want to leave you alone anyway," Phil said. "We're just gonna have to wait. Hmm, and I guess we'd have heard gunshots if there was any real trouble. Maybe they just caught sight of that freak who's been running around in the dark."

"Maybe honey," Alice said, distracted by the task she needed to complete, "maybe…"

David and Wyatt, meanwhile, were coming to upstairs. They did not awake near the vending machine where they'd been knocked out, however. Instead, they found themselves in an office, lying on their stomachs on the ground, with their hand zip-tied behind their backs. A candle, giving off a dim orange light, was burning in the office, which seemed to be the principal's or vice principal's office, from what David could see. Two pairs of shoes—both large men's shoes—stood in front of their faces.

"What…the hell?" Wyatt groaned as he awoke. Both he and David were feeling groggy and disoriented and had throbbing headaches pounding through their skulls.

"Thieving scum," one of the men standing over them growled.

David couldn't see much of him beyond his pants, but he seemed to be a large, heavyset man and sounded as if he were in his fifties or sixties. The other man, who, judging by the style of his shoes and pants, was a lot younger, perhaps college age, didn't speak. "I suspected," the older man continued, "that some no-good assholes would come in here and loot the place before long, with all this power-outage craziness, but I didn't figure it'd happen so soon. Well, me and my boy, we were ready for punks like you."

"We're not looters," Wyatt growled. "Now get these zip ties off my wrists before I get *real* mad."

"Ha!" the man scoffed. "You ain't in any position to be making demands. We didn't have guns before...but now we do, thank you very much."

"Look, uh, my friend Zack goes to this school, okay," David stammered, anxious and fearful. "We just, look, my mom, she's hurt bad, she needed to stitch up her wound, and, uh, um, we just needed—"

"Shut up!" the man snapped. "It's my job to protect this school from thieving scum like you, and that's what I'm gonna go! My boy and I are gonna go get your friends next, and y'all can spend the night tied up in here. We'll turn you thieving pricks over to the cops tomorrow morning. I don't care about your lies and excuses, so shut your goddamn mouths!"

"There won't *be* any cops, you idiot, not tomorrow, not next goddamn week!" Wyatt said. "This was no simple power outage. The power's never coming on again! This is how things are gonna be from now on, do you understand?"

"Bullshit!" the man snapped, but there was a hint of uncertainty in his tone.

"There's been an EMP attack," Wyatt explained, trying to rein in his flaring temper, but not quite succeeding in eliminating the growl from his voice. "Do you know what that means?"

"EMP? Uh...yeah, nice try, asshole. Making up bull-shit to try to confuse me!"

"Maybe we should listen to 'em, Dad," said an uncertain new voice, that of the younger man. "You said yourself that this ain't like any power outage you've ever seen."

"Shut up, Jason!" the older man yelled. "You do what I say, boy, and you don't listen to these assholes' lies! Come on, now that we've got us some guns, we gotta go get those other two. It'll be a lot easier than what we had to do to get these ones."

"But Dad—"

"No! We do things my way, boy! Now get these assholes up into the chairs so we can go get their friends."

"Uh, okay, Dad," the young man said nervously. He sounded even more frightened and anxious than David was. "You heard him," he said to David and Wyatt, trying to sound more confident. "Stand up, do it nice and slow. We've got your guns, and we'll use 'em if you try anything."

Wyatt and David struggled to their feet, which was a difficult job with their hands bound tightly behind their backs, but they finally managed to stand up. When they did, they were able to see their assailants. The older man was dressed in a janitor's uniform, while the younger man was dressed like a college student. What was most immediately striking about the younger man, however, was his eyes. Even in the dim candlelight, Wyatt and David could see that he was completely blind. This, they suspected, was why he'd been able to sprint around in the complete darkness to frighten and unsettle them. The darkness made no difference to his abilities of perception, and since his father was the janitor here, and likely had been for a long time, both the young man and the older one likely knew the layout of the school like the backs of their hands.

The younger man was holding a .45 he'd taken from Wyatt, while the older man had the .357 revolver in his hand. They'd also taken Wyatt and David's backpacks, and were wearing them. Both of them were pointing guns at Wyatt and David. "Sit on them chairs there," the older man said, pointing at two office chairs in the corner and keeping a good distance between himself and his prisoners. "Move slowly, or I'll put some goddamn holes in both of you."

Glaring at the two men with naked wrath in his eyes, his jaw clenched with anger, Wyatt strolled over to the chairs and sat down in one of them, while David followed and meekly took a seat in the other.

"Zip tie their legs to the chairs, boy," the old man said. "And you two, don't try to kick my boy or head-butt him or do nothing stupid like that, coz I'll blow your goddamn brains out if you do."

The younger man tucked the .45 into his belt and nervously approached Wyatt and David, picking up a bunch of thick cable-ties from the large desk in the room as he did. It was amazing how precisely he could orient himself using only sound, and he didn't have to do much fumbling despite his disability. "Don't try nothing," he said, trying to sound threatening and intimidating, but failing rather miserably.

The older man was jumpy and twitchy, and from

171

the way he held the gun, Wyatt knew he was not familiar with firearms and was likely no fighter, but also feared that he might squeeze the trigger by mistake if he got a fright. Wyatt didn't want to get anyone accidentally killed here—least of all himself—so he allowed the younger man to zip tie his ankles to the legs of the chair. David did so as well.

"Done, Dad," the young, blind man said after a bit of fumbling and feeling around.

"Good. Let's go get them other two. Remember the plan."

"Yeah."

The young man took out the .45, and then both of them walked out of the office and closed the door. After they'd closed it, Wyatt and David heard a key turn, after which came the sound of the click of a lock, and they realized that they'd been locked in, on top of being tied to the chairs.

"What are we gonna do?" David asked, his voice cracking with fear.

"Just relax, kid," Wyatt said. "They didn't get all of our guns."

"Yeah, they did!"

"I can feel the little .32 in my boot," Wyatt said. "They didn't know that one was there."

"It doesn't matter," David said, his head drooping onto his chest. "We're all tied up. You can't even get it out."

Wyatt chuckled. "Gimme about twenty seconds, kid. These chumps are amateurs." He leaned forward in the chair, clenched all of the muscles of his upper body and arms, and then raised his arms as high as they could go before bringing them down hard and fast, as if he was trying to reverse-hammer-punch his butt. He did this a few times, and on his third try, the zip tie around his wrist snapped.

"Whoa," David said, impressed.

"They taught us that in the army," Wyatt said.

"Quick, cut me loose too!" David said.

Wyatt hastily looked around the office. The janitor and his son had taken all their weapons, but he found a pair of large scissors easily enough. He cut the zip ties off David's wrists and ankles but put his hand on David's shoulder to prevent him from standing. "Hold up there, kid. You need to pretend to still be zip tied so they don't suspect anything when they come back in. Keep these behind your back…hopefully, you won't need to use 'em."

"What are you gonna do?" David asked.

"Wait behind the door and jam the muzzle of this .32 into the back of that janitor's skull as soon as he steps into the room. He won't see my chair is empty until he's inside the room…by which time it'll be too late for him. If you can jump up and grab the gun outta the blind kid's hand and get those scissors pressed up against his throat, we'll have 'em beat. You gotta move real fast, though, okay? Real explosive. Only do it after I've acted, okay?"

"Um, okay, okay, I'll do it," David said, doing his best to sound confident.

"Remember, act like you're still tied up until the time comes to act."

"Yeah."

Wyatt took the .32 ACP out of his boot, where it had been wedged since he had left the ranch, and pressed himself up against the wall to wait for the janitor's return. After around five minutes, the janitor and his son returned, but they weren't alone. The door opened, and Wyatt held his breath and tensed his muscles, ready to explode into action, but it wasn't the janitor or his son who stepped into the room first. Instead, it was Phil, whose hands had been zip-tied behind his back, followed by Alice, whose wrists were also tied. Right behind them came the janitor, and behind him was his son.

Wyatt had to change his plan a little, going for the young man instead of the janitor, but he acted swiftly and effectively, slipping out from behind the door as soon as the young man entered. In one smooth and brutally efficient maneuver, he yanked the young man's arm behind his back, causing him to drop his gun, and pressed the .32 into the back of his skull. The young man yelped with surprise but didn't attempt to fight back; he was too shocked and frightened.

"What the hell?" the janitor yelled, swinging around, but before he could even attempt to fight back, David moved with the explosiveness of a mountain lion, bursting up from the chair and aiming a rapid karate kick at the janitor's wrist. His kick hit home with perfect accuracy and vicious force, and the .357 went flying. The janitor cried out in pain and stumbled forward, but before he could reach for any of the other guns he'd taken from them, David had the scissors pressed up against the side of his neck.

"You messed with the wrong people," Wyatt growled, shoving the .32 more forcefully into the back of the young man's skull. "Get your asses onto those chairs, both of you! Now!"

There was now a complete reversal of the janitor's attitude. He looked as if he was about to burst into tears. "Don't hurt my boy, please, please, don't hurt him. He's all I got in this world," he pleaded.

"Sit down!" Wyatt roared.

"Okay, okay," the janitor whimpered.

David kept the scissors pressed against the janitor's neck until the man and his son had sat down.

"Zip tie their hands and ankles," Wyatt said to David, keeping his gun aimed at the janitor's face as he spoke.

David put the scissors down on the desk, took a bunch of the zip ties, and tied up the janitor and his son. Once he'd done this, he freed his mother and father from the zip ties around their wrists.

"They ambushed us right outside the nurse's room," Phil said, shaking out his aching wrists. "The moment I stepped out of the door, this guy pressed a gun against my head," he continued, pointing at the janitor.

"Yeah, they whacked Davey and me over the head with something heavy up by the vending machine, after this kid ran past to freak us out," Wyatt muttered, rubbing the painful bump on his head where they'd knocked him out.

"Please, please don't hurt us," the janitor pleaded. "Take whatever you want. Just don't hurt us."

"We're not criminals, you idiot!" Wyatt grumbled. "I've been trying to explain this the whole damn time."

"My wife desperately needed medical attention," Phil said to the janitor. "And she's a trauma nurse. Show him, Alice."

Alice lifted up her blouse, showing the janitor the fresh dressing she'd just put on her wound after stitching it back up.

"Well, but, uh, these two, they was breaking into the- the vending machine!" the janitor protested.

"Look at her face, asshole," Wyatt growled. "Can't you see how weak she is? We still have a long walk ahead, and the only way she's gonna get to where we're going is with the help of some sugar and caffeine. And in case you haven't noticed, the vending machines, like everything else electronic, are dead and will be dead pretty much forever. But here, take this if you're so damn concerned about a few missing Red Bulls and candy bars." He took ten dollars out of his pocket and threw it down on the table.

"We're going to leave now," Phil said. "All we needed here was to get my wife's wound stitched up and get a bit of caffeine and sugar in her to help her get to where we need to go."

"You can't just, l- leave us here like this!" the janitor said.

"Davey, get all the guns and the rest of our stuff back," Phil said. "After that, we'll cut you two loose."

David gathered all the weapons and backpacks and handed them back to their rightful owners. Once they were ready to go, Phil gave David the go-ahead to cut the janitor and his son free. Phil, Alice, and Wyatt kept their guns trained on the men the whole time, and David stepped quickly away from them once he'd cut them free, wary of them trying to grab him and reverse the situation. He didn't need to be too cautious, though; the janitor and his son had had all the fight taken out of them.

"We're gonna go bust that lock off the vending machine now," Wyatt growled, "and you two are gonna come with us, so I can make sure you don't try any other shit."

"You don't need to break into it," the janitor said. "I've got the keys. I'll open it up for you." He opened a drawer in the desk and took out a huge bundle of keys.

"Thank you. We'd appreciate that," Phil said. "No hard feelings, right?"

The janitor nodded reluctantly. "No hard feelings."

Phil nodded to the others; they could lower their guns now. He could see that the janitor was a broken, defeated man, and would not try anything else. His son was looking glum and defeated too.

They headed back up to the vending machine, and the janitor opened it up for them. Alice downed a Red Bull on the spot and ate a candy bar, and immediately felt a boost of energy invigorating her. "We'd better move fast," she said to Phil. "When this temporary boost wears off, I'm gonna crash hard."

"I'll let you out the back door," the janitor said.

"Thank you, friend," Phil said gently.

Wyatt scowled, rubbing the bump on his head, but said nothing. The janitor and his son, looking sheepish, led them through the school and let them out of the back door.

"Good luck," the janitor said to them as they left. "I hope you make it to where you're trying to go."

"Good luck to you, too," Phil said. "In the days ahead, you're gonna need it, believe me."

The walk to the truck, half through the quieter backroads of the northern suburbs and half through the woods, was mostly uneventful, for which all the members of the group were grateful. Alice's stitches held, and although the temporary energy boost from the sugar and caffeine started wearing off quite rapidly once they got into the woods, it was enough to get her to the truck.

Phil, Wyatt, and David got to work getting the branches and foliage off the truck while Alice rested. She was crashing hard and knew that she would pass out any second. Still, she didn't believe her life was in danger. She'd need a lot of rest and good-quality nutrition over the next few days, but as long as she was able to get these things, she was sure she'd be fine.

"We're ready to go, honey," Phil said to her. "Come on. We're about to start the truck. You ride up front with Wyatt and me, Davey can go in the back."

Alice nodded and mumbled a barely intelligible reply. She couldn't get up, so Phil helped her and carried her over to the truck. He got her into the passenger seat, tightened the seatbelt around her so she wouldn't be jostled around too much while the truck was moving. He then squeezed between her and Wyatt, who was in the driver's seat again, while David climbed into the bed of the truck. David rapped on the back window, signaling that he was ready to go.

"Take it easy on the way back," Phil said to Wyatt. "We're in much less of a rush now. Obviously, we want to get back before the sky starts getting light, but there's no need for any of that rally-style driving, buddy."

Wyatt flashed him a grin in the dark. "Don't worry. I'll make this ride real smooth. It'll be like gliding on air, brother!"

They both chuckled, feeling a lot better now that they were all in the truck. Everything they'd been through felt like some sort of horrendous nightmare they'd just woken up from...but both of them knew that it wasn't over yet, not until the truck was back at the ranch and the gates locked behind them.

Wyatt kept up a brisk pace but was by no means racing. They got to the river without incident, but Wyatt stopped at the water's edge. Crossing the water would be a lot more difficult in the dark, but there was another problem too.

"We've got over two hundred pounds of extra weight with your wife and son," Wyatt said. "And the truck was barely able to get across the river with just you and me in it. We're not gonna make it fully loaded."

"That's okay," Phil said. "We've still got those air mattresses we took from the sporting goods store. Davey and I will get across on those. And if push comes to shove, he and I could swim across, but that'll make for a freezing ride back if we're soaked to the bone in icy water."

"All right," Wyatt said. "With just Alice in here with me, the truck'll be lighter than when you and I crossed, so we should make it without any problems."

"There's some rope in the back," Phil said. "I'll get the mattresses inflated, and tie 'em to the back of the truck, so you can pull us across."

"Sounds good."

Phil jumped out and told David about his plan. They got the air mattresses out and inflated them, and then Phil tied both of them up to the rear of the truck. "All right, son," he said to David, "just try to stay on top of the mattress. I'm sure you don't wanna ride the rest of the way back dripping wet and freezing cold, right?"

"Hell no," David said, staring warily at the rushing black water.

"Lie on your stomach and spread out like a starfish so you can distribute your weight as evenly as possible across the mattress," Phil said. "Wyatt will cross the river real slow, so I think we'll be okay on the mattresses, they won't flip or anything as long as we keep our weight properly distributed."

"Okay, Dad."

When the mattresses were inflated and securely tied to the truck, Phil gave Wyatt the go-ahead to enter the river. He drove in cautiously, dragging the mattresses over the rocks until they were both floating in the shallows. When the mattresses were afloat, Phil called out to Wyatt to stop. Wyatt waited until Phil and David were safely on the mattresses, and then he set off, driving slowly and cautiously across the river.

The water level had dropped a little, and this, combined with the fact that the truck was lighter, made Wyatt's second crossing of the river easier than the first. Phil and David, spread-eagled on the air mattresses, were pulled gently across, and while a few small waves from the rushing current splashed over the edges of the mattresses, the two of them were mostly dry by the time they got to the other side.

"What should we do with the mattresses, dad?" David asked when he was on the riverbank.

"Let's keep 'em, son. I told my workers that if anyone needed to come and stay at the ranch, they could, so we might have more guests than we have beds for in the coming days and weeks. These'll come in handy, I think. Deflate yours and toss it into the truck."

While they were deflating their mattresses, David finally got the chance, after everything they'd been through since the EMP attack, to ask his father some of the questions that had been troubling him since that fateful moment. "Dad, what's gonna happen now?"

"Well, we're gonna go back to the ranch, make sure

your mother is okay, and then get some well-earned sleep."

"No, I mean…in the future. I'm talking about everything, our whole lives. Nothing's ever gonna be like it was before, is it? The world's changed, like, completely and irreversibly, hasn't it?"

Phil sighed. "It has, son. But I don't know if this is a statewide thing, a countrywide problem, or even an international one. For all we know, this could be a small, localized event just affecting this state, or only this county. Then again, this could be the start of World War Three…or the end of it; it may have lasted all of two minutes. I wish I could give you clearer answers, Davey, but for the moment, I really can't."

"Will we be okay on the ranch?"

Phil smiled reassuringly and leaned over to ruffle David's hair as if he were still a little boy. "We'll be just fine, son. You know how well-prepared your mother and I are, and how we've been putting together contingency plans for something just like this for years. Remember, when our ancestors came to this land hundreds of years ago, they survived just fine without electricity, motor vehicles, oil, running water, computers, all that stuff. Now on the ranch, even with all the electronic stuff that's dead forever, we've still got way more advanced stuff than our pioneer ancestors had. And you know how hard I've worked all these years to make the ranch completely self-sustaining. We've got purified water from the river, plenty of food, livestock, guns, and ammo in case of trouble…we'll be just fine."

David nodded, seemingly satisfied with this answer, and continued deflating his mattress. After he'd packed it into the truck, though, he looked up at Phil and asked him one more question. "Will I ever get to go to school again?"

Phil smiled sadly; he'd loved his own school days, and he could feel his son's pain and worry over the prospect of never being able to experience those life-defining moments like graduation, senior prom, and everything else David would be missing out on now that normalcy had been yanked like a rug from under their feet. "I don't know son, I'm sorry, but I really don't. I hope you'll be able to...but I just don't know. Come on, let's get moving, we need to get home. Try not to think too much about that stuff."

Phil climbed into the front of the truck, where Wyatt, stoic and grim, was waiting behind the wheel and Alice was passed out. David climbed into the bed of the truck. They headed off into the night, each silently lost in their own troubled thoughts and worries about the dark and uncertain future.

25

*W*hen Wyatt finally pulled up to the familiar main gate of the ranch, the sky was growing light on the eastern horizon with the coming dawn. Having been awake for almost twenty-four hours now, and with much of that time having been spent in situations of extreme stress and danger, everyone in the truck was beyond exhausted. There was nothing they wanted to do more than dive onto the nearest bed and fall asleep, but Phil knew he had to take care of a few things first.

First up was Alice. Phil needed to get Doc Robertson to look her over and make sure she didn't need a blood transfusion after all the blood she'd lost. Then he'd need to take care of all the early-morning ranch jobs that simply had to be done every day. He wondered if any of his workers would show up at the ranch to help out with any of this. Considering the events of the last twenty-four hours, he wasn't so sure and figured that he'd have to get Wyatt and David to help him with most of it.

Wyatt stopped the truck right alongside the front porch of the farmhouse. He helped Phil get Alice out of the truck, and she opened her eyes, looking around in bleary confusion.

"Where are we? What's going on?" she croaked.

That fact that she had woken up was good, Phil thought, but he needed her to rest and get back to sleep. "Don't worry, honey," he said in a soothing voice, gently stroking her hair, "you're home now, and you're safe. I'm gonna put you to bed, and you're gonna get some rest."

Phil planned on taking one of the dirt bikes and racing over to Doc Robertson's house—which was a mere two or three miles away, thankfully—to bring him over the instant he'd put Alice to bed. When he carried her through the living room, however, he found Doc Robertson curled up on the sofa with a blanket, snoring. While whispered a silent prayer of thanks, took Alice up to the room and put her to bed, and then went downstairs and woke up the old veterinarian.

"Boy, am I glad to see you, Phil McCabe," Doc Robertson said, rubbing his eyes. I wasn't sure anyone was coming back to the ranch at all, with you all being gone all night." He lifted up the blanket, and Phil saw that the old man had been sleeping with a shotgun next to him. "Figured I'd stay here and protect the ranch, just in case," Doc Robertson continued, patting the shotgun, and then stretching and groaning as he got up.

"Thank you, Doc," Phil said. "I really appreciate that. Look, Alice got herself injured pretty bad in the city. She stitched up her wound, but she lost a lot of blood. Can you look her over and make sure she's okay and see if you think she'll need a blood transfusion?"

"Well, I'm just a vet, Phil, but I'll see what I can do. Get my medical bag for me, will ya? It's in my car. I'm parked around back."

Phil retrieved the medical bag, and Doc Robertson headed up to the main bedroom and checked over Alice. He made a more detailed inspection once Phil had handed him the bag. When this was done, he gave Phil a satisfied nod. "She's weak, but not in any real danger. I'll hook up an IV drip to keep her hydrated, but I think a blood transfusion would be overkill. With good rest and nutrition, she'll recover in a few days. The wound's clean, and she did a great job of dressing it. I don't think there's any danger of infection there either."

"I'm very relieved to hear that, Doc. Thank you."

"No problem. You look like you could use some rest yourself, Phil. I suggest you get some. Let me take care of Alice. I've had a good night's sleep, and I'm full of beans now."

"I can't just yet, Doc. There's still a lot I have to take care of."

Phil went downstairs to the kitchen, where Wyatt had brewed up a pot of strong coffee.

"Figured you could use some concentrated caffeine," Wyatt grunted. "I know I sure as hell could after the shitstorm of the last twenty-four hours."

"Thanks, Wyatt," Phil said, taking a cup of coffee from his faithful right-hand man. "Let's just get through what needs to be done as quickly as efficiently as possible, and then we can hit the hay for the rest of the morning."

"Damn straight."

They went about their tasks, with David and Doc Robertson helping out, too, and managed to get everything done by mid-morning, which was impressive given how much needed to be done.

Phil was utterly drained by the end of it, so once he'd completed the final task of the morning—leading his horses to one of the pastures to graze—he staggered into the farmhouse, his head spinning, almost on the verge of hallucinating from all the stress, exertion, and lack of sleep, and collapsed onto the large sofa in the living room. He didn't even have the energy to get upstairs to his bedroom. The moment he laid his head on one of the cushions and closed his eyes, he drifted into a deep and restful slumber.

It felt as if he'd only just closed his eyes when urgent hands shook him awake.

"Dad, Dad, wake up, wake up, quick!"

Phil groaned and opened his eyes and saw David standing over him. His son's eyes were wide with fright, and in the background, Phil could hear people yelling, and someone crying, while someone else appeared to be moaning in agony. Despite how disoriented and weary Phil still felt, he scrambled to his feet. "What's going on? What time is it?" he demanded.

"You gotta come quick, Dad. Debbie's been shot!" David exclaimed frantically.

"Debbie? Shit, where? How?"

"Just come, Dad, hurry!" David turned around and ran out of the house.

Phil followed closely behind him, rubbing his eyes and trying to push the groggy fuzziness out of his weary head.

Anthony and Debbie were a middle-aged married couple who worked on the ranch. The previous day they'd used some of Phil's spare bicycles to get to their home, which was over ten miles from the ranch and near the closer of the two small towns. When Phil rushed out onto his porch, he saw Doc Robertson and Wyatt kneeling over Debbie, who was lying on the ground, groaning with pain, only half-conscious. Anthony was pacing up and down the length of the porch, his haggard face a mess of anxiety and worry. An old woman who Phil had never seen before was sitting on the porch steps, weeping, and a Ford truck from the late 60s, which Phil had also never seen, was parked in front of his house.

"What's going on here? What happened?" Phil asked, hurrying over to Doc Robertson and Debbie.

"Dammit, I wish Alice was strong enough to help me," Doc Robertson muttered. His blood-covered hands were pressed up against Debbie's abdomen. Her white T-shirt was mostly dark red, clinging to her plump form and drenched with blood. "I don't know if I can do this on my own."

"She's been shot," Wyatt said grimly. "That old lady there, she's Debbie's mother. She drove her and Anthony over here; it was just dumb luck that she'd insisted on driving that old Ford for all these years. The only working vehicle for miles, outside of what we've got on this ranch anyway."

Now Phil understood why the old woman was weeping so plaintively. He couldn't imagine how awful he'd be feeling if it were David lying on the ground with a gaping gunshot wound in his abdomen. "What does she need, Doc?" he asked. "Just tell me what you need to save her, and I'll get it."

"First up, I need an operating table," Doc Robertson said. "And whatever surgical supplies y'all have. I know Alice has a lot. Get 'em all out. Debbie's gonna need a blood transfusion at the very least. I've done it plenty times on animals, but never on a person. I'm sure I can get it right, though. What blood type is she?"

"Anthony, what blood type is Debbie?" Phil asked Anthony.

Anthony didn't answer; instead, he simply kept pacing up and down the porch, looking as if he'd seen a ghost. Phil wondered if he could even hear him.

"She's B-positive," the old woman sobbed. "My little girl is B-positive."

"Thank you, ma'am," Phil said, walking over to the elderly woman and sitting down next to her. He took her hand and gave it a gentle squeeze and smiled as reassuringly and sympathetically as he could. "Your daughter's gonna be okay. Doc Robertson knows what he's doing, trust me. He's gonna take good care of your daughter. Doc!" he called out. "What blood type can she receive if she's B positive?"

"O-positive—" Doc Robertson began, but David cut him off right away.

"I'm O-positive," David said. "I'll do it. I'll donate my blood."

Phil flashed his son a broad, warm smile. He felt immensely proud of him at this moment. "That's my boy," he said. "That's the spirit, Davey! Doc, is that okay?"

"Okay?" Doc Robertson asked. "It's perfect! David's young and strong, and I couldn't ask for a better donor. But hurry, we have to get that blood in her fast. And then I'm gonna have to try to get the bullet out and stitch up the wound."

"Got it," Phil said. "Will the kitchen table do?"

"Sanitize it and put a fresh sheet over it, and it'll be fine," Doc Robertson said. "But you have to hurry."

Phil hastily delegated a number of tasks to the people around him, ensuring that a makeshift operating table could be set up as quickly as possible. While everyone got busy with what he'd told them to do, he then went to gather all the medical equipment he and Alice had accumulated and set aside for an emergency just like this, not to mention the livestock on the ranch. He went and checked on her and was relieved to see she was sleeping soundly. He wished he could get her up and take her downstairs to help out Doc Robertson, but then he'd be putting her life at risk in addition to Debbie's.

He grabbed as much of the medical equipment as he could carry and took it to the kitchen, where the long table had been cleared and turned into a makeshift operating table.

"Get a camping cot or easy chair in here for David here, please," Doc Robertson said. "He's going to need to be comfortable while we do the transfusion."

"I'm on it," Wyatt said. He went over to the living room and began dragging Phil's favorite easy chair toward the kitchen.

Phil, meanwhile, got a bottle of whiskey out of his liquor cabinet and poured a glass for Anthony. He needed to calm the man's nerves before talking to him because he was worried about how and where Debbie had gotten shot and what this attack could mean for the safety of his friends and family on the ranch. He poured two shots into the glass and handed it to Anthony. "Here, buddy, this'll make you feel a little better," he said gently.

Anthony downed the liquor right away, and then wiped his mouth with the back of his hand, which Phil noticed was shaking violently.

"You want a little more?" Phil asked.

White-faced, Anthony nodded, so Phil poured in another two shots, which Anthony downed just as fast. After this, his hands stopped trembling so terribly, and he became visibly calmer. Phil put his arm around Anthony's shoulder and led him outside, where they could talk in relative quiet. He only noticed now that the sun was getting low in the sky. It was already late afternoon.

"Are you able to tell me what happened, Anthony?" Phil asked.

"Everything was such a mess yesterday, with all the panic and craziness," Anthony said, "and we didn't do much after going home yesterday but hole up and read books and stuff by candlelight. We clean forgot about Debbie's insulin for her diabetes, and only realized this morning she'd forgotten to go to the drugstore yesterday to pick up her prescription. She can't do without the insulin, as ya know, Phil, so we had to go into town to try to get it. Well, I guess I didn't really think things would get so crazy so quickly. I mean, sure, we saw the smoke on the horizon from the city, but we didn't think the madness would have spread to these small towns here in the mountains. I've only got a nine-mil pistol at home but didn't even think to take it into town. I keep it in my bedside drawer, and mostly just forget it's even there. Anyway, around lunchtime, we took those bicycles you loaned us into town, praying that somehow the drugstore would be open. It wasn't, of course. Nothing was open...but there were plenty of people in town. It was chaos. Half the stores were boarded up. A few had already had their windows and doors busted and had been looted. Debbie had to get that insulin, though, so we tried to get through the chaos. That was when these assholes held us up."

"Held you up? They robbed you?" Phil asked.

"Yeah. City people, I think. I never seen 'em in town before, and I know most faces in that town well. Guys with masks and guns—they wanted our bikes. I tried to fight 'em off; without those bicycles, Debbie would have been trapped in town. Without her insulin and a bike, there's no way she would have made it back home. While we were struggling, one of the bastards sh-sh-shot her." Anthony's voice cracked with emotion, and his lower lip started quivering. A tear rolled out of his left eye, and Phil put his hand on Anthony's shoulder.

"You don't have to tell me any more," Phil said gently. "Just one more thing, though. Did you end up getting any insulin for Debbie?"

Anthony put his face in his hands and started weeping as he shook his head. "None, Phil, we didn't get none at all," he sobbed. "So even if she makes it through the surgery alive, she's gonna die anyway. My wife is gonna die..."

Phil wrapped his arms around Anthony and hugged him tightly. "Not on my watch, she ain't, my friend," he said determinedly. "Not on my watch, she ain't." He comforted Anthony for a while longer, and then left him and took Wyatt aside.

"What's going on?" Wyatt asked.

"Load up your guns, brother," Phil said grimly. "We have to head into town..."

26

"*H*ow's she doing, Doc?" Phil asked.

Doc Robertson had just finished sewing up Debbie's wound. He'd successfully extracted the bullet and had completed the blood transfusion too. "She's stable," he said to Phil, "but without insulin, she'll be in bad trouble real fast."

"Wyatt and I are about to leave for town now. Is there anything else you think we'll need from the drugstore? You've seen our current store medical supplies."

Doc Robertson chuckled darkly. "I'd be happiest if you could bring back every damn item in that drugstore," he said. "Lord knows how long this state of affairs is gonna last, and while you can grow plenty of food on this ranch, you can't grow medication."

"I know, Doc. We've done our best to prepare for that, though," Phil said.

"I can see that, and I'm impressed!" Doc Robertson

said. "Nonetheless, there are a couple of things you may not have enough of and some other stuff I think we might need in the months to come. I'll write it all down on a list for you. Get as much of what's on this list as you possibly can; this'll probably be the last chance y'all will have to get medication and medical supplies...if the whole drugstore hasn't been cleaned out already."

"I'll do, that Doc. Get the list ready. Wyatt and I will be leaving in five minutes."

"Will do."

Phil headed outside to talk to Wyatt, who had stocked up with more ammunition from Phil's bunker. Phil had also instructed him to bring out some extra equipment: tactical belts, bulletproof vests, flares, smoke grenades, and other items. He'd also brought out the modified AR-15 rifles. They no longer needed to look like ordinary, unarmed people; the time for that had passed. Stealth, however, would still need to play a major role in how they operated, and Phil was praying that they could pull this mission off without having to fire a single shot.

"Are we taking dirt bikes or the truck, or the Humvee?" Wyatt asked.

"None of those," Phil answered. "We'll go on horse-back. We can move quietly through the woods on horses, stay off the roads, and get right up to the outskirts of town. It'll be dead quiet out there without any machinery or any of the usual sounds of civiliza-tion, and the truck and the bikes will draw unnecessary attention. We wanna do this as quietly as possible."

"Understood," Wyatt said. "I'll go saddle up two horses."

"Great. I'll meet you at the stables in five minutes. Throw some saddlebags on the horses too. We have to try to get as much medication and supplies as we can carry."

"And lights?"

"We'll use the same ones we took from those bikers. I've got a bunch of LED lights and other electronic items in a Faraday cage, but I wanna keep 'em here on the ranch."

"Got it," Wyatt grunted, stony-faced.

Before Phil left, he went to check on Alice. She was sound asleep, and he didn't want to wake her; she needed as much rest as she could get. He knew he was heading into a perilous territory and didn't want to leave without saying goodbye. He kissed her softly on her cheek and lips and ran his fingers through her hair. "Sleep well, honey," he whispered. "I'll be back before you know it."

She stirred in her sleep but didn't open her eyes. Even so, Phil felt as if she knew he was there. He took one more look at her and then headed across to David's room. David had just climbed into bed, where he was eating a big meal and drinking a tall glass of juice, on the recommendation of Doc Robertson.

"How are you feeling, son?"

David smiled, proud of what he'd done. His face

was pale. He'd given a lot of blood, and he was exhausted from the last twenty-four hours on top of that. Even so, vitality sparkled in his eyes. "Real tired, Dad," he said, taking a swig of juice. "But, I'm glad I got to help Debbie."

"And I'm real proud of you for doing that," Phil said. "You need to get some rest now, y'hear?"

"Sure thing, Dad. I could do with a good, long sleep."

"I'm sure you could," Phil said. "Now listen, Davey, Wyatt, and I, we have to go into town to get some medication."

David immediately set the glass of juice down and made as if to get out of bed. Phil stepped over to him and put his hand on his son's shoulder, keeping him in bed, and shook his head.

"I appreciate your wanting to come with us, Davey," he said, "but you need rest, son. Besides, I need someone to be in charge while I'm gone. Can you do that? Can you look after the place until I get back? It's a really important job."

"I…yeah, I can do that, Dad." David looked disappointed at not being able to come along, even though he desperately needed sleep. Even so, he was happy that Phil had asked him to be the man of the house in his absence.

"Good. You get some rest. Then when you're feeling better, you make sure everything gets done as it should, okay? You know all the jobs that need doing, so make sure the people who are here do 'em right."

David smiled. "I'll do that, Dad. I just need a couple of hours of sleep first."

"You sure do. I'll see you later this evening, okay?"

"See you then, Dad...and good luck."

"I'm sure we'll be fine," Phil said, even though he wasn't entirely certain of this. "We'll be back in no time."

He gave David a tight hug and then left, heading straight for the stables. Wyatt had two of the best horses saddled up and ready to go. Phil put on a bullet-proof vest and a backpack, slung an AR-15 over his shoulder, and then climbed onto his favorite chestnut stallion. Wyatt, meanwhile, was mounted on his own favorite horse, a somewhat cantankerous dun mare.

"We'll go out the main gate," Phil said to Wyatt, "and head along the road for a mile, then head into the woods from there."

"Sounds good," Wyatt said.

When they got within sight of the main gate, however, Phil saw a group of people gathered outside it. "Shit," he muttered. "I hope this isn't trouble. Hold up, brother." Phil raised his AR-15 to his shoulder and peered through the telescopic sight. He was then able to see the faces of the people at the gate clearly, and when he did, he breathed out a sigh of relief.

"Who are they?" Wyatt asked.

"More of our workers and their families," Phil said, lowering the rifle and breathing out a sigh of relief. "I'm not surprised to see 'em, but I am a little surprised that they're coming back to the ranch so soon, though."

"Guess they got nothing at home," Wyatt said. "Most people didn't have a goddamn clue what was about to hit 'em."

"Come on, let's go. I'll talk to 'em when we pass 'em."

Wyatt and Phil rode up the long drive, and the crowd of people let themselves in. They saw Phil and Wyatt coming, so they kept the gate open for them. Phil stopped and spoke to them; he was not surprised to find out that their homes had quickly run out of the water, and that rumors of violence and looting in the nearby towns—not to mention the ominous glow and blackened skies of the burning city on the horizon— had prompted them to flee. Phil told them they were welcome on the ranch, and that he'd address everyone properly when he got back. In the meantime, they were to do their usual jobs, where possible without electricity, of course.

Once the two of them were out, Wyatt locked the gate behind them. The gates were heavy, wrought-iron items over ten feet tall, and the chain that kept them locked was thick and impossible to cut with bolt-cutters. The weak link, though, was the lock. If the combination got out, anyone could get in. Phil made a mental note to change the lock to one with a key once all the workers had come to the ranch.

The road that ran past the ranch was dead quiet, but there was nothing unusual about that; there was barely any traffic here on a normal day. Phil wondered if there would ever be any traffic here again. Even though there was no traffic, Phil didn't want to be on the road for any longer than absolutely necessary. He spurred his horse into a run, and Wyatt followed him. They raced down the side of the road at speed, covering a mile quickly. After that, Phil reined in his horse and led the stallion down a winding footpath into the woods.

A sense of relief settled over Phil once he was in the woods. Among the trees, with birdsong and the sounds of nature all around him, it was almost possible to believe that nothing had happened and that everything in the world was fine. The birds and insects here certainly didn't realize that the world of human beings had been flipped on its head. These little creatures simply carried on with their lives, the way they had for millions of years.

Phil and Wyatt rode through the woods for around two hours before reaching the hill that overlooked the first of the two towns, the one they'd sped through in the truck the previous day. When they got to the top of the hill, they were able to get a good look at the town. Phil needed a clearer look that that his rifle scope could give him, so he took out a pair of binoculars and surveyed the town.

From what he could see, most places had been boarded up. The streets looked eerily like those of the city; plenty of abandoned vehicles, trash, and debris were strewn about. The only difference was that no bombs seemed to have gone off here. At least two buildings were on fire, though, which hadn't been the case when they'd driven through this town the previous day.

As for people, the streets seemed eerily deserted. It was hard to tell for sure, though, because only a few streets and buildings were visible from this vantage point. Since it was late in the afternoon, though, Phil guessed that most people would have retreated to their homes by this time. Even so, he planned to be extremely cautious when entering the town; there was no telling who was roaming the empty streets, nor how many dangers were lurking there in wait for unsuspecting victims.

"What do you see?" Wyatt asked.

"The place looks deserted, mostly," Phil said. "There are signs of looting, though; be on your guard and keep your eyes and ears open."

"Will do. Should we head down?"

Phil drew in a deep breath before replying. "Yeah. Let's do this."

---

*P*hil and Wyatt tethered their horses and went the rest of the way on foot. The sun was low in the sky, and the shadows were long, and the chill of the evening air was settling in among the trees. When they reached the houses that bordered the woods, they faced a somewhat difficult choice. They could take a direct route by cutting across a few people's backyards, or they could go all the way around and get onto the main road that ran through the town.

"What do you think, Phil?" Wyatt asked, whispering; in the eerie silence close to the houses, his normal speaking voice sounded alarmingly loud. "I know it's a lot quicker to cut across these yards, but we don't know who's camping out behind these drapes and shutters in the windows with rifles in their hands."

"You're right," Phil whispered back. "It'll save us a lot of time, but we do run a real risk of having someone take potshots at us."

"Then again," Wyatt whispered, "if we go strolling into town on the main road, we might be setting ourselves up to get ambushed by whatever criminal scum shot Debbie."

"That's true as well," Phil said. "Given the risks of both scenarios, I think we go through the yards."

"You sure? I'm willing to bet there are some eagle-eyed marksmen sitting in their windows with itchy trigger finger, just waiting for someone to dare trespass on their properties."

"That's why we use the element of distraction," Phil whispered with a smile. "I knew these smoke grenades would come in handy."

"Are you sure a smoke grenade will provide enough of a distraction?" Wyatt asked.

"Not just a smoke grenade, brother," Phil said, his smile broadening and taking on the quality of a boyish grin. He took his backpack off, opened one of the side compartments, and took out an M-80 firework.

Wyatt chuckled. "Illegal fireworks, huh?"

"You and I have both got good arms," Phil said. "We toss the M-80 and the smoke bomb right over this house into the front yard, and the bang and the smoke will get whoever's inside this place and all the neighboring houses to go check it out. We'll be able to move through their backyards without 'em noticing."

Wyatt flashed Phil a rare, impish grin. "I think this is just crazy enough that it might work. Here, I'll toss the smoke grenade. I always did have a good arm when it came to slinging footballs."

"Once these things go off, we have to move fast," Phil said. "Rifle in your hands and keep your head low."

"Just like they taught us in the army," Wyatt said. "Hand me that grenade, and let's hit it."

Both men leaned their rifles against the wooden fence and got ready to throw their respective projectiles. Phil got his Zippo out and flicked it on. The instant the flame touched the M-80's wick the fuse hissed to life, spitting out sparks. Wyatt saw this and pulled the pin of the smoke grenade, and then hurled it as long and far as he could. It sailed over the roof of the house and was followed by the hissing M-80, which Phil had flung in the same direction. Both men snatched up their rifles and tensed their muscles, ready to go.

There were a few moments of tense silence, but then a tremendous boom ripped through the neighborhood, startling flocks of birds, that all flew out of the nearby trees in a panic. Soon afterward, plumes of smoke from the smoke grenade could be seen billowing across the front yard of the house.

"Go, hurry!" Phil urged, hopping over the fence. He and Wyatt raced across the backyard, then clambered over the next wooden fence and sprinted across the next yard, keeping their heads low. They jumped one more fence, ran down a drive, and then found themselves on the street. They hastily scanned the street, making sure they were alone, and then jogged down it. They rounded the corner and found themselves on the edge of the town.

"Made it," Wyatt said, breathing hard.

"It'll be dark by the time we come back this way," Phil said, also panting from the exertion of the sprint, "so we won't need to do anything like that again. Come on, let's get to the drugstore."

The red sun was touching the tops of the distant mountains now; the town would be shrouded in complete darkness soon. The men moved swiftly through the streets, using abandoned cars for cover, darting from vehicle to vehicle, and stopping at each one to carefully survey their surroundings and make sure they weren't being watched or stalked.

They got to within a block of the drugstore when they heard an ominous and familiar sound in the distance—a large number of two-stroke dirt bikes. Phil and Wyatt glanced at each other with looks of concern writ plain across their faces, and the unspoken question on each man's lips was the same. Were these the same violent raiders who had chased them down in the city the previous night?

"Sounds like they're heading toward the town," Wyatt growled, gripping his AR-15 tightly.

"I'm sure they are," Phil said. "And I doubt their intentions are friendly. We have to try to get in and out of the drugstore before they get here."

"Agreed. Let's hustle."

The men ran to the drugstore. It was on the main strip, and it was inevitable that the bikers would at least pass by the drugstore. A roll-down steel grille had been used to protect the large, vulnerable storefront window of the drugstore from looters, but because of how dark it was inside the store, the men would have to use their lights, which would be seen clearly by anyone outside in the street through the gaps in the security grille. It was a risk they would have to take, though; without the insulin, Debbie was as good as dead.

"No surprise that this place is locked up tight," Wyatt remarked, looking up and down the main strip, which was strewn with abandoned vehicles but seemingly deserted.

The steel grille was badly dented in many places, evidence that people had been trying to break in, but nobody had succeeded thus far, it seemed—at least not via the front of the store.

"Let's check around the side," Phil said, pointing to a small alley on the side of the drugstore.

They headed into the alley and saw that there was a side door that had previously been boarded up, but someone had smashed off all the boards. They walked up to the door and saw that the heavy security gate in front of it had been attacked and dented, but not yet defeated.

"Looks like someone tried taking an ax to this security gate," Wyatt said.

"And the lock," Phil said. Securing the gate was an extremely hefty padlock, which had been battered by hammers and axes, but which was still holding strong.

"What are you gonna do?" Wyatt asked.

Phil rummaged around in his backpack. "Use

science against this thing," he said. "I figured we might have to defeat a lock or two, so I came prepared. He handed Wyatt a portable propane torch, and a secure bottle of liquid nitrogen. "I'm gonna heat this thing up until it's red-hot," he said, "then I'm gonna give it a dose of liquid nitrogen. The rapid changes in temperature should make it brittle enough to shatter."

"All right," Wyatt said. "I'll watch the alley while you take care of that."

The sounds of the motorcycles were getting closer, and both men were aware of the immense danger they represented. Breaking the lock, though, was a task that couldn't be rushed. Phil got busy with it right away while Wyatt stood sentry. Phil slipped on a pair of safety goggles and ignited the propane torch. Then he blasted the lock with the flame for a good minute or so until the whole lock started to glow bright red. He ditched the torch and then started pouring liquid nitrogen all over the glowing lock, which hissed and crackled. After dumping all of the liquid nitrogen onto the lock, Phil took out a hatchet and whacked the lock with the back of it. The shackle snapped, and the broken lock fell to the ground, and Phil breathed out a sigh of relief.

"Come on, let's get in and out of this place as fast as we can!" Phil urged, yanking open the security gate. Beyond it was a locked door, but with a few powerful kicks, they were able to kick it open.

The sun was gone, and the alley and the street beyond were gloomy with thick shadows, and the inside of the drugstore was pitch-black. The men had no choice but to use their headlamps, even though they could hear that the bikers were getting dangerously close. Phil flicked his headlamp on, ripped Doc Robertson's list of medication in half, and handed half of it to Wyatt. "You get what's on this section of the list. I'll find the stuff on mine," he said. "Hurry!"

The men split up and dashed through the drugstore, racing against time to try to grab what they could from Doc Robertson's list. Phil made a beeline for the insulin and diabetic supplies; if they only got this and nothing else, then at least he would be able to save Debbie's life. He was relieved to find a large store of insulin in one of the back rooms of the drugstore, and he took as much of it as he could safely carry. After that, he got busy grabbing what he could of the other items Doc Robertson had written down.

He'd gotten about half of what was on the list when he heard the dreaded sound of dirt bikes rolling down the street; the bikers had arrived. He ran out to the front section of the drugstore, where Wyatt was still gathering supplies. "Time's up, brother, let's get the hell out of here!" he yelled.

"Dammit!" Wyatt yelled. "I've only got half the stuff on the list!"

"It doesn't matter. They're outside. We gotta go!"

"Shit," Wyatt growled, stuffing the last few items he'd grabbed into his backpack before pulling it over his shoulders. "Okay, let's go!"

As they bolted for the rear door, though, they heard

boots running up the alley, along with shouts of aggression and wild, almost maniacal whoops. The bikers had moved faster than they'd thought, and now there was only one way out of the drugstore…and that was *through* the bikers.

here was no time to argue or debate or try to figure out a way to escape. They were trapped in the drugstore, and the only way out was through the rear door to the alley—the same door the bikers would be charging through in seconds.

"Shut off your headlamp!" Phil instructed urgently.

"Take cover behind that shelf," Wyatt responded, after turning his headlamp off. "That way we're covering the door from two wide angles."

Phil scrambled to get down behind the shelf, then kneeling, he aimed his AR-15 at the door, resting his finger lightly against the trigger. He had a clear shot at anyone who tried to come into the door from here.

"Yo, whoever the fuck is inside the drugstore, drop your weapons and come out now with your hands up!" a voice from just outside the door roared. It was a strangely familiar voice, one Phil was sure he'd heard before. He couldn't quite place it, though.

"We'll come out," Phil yelled back, "but you allow us to leave on our terms, with our rifles in our hands!"

"Fuck that! You get the fuck out right now, hands empty and above your heads, or you don't come out alive, motherfucker!"

Phil knew he'd heard this man's voice somewhere before, but he couldn't work out where. It didn't really matter, though; it was clear that they wouldn't be leaving the drugstore without a fight.

"No deal!" Phil yelled.

There was no response from the alley. Instead, a hard, round object was hurled through the door into the drugstore. From the sound it made when it bounced, Wyatt knew exactly what it was. "Grenade!" he roared, diving for cover.

Phil couldn't see where the grenade had landed, but he could hear it had bounced somewhere alarmingly close to him. He dropped his rifle and desperately dived over the nearby counter, only just clearing it before a deafening explosion ripped through the drugstore. Wyatt yelped with pain, and from outside came furious howls of aggression. Through the billowing clouds of smoke and debris that were making the already dark interior even darker, Phil, whose ears were ringing with a shrill whine, saw shadowy figures wearing headlamps come charging through the door. While he no longer had his rifle, he did have his .45 in a holster on his hip, and he whipped out the pistol and started firing at the intruders.

From the other side of the drugstore came a burst

of AR-15 fire; Phil knew that Wyatt was still alive and kicking. Two of the invaders dropped dead, while another howled with pain and careened into a shelf when one of Phil's .45 rounds caught him in the leg.

Someone outside the door pointed an AK-47 in and blindly unleashed spray of automatic fire in an arc across the store, and Phil barely managed to duck under the counter before two of the AK rounds smashed into the cash register, in front of which his head had just been. With the man firing the AK-47 covering them, two more invaders scurried into the store, these two armed with shotguns. They fired a couple of shots in Phil's direction, keeping him pinned down and took cover behind a few shelves.

"You're dead, you fucking assholes!" the man outside the door roared. "You're fucking dead!"

Neither Phil nor Wyatt said anything in response. While their hearts were pounding in their chests and adrenalin was coursing through their veins, they were both utterly focused on dealing with and eliminating the threat the attackers presented.

Phil was coldly thankful that the attackers hadn't thought about the fact that their headlamps made them perfect targets in the dark. When one of the men with shotguns popped up from behind a shelf to fire at Wyatt, Phil got a perfectly clear shot at his head and took it. Before the man could even squeeze his trigger, his head snapped back, half his skull blown out by the .45 bullet.

The other biker, realizing his headlamp made him

an easy target, pulled it off, flung it across the store, and started crawling across the floor. "Take your head-lamp off, Jackson!" he yelled. "These assholes can see us like that!"

Phil saw the shadowy silhouette of the man with the AK-47—the one called Jackson—slip into the store sans headlamp. Another man, this one armed with a pistol, crept in after him. Phil got a good shot at him, though, and dropped him with a single shot to the torso. Jackson responded by popping up over a shelf and spraying a burst of AK fire in Phil's direction.

"Suck on that, motherfucker!" Jackson roared. The bullets peppered the counter and blew holes through the cash register, but Phil was safe.

Suddenly, something clicked in Phil's mind and realized where he'd heard Jackson's voice before. He had been one of the men who tried to break into Alice's apartment, and who had then tried to trap Phil and his group in the burning building. A burst of fresh anger ripped through Phil; this evil criminal had tried to kill him once before, and now he was trying again. This time though, Phil decided, this psycho wouldn't escape.

He knew that Jackson and the other bikers who were in the drugstore knew he was behind the counter, and they would keep on sending fire his way. He took out his headlamp and grabbed a nearby broom from the floor. He hung the headlamp on the end of the broom, then raised it above the counter, moving it as if it were a man trying to run.

A blast of shotgun fire came from the floor nearby,

and Phil knew it was one of the bikers shooting at the headlamp. Before he could fire at the man, though, Wyatt, who'd also seen the shotgun blast in the dark, took out the man with a burst of AR-15 fire.

"Fuck this!" one of the bikers yelled from near the door. "You're on your own now, Jackson. This ain't worth it!" The man fled, running out of the rear door, and Phil heard him yelling in a panicked voice to his comrades.

"Sons of bitches!" Jackson howled. "Cowardly motherfuckin' sons of bitches!"

From outside came the sounds of motorcycle starting up and then riding away as the gang rode off to find an easier target. A burst of triumph ripped through Phil's veins, but he knew the battle wasn't won just yet—there were at least two bikers still in the store, and Jackson, at least, seemed prepared to fight to the bitter end.

"To the bitter end then, asshole," Phil whispered, popping the empty clip out of his .45 and loading a fresh one.

"Rraahh!" one of the bikers screamed wordlessly, jumping up from behind a shelf and blindly firing into the dark, overcome by panic.

Wyatt popped up from behind cover, unloading a couple of rounds into the man's chest and face, but this was what Jackson had been waiting for—he too popped up and unleashed a burst of AK fire in Wyatt's direction. The bullets slammed into Wyatt's chest, and he dropped to the ground with a grunt.

"No! Wyatt!" Phil roared, jumping up on top of the counter, his heart racing.

"Fuck you!" Jackson snarled, coming up to blast another burst of AK-47 fire, his rifle aimed squarely at Phil's silhouette...but when he squeezed the trigger, there was nothing but an empty click—he was out of ammo. Phil fired a couple of rounds in quick succession, and all of them slammed home into Jackson's torso. He dropped his AK and crashed through a flimsy shelf.

That was it, the battle was over, but the only thing Phil cared about was Wyatt. He grabbed his headlamp from the ground, put it , and raced over to Wyatt. He found him lying on his back, wheezing and gasping for breath.

"I'm...okay," Wyatt managed to gasp. "Vest...saved me...but...wind knocked outta me...gimme...a minute."

The front of Wyatt's bulletproof vest was all torn up, but the plate inside, while badly dented, was intact. Phil whispered a prayer of thanks, then hurried over to check on the bikers to make sure none of them were alive. Every one of them that Phil came across was dead, but when he got to Jackson, his enemy looked up at him with life still burning with a bright and hateful vigor in his eyes. Phil saw that Jackson was also wearing a bulletproof vest, which had saved his life. One of Phil's bullets had done some damage, though. It had hit Jackson in his left shoulder, and the wound was oozing blood. Phil recognized Jackson's powerful build, his tattooed arms and neck, and his ugly, coarse-featured face from Alice's apartment building.

Now that there was some light in the dark store, Jackson was also able to recognize Phil. "Ahh, it's you, cowboy. I thought you and your bitch wife burned to death in that building yesterday," he growled, smiling evilly. "Guess I was wrong." His AK was empty, and he didn't have any other guns on him.

Phil pointed his pistol at Jackson's forehead, and cold rage was flowing through his veins.

"Go on, do it," Jackson taunted, grinning. "Put me outta my fuckin' misery. Do it, go on cowboy, do it!"

As much as Phil hated this man, he couldn't bring himself to execute an unarmed man. The battle was won, and pulling the trigger now would be murder, not self-defense.

"What're you waitin' for, cowboy?" Jackson growled. "Come on, put a bullet in my head. Do it! Fuckin' pussy, do it! You piece of shit, son of a."

Jackson's taunting was cut short by a heavy thud; Wyatt had gotten up and had just punted Jackson in his jaw with a heavy boot, knocking him out cold.

"Come on, Phil," Wyatt muttered, staring down with contempt at the man he'd just knocked out. "Let's get the hell out of here."

Phil slowly lowered his pistol and then holstered it. He took one last look at Jackson's ugly face, and then picked up his backpack and followed Wyatt out of the store into the pitch-black alley. It was time to go home.

29

"*I*t's been a month now since E-Day, Dad," David said to Phil. "Do you think things are ever going to go back to being the way they were?"

E-Day was what Phil and everyone else on the ranch had started calling the day of the EMP attack. "I don't know, son," Phil replied. "I mean, I know everyone hopes things will eventually return to normal, but don't get too attached to hope like that. It can be a dangerous thing."

David sighed, and Phil felt a sharp pang of empathy. He knew how much David missed school and his friends, and the old electronic things he'd loved so much before E-Day: video games, TV, phones, computers. Phil was sure that none of that sort of stuff would be coming back any time soon, though, not in this strange and uncertain new world they had found themselves in. He put down his shovel, stepped over to David, and gave him a hug.

"I know you're missing the old days, son. Believe me; I am too. And it's perfectly okay to be sad about those times and to want 'em back. But we have to live in the present, and prepare for a new future, one that's very different from how the old future was gonna be."

"I know, Dad, I know," David said sadly. "I just…it's hard sometimes."

"I know that, son. But come on, let's get back to work. These seed potatoes aren't gonna plant themselves, and we're running out of daylight. There's nothing like a bit of good old hard work to take your mind off sadness, trust me on that."

"Okay, Dad." The two of them got back to digging and planting potato seed.

They did this for around twenty minutes, working in silence until the sound of approaching hoofbeats caught their attention. They looked up and saw Wyatt approaching on his dun mare. On his usually stony face was an expression of concern, which worried Phil. He put down his shovel as Wyatt trotted his horse over to him and David.

"What's up, buddy?" Phil asked. "Did you finally pick up a non-military signal on the ham radio?"

"Nope, still the same old military garbage on the ham radios," Wyatt said. "Nothing new there. But you better come over to the farmhouse. The workers have called a meeting, and they wanna speak to you."

"All right, right now?"

Wyatt nodded. "Right now, yeah."

Phil and David's horses were tethered nearby.

"Come on, Davey," Phil said, "let's saddle up and go see what's going on. Leave the shovels here. There's still plenty of daylight left. We can come back and finish up the tater planting later."

Phil and David mounted their horses, and they and Wyatt rode the mile or so from the potato planting area to the farmhouse at a brisk pace. Outside the farmhouse, Phil saw a group of ten or eleven people gathered. This was about half his workforce. In the first few days after E-Day, all of his workers and their families had come to the ranch, driven out of their homes either by the danger of looters and raiders or because of running out of food and water. Phil had welcomed them all, had given them shelter in the many outbuildings on the ranch, and had divided the food up equally for them. He had assured them that as long as they all worked hard on the ranch and pulled their weight, they could stay on as long as they liked. He needed the labor to keep the ranch running optimally, and they needed the food and water the fertile, well-managed homestead provided. It was a positive arrangement for everyone, and Phil wondered why there was discontent. Everyone had seemed happy enough with the status quo over the past month, and everybody got their fair share for the work they put in.

Anthony and Debbie seemed to be the leaders of this group of workers. Debbie had recovered well from her surgery after the E-Day shooting, and thanks to the insulin Phil and Wyatt had taken from the drugstore, she was healthy and energetic. Anthony had recovered well from the trauma of seeing her shot too. Phil wondered why these two, of all people, seemed to be agitated about something. He walked up onto the porch steps to speak to the group. "Good afternoon, my friends," he said, smiling amicably. "What can I do for y'all? Is there anything I can help with?"

Anthony, looking a little nervous, got up onto the porch to speak to Phil on the group's behalf. "Phil, first up, we wanna say that we appreciate everything you and your family have done for us in these difficult times. Especially with what happened to my wife right after E-Day."

Debbie nodded, wordlessly expressing her gratitude.

"We aren't unhappy with anything about you or your family or the arrangement we've got going here on the ranch."

"Okay," Phil said, feeling a little confused. "So… what exactly is the problem here, if everyone's happy with how things are working?"

"We just…we think there has to be some sort of government station set up," Anthony said, looking a little guilty, "some sort of place we can go where they'll evacuate us and take us to a part of the country where, where things still work like they used to."

Phil sighed. "Anthony, we've been over this. Have you seen a single aircraft in the sky since E-Day? Any sort of aircraft at all? Besides the truck and dirt bikes here on the ranch, have you heard any kind of vehicles moving around?"

"Well, we couldn't even if there was any," one of the workers from the group said. "You guys dynamited the road leading to the ranch, so nobody could get here."

"And we destroyed the road to keep this place safe," Phil said calmly. "You all know about those biker gangs; some of you almost killed by 'em."

Debbie looked guiltily down at her feet when Phil said this.

"We had to cut ourselves off, people. We've been over this. We keep this place secret and remote, we keep it inaccessible from the outside world, and we stay safe. Look, I understand that some of you might be feeling a little stir-crazy. None of us has left the ranch, as big and expansive as it is, for almost a month. But we've got food and water and shelter here, people. This place is self-sustaining. We can live here indefinitely, independently. And we've been monitoring the ham radio every day, non-stop. Throughout the whole month, there's been not one broadcast from any sort of government. It's all military stuff, and from what I can hear, they don't know what's going on or have any sort of plan either."

"We realize that, Phil," Anthony said, unable to make eye contact with Phil. "And I'll say it again. We are super, super grateful for everything you've done for us. But some of us, we just can't live like this. This place is starting to feel like a prison—and that's got nothing to do with you or your family, Phil. I'll just say that as plainly as I can. You guys have been nothing but generous and loving to us…but we can't help the way we feel. We feel very strongly that the government of the United States still exists, and that they're doing their best to help survivors. We think that there's no way the EMP could have destroyed all technology across the whole nation, and we're sure there are town, cities, hell, maybe even whole states, where life has continued as normal."

Phil breathed in a long, deep breath and held it in for a while before releasing it in a slow sigh. "So what you're trying to tell me, Anthony, is that you're leaving?"

Anthony nodded. "We want to head out and find government help. We know it's out there. We just want to have normal lives again. I mean, what you've got going on the ranch is amazing, Phil, and we think it's wonderful that you've made this self-sustaining place… but we can't live like this forever. Maybe you can, but we can't. We have to try to get back to normal lives. And we're prepared to take whatever risks we have to to find that."

"Well, you're all free folk," Phil said. "And I can't stop you if you want to leave. For the record, I don't think you're making a wise decision at all, but if this is truly what you want to do, I won't stand in your way. Where are you going to go, anyway? Back to the city? You know it'll take you days of walking to get there because of the roads we destroyed."

"Yeah, back to the city," Anthony said. "We figure the violence has died down there now and the raiders have moved on or been driven out by the military.

We'll walk through the woods, the long way round. We don't mind that."

"Very well, then. I'll give you all a few days' worth of supplies and some spare tents we've got," Phil said. "I'm just going to ask you all for one thing, though."

"Sure, Phil," Anthony said.

"Don't tell anybody about this place, please. Not civilians you meet, not military, not government people, if there are any of those. That's all I ask: please, please keep this place a secret."

"Don't worry," Anthony said. "We won't tell a soul."

Phil extended a hand, and Anthony shook it. "Thanks for all the work you've done on the ranch, guys," Phil said. "I really appreciate it, and we'll miss you all when you're gone."

"We'll miss you, too, Phil," Anthony said. "But we have to do this. I hope you understand."

After the meeting, Phil, his family, and the workers who were staying on at the ranch said their farewells to the group that was leaving. They wished them luck, and Phil assured them that if they changed their minds, they were welcome to come back. After the group had departed, Phil had a meeting with those who were staying behind to reorganize shifts and duties. Now that a bunch of people had left, everyone would have to work harder, and their hours would be longer. Nonetheless, Phil still had everything under control, and the workload was by no means unmanageable. As long as another group didn't decide to leave as well, Phil was confident that the ranch could keep running as normal.

After the second meeting, Wyatt took Phil aside. "Brother," he said, "can we have a word in private?"

"Sure," Phil said.

They walked down to the stables to talk. "I'm worried about the safety of this place now," Wyatt said when they got there.

"You think someone in the group who left is gonna spill the beans about this place?" Phil asked.

"Not necessarily," Wyatt answered. "But I think there are gangs of real bad people out there, prowling the wastelands of the dead cities and towns. Think about it. It's been a month, and most people out there in the rest of the county probably ran out of food and water weeks ago. Shit, most of 'em probably ran out in the first few days after E-Day. Most people out there—those who survived, anyway—are gonna be looking dirty, disheveled, starving, ragged. Our people who just left, they're all well-fed and healthy. What do you think's gonna happen when these bandits and marauders see a group of well-fed, clean, healthy people?"

"I did warn them about the dangers of being attacked and robbed out there," Phil said.

Wyatt shook his head, and a dark look came across his craggy face. "It's not just about 'em getting robbed, Phil. The kind of people who are gonna be robbing people and marauding—like those bikers we fought off on two occasions—are not just gonna rob our people. They're gonna want to know *where they came from*, how they ended up being so well-fed and healthy in a time like this."

The color drained from Phil's face. "I can't believe I didn't think about it like that," he murmured. "But there was nothing I could do. I couldn't hold 'em here against their will."

"I know that. You had no choice. The people who left are good people," Wyatt said. "They wouldn't willingly divulge any information about this place...but these are dark times. In the Gulf War, I saw men who'd been tortured. The things that were done to 'em would have made them confess anything. And the bandits out there like those bikers, you think they wouldn't stoop to torture to get information? To starving people, this ranch is a goldmine. We need to be extra vigilant from this point on."

"You're right," Phil said, feeling determined. "We have to protect this place at all costs, and to do that best, we need an early warning system to detect any possible threats. Come on, there's plenty of wire and fishing line in the barn, and I've got a bunch more fireworks. For the rest of the day, we're gonna rig up some tripwire systems around the perimeter and in the woods nearby."

30

*J*ackson shoveled another mouthful of pork and beans into his mouth, chewing mechanically and staring at the fire. Black smoke billowed up from the fire, which was surrounded by old car tires, but the roof of the abandoned warehouse in which he and his gang were camped out was high, and the fire would have to burn for a long time before smoking the place out.

His jaw clicked every time he chewed, and it had been doing this ever since the Native American man had kicked him in the face, when he'd fought him and his cowboy friend back at the drugstore. Jackson had gotten used to the dull pain that throbbed in his jaw whenever he ate and had become accustomed to the lowered strength and mobility in his left arm after the cowboy had popped a .45 round into his shoulder. But what hadn't lessened over the five or six weeks that had passed since that fateful evening in the drugstore was his hatred for these two men. Every time he tried to chew anything hard or tried to pick up something heavy with his left hand, he was reminded of how those two had defeated him. And defeat was not something that Jackson Miller could tolerate being reminded of. As he ate his pork and beans, he played out dark scenarios in his mind, in which he slowly dismembered the two of them, or poured acid over their faces, molten metal down their throats, raped the cowboy's wife in front of him, and beheaded his teenage son while he was forced to watch...if only he'd succeeded in burning them all to death in that apartment building on E-Day, he thought, he'd still have a fully functional left arm and a jaw that didn't click. More than anything, he wanted to find the cowboy and make him pay for what he'd done to him.

"Yo, Jackson," one of his henchmen said, emerging from the thick darkness beyond the firelight, interrupting these sadistic thoughts. "We caught some stragglers."

"So?" Jackson growled. "Take their shit, kill 'em, keep any pretty women and girls for me...you know the fucking drill, numbskull. Fuck off, and don't interrupt me when I'm eating again if you want to keep that stupid tongue of yours attached to your mouth."

"Uh, yeah, man, trust me, I wouldn't have interrupted you if it hadn't been something big. And believe me, Jackson, this shit is big."

"As big as the bunker on Judgment Day?" Jackson put down his plate of food and looked up at his henchman, a heavyset man who wore an eyepatch, after losing his eye in a street battle a few weeks ago. His interest was now piqued.

"Maybe. That's why I came to call you before we interrogate the fuckers."

Jackson and his goons referred to E-Day as Judgment Day, and the big find he was referring to was when he and his gang—formerly a street gang of drug dealers and auto thieves—had raided a government warehouse shortly after the madness had started in the city. Jackson and his gang had been well-placed to take advantage of the chaos in the city. They already had a large cache of illegal arms and were accustomed to fighting in the streets, with the disputes and gang wars they'd had with other drug pushers. After killing the soldiers who were protecting the government warehouse, they had discovered a secret underground bunker beneath the facility. In the bunker had been a large collection of vintage dirt bikes, a couple of vintage trucks, and Faraday cages in which there had been a number of electronic items protected from the EMP. Jackson and his gang had hit the jackpot, and it was because of what they'd found in that bunker that they'd been able to thrive during this period of anarchy, in which most other people were starving and dying on the streets.

"Bring 'em here," Jackson said, smiling malevolently. "I'll get some of the branding irons nice and warm in the fire…" Jackson had taken some livestock branding irons from a farm they'd looted, and these items had turned out to be some of his favorites when it came to interrogating people and torturing information out of them. He stuck a few of the irons in the fire and watched them growing red hot, his smile broadening as the branding irons' glow brightened.

When he heard footsteps approaching, he stood up, clipping his sword onto his belt. The Civil War-era cavalry saber was another looted item he was fond of using to get information out of people, and he enjoyed wearing it for its symbolic role. He felt like a true, powerful general with his sword on his hip, rather than simply a gang kingpin.

His henchmen brought two people before him. They were a middle-aged couple, and their faces were purple and swollen from the beatings they'd already received at the hands of Jackson's thugs. A look of surprise registered on Jackson's coarse-featured face when the couple, whose hands were tied behind their backs, were shoved into the area of light around the fire. These people looked far healthier and well-fed than anyone he'd seen since before Judgment Day, and this immediately triggered a bunch of burning questions in his mind.

"What's your name, friend?" he asked the man, speaking in a friendly tone and smiling at him. He always used this tactic, catching his victims off their guard with unexpected kindness and gentleness before abruptly switching to his true, far darker self.

The man looked sullenly up at Jackson through

swollen, purple eyelids, and said nothing, his jaw tight with defiance.

Jackson grinned amicably and nodded. "All right," he said, "you don't feel like talkin'. That's understandable. It looks like you've had a rough time with my boys. I apologize for their behavior. Sometimes they can get a lil'...carried away." He slowly circled the prisoners, keeping his hands behind his back in a nonthreatening way. "How about you, ma'am?" he said to the woman. "Feel like telling me your name? My name is Jackson, Jackson Miller."

The woman stared at him with fear-bulging eyes. Her whole body was trembling with fear. She was a plain-looking woman, but every bit as healthy and well-fed as her husband, or boyfriend, or whoever this man was. She didn't say anything and only whimpered wordlessly.

"Cat got your tongue too, ma'am?" Jackson said, nodding and smiling. "That's okay, that's okay. Don't worry...it's all gonna be okay." He went and retrieved one of the branding irons from the fire. The branding end was glowing bright red. "You folk look like you may have worked on a farm, so I'm guessing you've seen one of these things before," Jackson said softly. "You know what it's for, don't you?"

The man gulped slowly, and Jackson felt a thrill rush through him as he saw the fear in the man's eyes. He was in his element now; he loved these interrogations. One way or another, these people would talk. They might be trying to act brave now, but they would eventually talk. They all did, in the end, when he was finished with them.

"Sir, is this woman your wife?" Jackson asked the man, standing in front of him with the glowing branding iron hanging loosely, almost casually from his right hand. "Your girlfriend, maybe, your lover?"

The man swallowed again and stared at the ground. Finally, he spoke. "She's nobody, just someone I...met on the road."

Jackson slowly circled the two of them again, smiling. "Just someone you met on the road, huh? Strange coincidence that both of you are so clean, healthy, nicely dressed, and well-fed in these...difficult times. Very strange, isn't it? Are you *sure* she's just nobody, just a stranger to you, friend?"

"She's...nobody," the man said, his voice cracking. It was painfully obvious that he was lying.

"Well then, friend," Jackson said, stopping next to the woman. "If she ain't nobody to you, then I guess it won't mean nothing to you if I do...this." He suddenly grabbed a fistful of the woman's hair and whipped the branding iron up. Before she could even react, he pressed the red-hot branding end into her cheek.

The scream that erupted from her lips was unearthly, and the terrible volume of pain in that animalistic howl of agony was music to Jackson's ears, even more so than the sizzle of burning flesh and the smell, disturbingly reminiscent of bacon, that wafted from her burning cheek as he pressed the branding iron in with more force.

"Debbie, no!" the man screamed hysterically, trying to charge over to her as she dropped to the ground, writhing and howling in sheer agony, smoke rising grotesquely from her burned cheek.

Jackson coolly sidestepped the clumsy charge and kicked the man's legs out from under him, causing him to crash face-first into the debris-strewn concrete floor of the warehouse. The man lay there, groaning in pain, while Debbie continued to scream her lungs out a few feet from him.

"Now I'm gonna ask you again, *friend*," Jackson said menacingly, dropping the branding iron and drawing his cavalry saber. "What's your name, and where have you and your fat, healthy friends come from?" He held the sharp tip of the sword in front of the man's eye, hovering the steel a mere sliver of an inch from his reddened eyeball. "You'd best tell me quick because I'm losing my patience, and when I lose my patience, I get nasty...*real* nasty. Now *tell me* your fucking name and where the fuck you came from because if you don't, the next question I ask you is gonna be which of your goddamn eyeballs I should gouge out first."

The man started weeping and shaking. "My name's...Anthony," he gasped. "I'll tell you whatever else you wanna know, just please, please don't hurt my wife again, please..."

Jackson smiled. They always cracked. Always. "That's the spirit, friend," he said, squatting down next to Anthony. He used the flat of the saber blade to force Anthony to look up into his eyes. "All right, Anthony, let's start at the beginning, now, shall we? We've got a long night ahead of us, and you're gonna do a lot of talking. Yeah, a lot of talking. Bill, hand me the other branding iron, would ya, and let's get this party started."

"*How* do you think Debbie and Anthony and their group are?" Alice asked, swirling her fork around her mashed potato in the manner she often did when preoccupied with worry.

Phil, sitting in his usual place at the head of the dining table, put his own fork down and shook his head, his face grim. "I pray every day that they find what they set out to find," he said, "but I've got a bad feeling about 'em, a bad feeling I just can't shake."

"Do you think they'll come back here?" David asked from the bottom of the dining table, his mouth full of half-chewed steak.

"I hope they do," Phil said, "but I hope that nobody else follows 'em."

In the days since Anthony's group departed, everyone on the ranch had worked hard to prepare for a possible threat. They'd started by installing early detection systems: a complex set of tripwires all around the perimeter of the ranch that was hooked up to fireworks with basic chemical ignition systems Phil had put together. If anyone set off a tripwire, it would detonate an M-80 firework and launch one of his orange signal flares into the sky. These signals would be seen and heard from anywhere on the ranch.

Phil and his workers had also dug trenches in the woods around the ranch, and they had destroyed all the bridges over the rivers and creeks, so if anyone did come, they would have to come on foot and wouldn't be able to get to the ranch with vehicles they could ram open the gates with.

They had also made contingency plans in the event that the perimeter did end up getting breached. Phil conducted emergency drills every day. Everyone was required to have a sidearm and two extra ammunition clips on them at all times, as well as keeping a bullet-proof vest and a rifle nearby. They'd also filled sacks with dirt and rubble to create sandbags and had piled them up around the walls of the house and the barn to reinforce them in case they had to fall back and defend these places.

Even while sitting around the dinner table eating dinner, the family kept their AR-15s and bulletproof vests close at hand. As Phil liked to say, it was better to be safe than sorry. All three of them shot furtive glances over at the rifles as they talked, each praying that they wouldn't have to use them.

Their conversation topic turned to lighter-hearted

subject matter, but in the backs of their minds, all three of them kept thinking about the unknown fate of Anthony's group.

The next day, everyone was up bright and early, but the day itself was gloomy, with dark, heavy clouds blotting out the sun. The rain started shortly after daybreak and only seemed to grow heavier as the morning went on. Phil and his workers put on ponchos and worked in the downpour; rain or shine, there were things that simply had to be done to keep food on the table.

Around late morning, the clouds coming over the distant mountaintops grew even darker, and there were flickers of lightning on the horizon. A storm was on its way. Phil moved around the ranch, encouraging everyone to work at double-time. As important as their respective jobs were, he didn't want anyone getting struck by lightning when the storm did hit the ranch.

Soon the wind began to howl through the trees, and crashes of thunder boomed across the meadows and fields. After everyone had got the horses in the stables and the cattle under shelter, they all went to find shelter themselves.

Phil, David, Alice, and Wyatt stood around in the kitchen, having coffee, after just having come in from the storm. They were chatting about how welcome the rain was after a long, dry spell when there was a loud boom that sounded quite different from the other thunderclaps.

"Shit," Wyatt grunted. "I don't think that was thunder…"

"Davey, run upstairs and look out the window, see if you can see anything!" Phil said, his voice low with urgency.

David raced up the stairs and yelled down the words that none of them were hoping to hear. "There's an orange flare in the sky, dad! Someone's set off the tripwires!"

"Where?" Phil yelled.

"From the direction of the main gate!"

Phil hung his head for a moment, massaging his temples with his hands. It was happening. He quickly forced the despair and fear out of his mind and took charge of the situation. "Wyatt, grab your rifle and put on a bulletproof vest. Alice, you tell everyone else that we've got company. Get into defensive positions, and tell everyone to get their walkie talkies out. I'll take one with me." Phil had saved a couple of walkie talkies in one of his Faraday cages; he knew they'd come in handy sometime.

"What should I do, Dad?" David asked, running back down the stairs.

"You know what you're supposed to do, son," Phil said. "Cover the drive with your rifle from the attic window."

"Can't I come—"

"No, you can't," Phil said firmly. "Up in the attic with your rifle, Davey. *Now*."

David looked disappointed, but he did what his

father told him. Once Wyatt and Phil had their bullet-proof vests on, Phil kissed Alice goodbye, and then they slung their rifles over their shoulders and headed outside.

Phil kept two dirt bikes—David's old Yamaha and an even older bike from the 60s—just outside the farmhouse in case he needed to get anywhere in a hurry. He and Wyatt hopped onto the dirt bikes, kicked them to life, and then, with their hearts thumping in their chests, they raced through the driving rain to the main gate.

When they got within sight of it, fear blasted through each man. It was worse than anything they could have imagined, for there was a huge mob outside the gate. Phil estimated that there were at least fifty people there, possibly more…and it was plain to see that all of them were armed.

When Phil got closer, his alarm grew more intense, for he recognized the man standing at the head of the mob: the huge, tattooed man he'd fought in the drugstore, the man who had almost burned them all to death in Alice's apartment building. He wished now that he'd executed the bastard when he'd had the chance. When Jackson saw him and Wyatt riding up to the gate on their bikes, he beamed out a broad, smug grin at them.

"Well, well, look who it is, the cowboy and the injun," Jackson said. He was holding his cavalry saber in his right hand, but he had an AK-47 slung over his shoulder and a pistol on each of his hips. "I was hoping to run into you two again."

Phil and Wyatt pulled up to a stop a couple of yards from the gate and stayed on their bikes, leaving the motors running. Sheets of rain beat down from the heavens, drenching everyone and soaking them all to the bone.

"There's nothing for you and your friends here," Phil said coolly. "You'd best leave."

"That's where you're wrong, cowboy," Jackson said, his grin broadening. "There's *everything* we need here. See, friend, we're getting real hungry out here, and a little bird told me that there's plenty of food beyond these gates."

"Not for you," Phil said. "There are plenty more of us here, and we're all armed and well-trained."

"I'm not here to talk to you or negotiate, mother-fucker," Jackson snarled, his grin disappearing in an instant. "I'm here to tell you that this fucking place is *mine* now. The rest of my army—yes, motherfucker, my *army*—will be here at sundown. And when they get here, you're fucked, all of you. I'm a fair man, though, and even though I'd like to skin you alive, nice and slow, like, I'll give you fucks the chance to leave peacefully. If you and whoever else is on this ranch leaves before sundown, you get to live. If you choose to stay, though..." He smiled again, picked up a backpack from the ground, and tossed it over the gate to Phil. "It's a little gift from me to you. Don't be rude and open it in front of me now Go on, take it back to your house and have a little look-see at what's inside."

"You aren't taking this ranch," Phil growled. "I don't care how many of you there are…you're not taking this ranch."

"Let's get out of here," Wyatt said. "There's no point in talking to these assholes."

"See friend," Jackson said to Phil, smiling. "The injun's got it right. There's nothing to talk about. This place is mine, and I'm taking it at sundown. Now take my gift and get the fuck out of here before our trigger fingers start getting itchy."

The mob raised their firearms and pointed them at Phil and Wyatt. Being outnumbered like this out in the open meant that they would be dead within seconds if they tried to fight. Wyatt got off his bike, picked up the backpack Jackson had tossed over the gate, and then got back on the bike and rode off, with Phil following close behind him.

When they were out of sight of the gate, both men pulled their bikes over to the side of the drive.

"I'm not taking that bag into the house," Phil said.

"I don't think it's a bomb or anything," Wyatt said. "He wouldn't have just tossed it like that if it were an explosive. I'm gonna open it up." Wyatt opened the backpack, and when he saw what was inside, he dropped it and staggered back, his eyes almost popping out of their sockets.

"What is it?" Phil asked, alarmed.

"It's…oh my God…it's…" Wyatt couldn't even

complete this sentence; what he'd seen was beyond horrific.

Phil walked gingerly over to the backpack, his heart in his mouth. And when he looked inside, he saw the severed heads of Anthony and Debbie.

*A*fter recovering from the shock of seeing what was in the backpack, Wyatt and Phil rode over to the barn, picked up a pair of shovels, and then rode out to a quiet, scenic spot and buried the heads. Phil said a quick prayer over the grave and then sent Wyatt off to round up everyone for an emergency meeting. He instructed him not to say anything about Debbie and Anthony just yet.

Phil debated over whether to tell the other workers about the severed heads. On the one hand, the knowledge of what Jackson had done to Debbie and Anthony may well fill the workers with righteous wrath, giving them fire in their bellies to fight off Jackson and his so-called army. On the other hand, though, it might traumatize them and make them panic. Phil thought about it for a long time, only making his decision on what to tell people once they were all gathered by the porch of the farmhouse.

"What's going on, Phil?" Doc Robertson asked as soon as Phil took his spot at the top of the porch stairs. "I could have sworn I saw one of those orange signal flares go up during the storm, around an hour ago."

"I've got some bad news, everyone," Phil announced gravely. "We're about to face a terrible threat…a direct threat to our lives and our very existence out here."

Gasps of shock rippled through the crowd of workers.

"A gang leader, warlord, whatever you want to call him," Phil continued, "has discovered this place. Most likely after he…after he killed Anthony and Debbie."

"Oh God!" Doc Robertson gasped, and other exclamations of shock and horror exploded from the crowd.

"Oh my God, Phil," Alice murmured, the color draining from her face. "Are you…are you sure they're…dead?"

Phil nodded grimly and exchanged a quick glance with Wyatt, who remained tight-lipped. "I know without a doubt that this man, Jackson, murdered Anthony and Debbie," Phil said. "He showed Wyatt and me irrefutable evidence of this. I'm not going to go into details about it…but we'll have a proper funeral for them and the other members of their group—who I think he murdered as well—if we survive the coming storm."

"What exactly do you mean by that?" Doc Robertson asked.

"Jackson already has around fifty thugs with him, all armed with firearms, and he says the rest of his 'army' will be here by sunset. He's given us until then to vacate the ranch peacefully before he takes control of this place. After that, anyone who's still here will be killed."

This time there were no gasps or exclamations of shock or horror. Instead, a deathly silence settled over the group. None of them had felt so frightened and worried since the initial EMP attack on E-Day.

Phil gave them a few moments to process what he'd just said before he continued. "I intend to stay here and fight," he said calmly. "This land has been in my family for generations, and if I have to die fighting to defend it from a murderous scumbag and his gang of looters, who'll just destroy everything I've spent my life working for, and leave it in a state of ruin when they abandon it in a few months to move on to the next place, then I'm prepared to die for that."

"My ancestors hunted and fished in this area for thousands of years," Wyatt added stoically, "and this ranch, this self-sustaining place where we live according to the principles of nature without raping and abusing the land, is as close a vision to how the land should be used as my ancestors had. They would turn in their graves if they saw me abandoning this place to scum who are nothing more than a plague of locusts. I'm staying, too, and I plan on fighting to the bitter end."

Phil exchanged an intense look with Wyatt, silently thanking him for saying this. Then he addressed the workers again. "I don't expect anyone else to stay and fight," he said. "I know that this ranch holds a special place in all of your hearts, but I don't expect anyone to die for it. If you want to pack your belongings and leave before sundown, I won't think any less of you. That goes for every single one of you, and I say this from the bottom of my heart. This is my fight, and the only life I'm willing to risk is my own. I'm not going to put you on the spot now. I'll let you talk among yourselves for a few minutes before you all come to a decision about what you want to do. When you're ready to tell me, I'll be in the kitchen with my family."

Without saying anything else, Phil turned around, took Alice's hand, and led her into the farmhouse. David and Wyatt followed them, and Wyatt closed the door behind him. Once they got to the kitchen, Phil could focus his attention on his wife and son. Both of them were understandably, immensely distraught.

"Dad, I'm staying here to help you fight," David said, doing his best to be brave.

Phil could see the terror in his son's eyes, though, and didn't want to subject him to the horrors of having to fight a monster like Jackson. Of course, he also didn't want to diminish his son's courage and make him feel as if his offer to fight was unworthy. "I really appreciate you saying that, Davey," he said, giving David a hug. "You're a brave kid, you really are. And that's why I need you to take on a really important role. You think you can handle some serious responsibility?"

"I sure can, Dad."

"In the event that things…well, go badly for us,

someone has to lead the women and children out of here and make sure they're safe in a retreat."

"Phillip McCabe," Alice said sternly, folding her arms defiantly across her chest, "you are *not* sending your wife and son away to hide while you recklessly throw your life away! David and I can shoot as well as anyone on this ranch, and we're *not* going to hide away like mice and let these violent thugs overrun you."

Phil had to chuckle at his wife's fiery attitude. He wasn't surprised that she refused to back down in the face of a threat. "I really appreciate you saying that, honey," he said, "but I'm not throwing my life away. I'm buying time for anyone else who stays to get away with their lives. And there's no use in all of us dying. David still has his whole life ahead of him. And I meant what I said; someone has to make sure that the women and children get away safely in the event that we lose this battle. Jackson is a cruel, evil monster, and if he gets hold of any women and children…I don't even want to imagine that. You two can take up sniper roles in the initial assault, but the instant that it looks like we're going to be overrun, you two *must* leave, and make sure that you take all of the other women and children safely with you. I'm sorry, but I'm putting my foot down about this."

"And if you two don't do that, I'll shoot you both myself," Wyatt said. "Trust me; this guy is a psycho. I couldn't die in peace knowing he'd got hold of you alive."

"All right, all right," Alice said, reluctantly giving in.

"But we *are* going to fight in the early stages of this battle. Neither of you two are going to stop us doing that."

"I'm okay with that," Phil said. "Come here, everyone."

Everyone huddled together and had a group hug. Before anyone else could say anything, there was a knock on the kitchen door. Phil opened it, and Doc Robertson was standing there with everyone else behind him, wearing expressions of grim determination on their faces.

Doc Robertson's message was simple and direct. "We're going to stay and fight, Phil," he said. "Every last one of us."

"*E*verything's packed and ready to go, right?" Phil asked.

The group, assembled before him below the porch, all called out cries of affirmation. Everything essential —the medical supplies and medication, the few working electronic items protected by the Faraday cages, long-life food, some fuel, ammunition and camping supplies—had all been packed into hiking backpacks, which would be carried by those who fled the ranch in the event that the defenders were defeated.

"Excellent," Phil said, looking down at the group with pride sparkling in his eyes. "And I'm doubly impressed at how fast you all managed to get it all together."

"Teamwork and a ticking clock," Doc Robertson said, grinning, "make for the most efficient work."

"Indeed they do," Phil said. "All right, the rain's

stopped, the sky's cleared up, and we've got the whole afternoon to get our defenses set up and get a solid plan of action together. Wyatt's got military experience, so he's going to be overseeing that."

"First thing we're gonna do is real simple but deadly effective," Wyatt said grimly. "And it's guaranteed to take out a couple of those bastards before they cotton on to what we've set up, especially seeing as they'll be coming in after sundown when it's getting dark. Jonathan, Eddie, and Rick, I'm putting you three in charge of this operation. Everyone else needs to listen up, though, and pay close attention, because you all need to know where these traps are so you can avoid 'em."

"What kinda traps are you talking about, Wyatt?" Doc Robertson asked.

"Tiger traps," Wyatt said. "Pits in the ground with sharp spikes in 'em. Primitive and crude, but extremely effective against an unsuspecting invader. We'll cover 'em up with straw, and I guarantee at least a few of those scumbags will step on it. Jonathan, you're gonna take the backhoe and dig trenches at least four feet deep across the drive here, here and here," Wyatt said, pointing at different spots on a map of the ranch he'd drawn up. The ranch still had a working tractor and backhoe, as both of those items, like the other vehicles on the ranch, were 60s-era machinery which hadn't been affected by the EMP.

"What do Rick and I do?" Eddie asked, studying the spots Wyatt had marked on the map.

"You're the strongest man on the ranch," Wyatt said to Eddie, a huge man who was close to seven feet tall and over three hundred pounds. "And you're gonna put that strength to good use. Get a couple of wheelbarrows, tanks of water, and bags of quick-dry cement. You're gonna be hauling the cement around, mixing it, and filling the bottoms of those trenches with it."

"And me?" Jonathan asked. In physical terms, he was the opposite of Eddie, a thin, wiry little man with quick, dexterous hands. "What's my role?"

"You're gonna cut a bunch of rebar into twenty-inch lengths, which you're gonna sharpen at one end. Stick a bunch of 'em into the cement with the sharp ends facing up once Eddie's laid it down. After that, cover up the pits with straw, branches, dry grass, anything flimsy that'll cave in right away as soon as any weight's on it."

Jonathan flashed Wyatt a wicked grin. "Can do, Wyatt."

"While you three are busy with that, Phil's gonna need some help setting up some other booby traps," Wyatt continued. "Phil, you wanna take over for a bit?"

Phil nodded. "My team is going to set up some more sophisticated traps," he said. "But before that, we need someone to double-check all the early-warning tripwires beyond the perimeters of the ranch. Davey, you're the fastest rider on the ranch. As soon as this meeting is over, you take your dirt bike and ride to each of those tripwires and make sure they haven't been tampered with. We need to know when this army arrives."

"I'll do that, Dad," David said, doing his best to sound confident and determined.

"Take an AR with you, and if you spot anyone suspicious, shoot first and ask questions later, son," Phil said gravely. "And don't hang around outside the ranch. Come straight back in."

"Okay, Dad."

Phil then addressed the others. "The last trap I'm gonna set up will likely do a *lot* of damage, and it'll be the second trap that goes off in the battle. Hell, in the best-case scenario, it might be enough to end the battle without a single shot being fired. It won't make for the first kill of the battle, though."

"What will set up the first kill?" Doc Robertson asked.

"I'll tell you about the big trap later, but as for the first kill, I'm gonna set up a car battery with a capacitor and hook it up to the main gate. I'm ninety-nine percent sure Jackson and his army are gonna come straight in through the main gate. They're overconfident, and it's the easiest point of access. I changed the code lock for a keyed lock long ago, but even so, they'll probably just shoot the lock off, and then they'll have access. Whoever touches that gate first, though, will get a lethal electric shock."

"From a car battery?" Doc Robertson asked, looking skeptical.

"With the right capacitor setup," Phil said, "a car

battery can deliver a charge high enough to kill a grown man. And that's exactly what I'm gonna set it up for."

"What about the big trap?" Alice asked.

"I'll get onto that, honey," Phil answered. "I'm going to have to spend some time tinkering with a few chemicals in the workshop to get everything set up just how I need it to be, but it'll be devastating when they set it off. Don't worry about that just yet. I've got a whole bunch of other traps I'm gonna need help from everyone getting set up."

"You just tell us what to do, Phil, and we'll do it," Doc Robertson said, curling his liver-spotted hands into fists, his jaw set with determination. "We'll stop these bastards in their tracks."

"I've got a job just for you, Doc," Phil said. "You know cattle better than anyone, and I'm gonna need you to get 'em all riled up in the pen. When I give the signal, you're gonna open the pen and spook 'em into stampeding, hopefully. The herd stampeding at the right time should flatten a few of the invaders."

Doc Robertson grinned. "Don't worry, Phil. I'll get 'em good and spooked and ready to stampede. Hell, if there's a bunch of gunfire going off, they'll be spooked enough without any encouragement from me. But I'll make sure the cattle get a little kick in the pants at just the right time."

"Perfect," Phil said. "Everyone else, listen up. We're going to have to approach this battle in stages. We must assume that these people will keep attacking, even if my big trap does a lot of damage. The truth is, I don't know how many men Jackson has in his so-called army. It may be a hundred. It may be two hundred, maybe even more. Even if my big trap takes out a few dozen of 'em, they could be desperate enough to keep coming. They'll lose a few more men to the tiger traps, and then maybe a few more to the stampede and our snipers, but even then, we have to assume they'll simply keep coming."

"So, what do we do if that happens?" Alice asked.

"We defend from the farmhouse first," Phil said, "but when they get too close—which they very well might—we have to retreat to the barn. That brings me back to you, Eddie, and the other men, when you're finished setting up tripwires and improvised bombs, like how I'm gonna show you."

"Just tell me what to do, and I'll do it," Eddie said.

"All the men need to build a sandbag corridor between the farmhouse and the barn," Phil said.

"Phil, that's a really long way, it'd take days to build that," Eddie said.

"I know that, and it doesn't have to be one long corridor. Just sections of sandbags that people can sprint between, rest at, then sprint to the next pile of sandbags, so that it isn't one long open run to the barn with no cover."

"Got it," Eddie said. "I can do that."

"And once we're in the barn, what then?" Alice asked.

"We shoot flares up to light up the battlefield," Phil

said grimly, "and fight until we either win or we can't fight any longer."

"And if the latter is the case?" Alice asked, looking worried. "What do we do then?"

"I've got one more major weapon to use that'll draw the heat from the attackers long enough to give you all the chance to flee. Below the basement, there's the old underground tunnel that comes out near the southern border of the ranch. If it looks like the fight is lost, Davey, you and Alice lead the retreat. You'll have to take the survivors out of the ranch through the woods to the south. Follow the river to the lake, and row out to the island in the middle, where you make camp. If I survive my last stand, I'll meet you there at sunrise tomorrow. If I'm not there by then, you'll know that I didn't make it. Row across the lake and head west. You'll be safest in the wilds there…and you'll have to look for a place to make a new start."

A somber silence settled over the group at this point. The reality of what was about to happen was starting to sink in, and everyone understood that there would likely be casualties on their side.

Phil, sensing this, cleared his throat and addressed everyone. "Regardless of how well-prepared we are, some of us are going to be hurt, maybe even killed. Jackson and his men have a lot of guns, grenades, and maybe even some other weapons we don't know about. We may well be able to do a lot of damage to 'em, but it's naïve for us to think that we'll come away from this battle—even if we're victorious—without a scratch. I'll say it again, at this point: anyone who wants to leave now, you're free to go. I won't think any less of anyone who pulls out right now. You've all been such heroes up to this point, and you've all already done so much more than I could ever have imagined. In fact, if any of you think you're not going to be able to handle the coming fight, I'd rather you left now. One weak link in our chain could result in disaster for us. Again, I just want to say that regardless of what you choose to do, you'll always be a hero in my eyes and my family's eyes for what you've already done."

"I'm staying right here," Doc Robertson declared, proudly and confidently. "I may not be young and strong no more, but I'll fight with every ounce of strength I have in these old bones. I stand against tyranny, thieving, and thuggery!"

"Me too!" Jonathan declared.

"You can count on me, Phil," Eddie said, folding his heavy arms across his broad chest.

Everyone else confirmed that they were in this fight until the end, and tears of pride rolled down Phil's cheeks. He could see the sincerity in everyone's eyes and hear it in their voices. A tight knot of emotion gripped his throat, and it was a few seconds before he was able to speak.

"Thank you, everyone," he said, still choking up. "You're true heroes, every last one of you, and you mean the world to me, all of you. And now…let's get everything ready for the coming battle."

34

*T*he sky had cleared completely from the earlier rain, and the sun was hovering close to the distant mountaintops. There was perhaps an hour of daylight left, all the traps had been set up, and the battle preparations had been laid out. Every person on the ranch was suited up in a bulletproof vest, and all of them were carrying a rifle—either an AR-15 or a semi-automatic hunting rifle—and a sidearm or two, along with plenty of ammo for both firearms.

There hadn't been time for anyone to make any food, but Phil insisted on sitting down for one last meal with everyone before sunset. Alice had some cornbread in the morning, and there were plenty of cans of food that were easy to heat up in a hurry. It wasn't exactly a dinner fit for a king, but it was hot, wholesome food, and after the hard work everyone had put in throughout the afternoon, they were all grateful for it.

Phil opened a few bottles of wine from the cellar

too. He certainly didn't want anyone to get drunk, because they all needed to be mentally alert and sharp for the coming battle, but a little alcohol would at least take the edge off their nerves. He even allowed David to have half a glass.

Before the meal, Phil said grace, and then raised his glass of wine. "I'd like to thank each and every one of you one last time, from the bottom of my heart," he said. "Here's to your courage and valor. I'm honored and humbled to have every one of you here with me. Thank you, all of you."

Everyone raised their glasses to Phil. "You've kept us alive these past few weeks, Phil," Doc Robertson said. "Most of these folks around this table didn't have no place to go, nor a crust of bread to chew on a couple of days after E-Day. Thanks to your foresight and this wonderful ranch, every person here has not only been able to survive but to thrive. We'll defend it to the last; I promise you that."

Everyone else added vocal and enthusiastic support to this statement, and another wave of intense emotion surged through Phil.

"Thank you, everyone," he said, his voice cracking, his heart swelling with pride in his friends. "Thank you all so much. For the rest of the dinner, let's just act as if it were an ordinary Sunday evening, how about that? In these last moments of peace we have together, let's look back at some good memories we've all had here. Let's smile and laugh and worry later about what's to come."

Everyone agreed heartily with this, even though there were tears in many of their eyes and fear in their hearts. Eddie stood up and smiled. "Hey Phil," he said, "remember that time one of the calves got out and got lost, and I had to go try to find him after dark, and I fell in the creek and got all covered in mud…"

"And my friends and I were camping down in the woods," David said, picking up the story, grinning, "and we'd just watched that documentary about sasquatches."

Phil chuckled. "How old were you, about nine or ten, right?"

"Yeah," David said.

"And I was all covered in mud and twigs, and I was mad as all hell after having been traipsing around the damn woods in the dark, soaked to the bone after falling in the creek," Eddie said, "and I came stumbling outta the woods just as your buddy got out of the tent to take a leak, Davey. I ain't never heard a kid scream so loud!"

Everyone laughed, and the tension and stress were lifted, at least temporarily.

"When you and your buddies ran into the house," Phil said to David, chuckling, "screaming about a sasquatch in the woods and looking like you'd seen a ghost, and I realized it was just Eddie all covered in mud and twigs, I almost bust a rib laughing!"

Everyone continued to tell amusing stories over dinner, and they got so lost in their memories and recollections that they almost forgot about the looming battle…almost. Soon enough, though, the sun brushed the tops of the mountains, and the air became thicker and thicker with bottled-up tension.

Phil looked out of the windows and saw that the sun had almost disappeared behind the mountains. The smile faded from his face, and it was replaced by a look of grim determination.

"All right, everyone," he said. "The time has come. The battle will be starting soon."

"Remember what I told y'all," Wyatt said. "Work in pairs, with one providing cover fire at all times, especially if the other has to reload. Don't pop your head out at the same spot every time when you're shooting from behind cover. They'll wait for you to do that and aim at that spot. Keep your bodies as low to the ground as possible; present as small a target to the enemy as you can. And follow orders! The rabble who'll be attacking us probably won't have any discipline, and that's one area we can beat 'em in, even with far fewer numbers. Well-disciplined sharpshooters in small numbers have overcome crazed masses of undisciplined rabble many times in military history."

"He's right," Phil said. "Each group or pair, you must keep your walkie talkies on at all times, and when we say retreat, retreat! Don't try to be a hero and ignore our orders to go out in a blaze of glory or anything stupid like that because you'll only be hurting the rest of us. The orders aren't about Wyatt and me having some sort of authority and power over the rest of you;

they're about winning this battle and suffering as few casualties as we possibly can."

"We understand that, Phil," Doc Robertson said. "Don't worry, we'll obey to the letter, just like real soldiers, won't we, everyone?"

Everyone gave an enthusiastic cheer.

"Excellent," Phil said. "Have faith, shoot straight, be disciplined and brave, and we can overcome this mob of savage criminals."

Everyone cheered again.

"All right people," Wyatt said, "you all know where your battle stations are. We've been over the positions for the first, second, and third phase of the battle a few times, and you all know where to retreat to when we give the orders. Let's move out. Everyone get over to your first phase battle stations!"

The defenders all picked up their rifles and moved out to their various battle stations. Phil was certain that Jackson would come through the main gate because the trees lining the long drive would give his army cover from fire. If he tried to attack from any other point, he'd have to move his troops across the wide-open ground with no cover at all, where they could be cut down in masses. Even so, Phil and Wyatt had made contingency plans in case Jackson tried to do something as suicidally stupid as this and had given everyone alternative battle stations in case the attack came from the south, east, or west.

Phil gave Alice a long, tight hug and a long kiss, and then he hugged David as well. Then all three of them hugged as a family. When they stepped away from each other, tears were glistening in all of their eyes.

"I love you, Phil," Alice said, choking up. "So much."

"I love you, too, honey. You keep her safe, Davey, you hear?"

"Yeah, Dad," David said, tears running down his cheeks and his lower lip quivering.

"Stay alive, both of you," Phil said hoarsely. "Whatever happens…stay alive."

"Come on, Phil, we gotta go," Wyatt said gently. "It's already getting dark out there."

Phil took one last emotion-drenched look at his family, and then turned and strode briskly out of the farmhouse, stifling the sob that was rising up his throat. He and Wyatt hopped onto the dirt bikes, kicked the motors to life, and then raced up the drive to take their first battle positions. Once Phil was on the bike, he began to feel less emotional, and a hard, fierce sense of determination took over. An image of Jackson formed in his mind as he rode through the dusk, and a vengeful loathing for this evil warlord burned in his belly. He growled wordlessly and cranked the throttle, accelerating ahead of Wyatt. A part of him that rarely awoke, a part that he'd only discovered a few times—in Alice's apartment building, in the motorcycle chase, and in the drugstore—was coming to life again. He knew that he had to fight, and he knew that he was fighting on the side of good against the forces of evil. These feelings of righteous aggression filled him with fresh energy and zeal, and he felt ready for the coming battle. All that mattered now was defeating their enemy.

He and Wyatt got to their battle stations after two or three minutes of riding. They'd chosen to begin their defense from two large boulders on either side of the drive, on top of a rise. From this vantage point, they had a clear view of the main gate, around three hundred yards away, and much of the drive, although the many trees along it would provide cover for the invaders.

Phil and Wyatt had Remington 700 rifles set up on tripods next to each of their boulders. These would be used for long-range, sniper-style shooting when the first wave of attackers came down the drive. If and when the attackers pressed on and got closer, the men would discard these rifles and use their AR-15 rifles instead and then retreat to the next position, where they'd be covered by rifle fire from multiple points. The attackers would be funneled through a killing alley if they continued to try to press on up the drive, and there would need to be hundreds of them to continue past this point.

Phil was still hoping that when his first big trap went off, it would cause enough damage to demoralize the attackers and dissuade them from coming any farther, but he knew that starvation and desperation would probably be enough to push them to continue their attack…and he was prepared for this.

The sun had disappeared behind the mountains already, and above them, the clear sky was dotted with hundreds of stars and was turning from deep blue to black. Dusk was giving way to night, but there was no sign of Jackson and his army yet.

"Where the hell is that asshole?" Wyatt asked, getting impatient.

"Maybe he was bluffing," Phil said. He doubted that this was the case, though.

A voice crackled through Phil's walkie talkie. It was Doc Robertson. "I'm getting these cattle pretty riled up, Phil," he said, "but soon enough, they're gonna become accustomed to what I'm doing, and they won't be spooked out anymore and won't stampede. Any sign of the enemy yet?"

"Nothing Doc," Phil replied. "And honestly, if they don't show up at all, it'll be the best outcome we could have hoped for. Be ready, though; I have a feeling they'll come eventually."

"All right but be aware that the cattle might not do what you're hoping they will."

"I'll take that into account. Over, Doc."

"Over."

Despite the chill of the evening air, Phil was starting to sweat. He wondered if Jackson was delaying his invasion just to mess with their heads. If that were the case, it was working.

"I really hate waiting around like this, not knowing when these assholes are gonna attack," Wyatt grumbled. "I wish they'd just come outta the woods with guns blazing, so we could get on with this damn fight."

"Be careful what you wish for," Phil cautioned, "because you just might—"

Before Phil could finish his sentence, a loud bang echoed from the woods beyond the gate, and an orange flare streaked up into the sky; one of the tripwires by the gate had just been set off. Jackson and his army had arrived.

"Here they come," Phil muttered grimly, pressing his eye up to the rifle scope and easing his finger onto the trigger. "Let's get ready to—"

Again he was cut off from finishing his sentence by a bang—but this one was a distant boom, barely audible, coming from far off. It was followed by another distant bang. Alarmed, Phil looked over his shoulder and saw two more orange flares shooting up into the sky in the distance.

"Oh shit," he gasped as he was hit by the realization of what these flares meant. "They're attacking from three different places at once!"

35

*P*hil and Wyatt hadn't been completely unprepared for a multi-pronged attack. Phil knew that it was dangerous to underestimate an opponent and knew that as loathsome as Jackson was, he had to possess at least some measure of intelligence to have risen to the position of leader, even if what he was leading was nothing more than a glorified gang of murderers, rapists, and thieves.

Therefore, they had a contingency plan in place in the event that Jackson split his force in two and attacked from two different spots. They knew that while this presented a danger for them, it was also risky for Jackson. By splitting up his force, he was weakening the strength of his superior numbers. However, it would also split the defenders' force, so Phil had figured that it would be a very real possibility.

What he hadn't prepared for was a three-pronged attack. He simply hadn't assumed that Jackson could have that many soldiers. Now the battle had started, and Jackson had taken the upper hand without a single shot being fired.

"They're coming from three directions!" Phil yelled into his walkie talkie. "Red team and blue team, move down to the barn and cut down anyone you see coming across the pasture! Yellow team, move to the stables, you're gonna be fighting from there because they're coming from the south as well! We'll hold them off as long as we can from this side! Everyone move now!"

Phil knew now that there was going to be a fierce fight regardless of what happened in this area, by the main gate. Even so, he knew that with his traps and sharpshooting, he and Wyatt would be able to decimate the segment of Jackson's force that was attacking the main gate.

"Stay calm, keep your wits about you," Phil muttered, half to himself and half to Wyatt. He peered through his rifle scope, watching as the first of the invaders emerged from the woods opposite the main gate. In addition to the damage that his traps would do, he was hoping that he could get a clear shot at Jackson early on in the battle. If he could take out Jackson, he hoped that it might demoralize the rest of the invaders.

The men who were emerging from the woods were all armed with firearms—there were shotguns, rifles, AK-47s, M-16s, and plenty of handguns—and most were wearing items of makeshift armor. Some were armored up in police SWAT gear, many had bullet-proof vests, and some were wearing football or baseball helmets and other protective gear. They had clearly come ready for a fight. Well, Phil thought, they're gonna get one.

He panned his scope across the gathering crowd but frustratingly saw no sign of Jackson. He wasn't too surprised about this; he knew Jackson wouldn't be standing out front when it was obvious that there would likely be traps and sniper fire to overcome. He had surely placed his more expendable men in the front lines.

"I've got clear shots at so many of these bastards," Wyatt growled from his boulder.

"Hold off, brother," Phil said. "We want 'em to come on confidently so the big trap can take out as many as possible. Any rifle fire will make 'em scatter and run for cover."

"I know, I know...it's just hard to refrain from taking out so many easy targets," Wyatt said.

Phil watched as a crowd of invaders gathered outside the gate. He could hear his pulse pounding in his temples, and his mouth was dry. A man dressed in SWAT gear holding a combat shotgun stepped forward and yelled something to the others. Phil couldn't hear what he said from this distance, but it seemed clear that this man was some sort of leader. It wasn't Jackson —this man was much shorter than he was, although he was broad and powerfully built too.

The man stepped up to the lock and blasted it twice with the shotgun. The lock shattered, and the thick chain holding the gate shut crashed to the ground. The crowd of invaders cheered, and one of them rushed forward to grab the gate.

The moment his hands came into contact with the steel, there was a dazzling burst of sparks and a loud bang, and the man was flung back with such force from the shock that his body bowled over two of the other invaders behind him. The man was dead before he hit the ground, the first casualty of the battle, which had now officially started.

"Zap!" Wyatt grunted, chuckling darkly.

The invaders hesitated, examining the smoking body of their dead comrade. The leader yelled something at them, and they seemed to get some of their courage back. A few of them broke off long pieces of grass and gingerly tested the gate, checking to see if any more deadly electrical current was flowing through it.

They quickly found out that it wasn't, so they grabbed the gate, and when nobody else was electrocuted, they roared out a cheer of triumph and yanked it open. The crowd of attackers surged, looking like they were going to charge through the gates in a raging mass of aggression, but the leader held them back, correctly suspecting that there were more traps laying in wait for them.

"You're right about that, asshole," Phil whispered, lining up a target in his rifle scope and easing his finger onto the trigger.

The leader tried to get the unruly men into a semblance of order—as Phil and Wyatt had guessed, they were completely undisciplined—and then started marching them along the drive slowly. The man was looking around suspiciously and was wearing a head-lamp, like many of them, so he was able to see through the gloom. He was presumably looking for tripwires and other such traps and did not notice that much of the earth along both sides of the blacktop drive had been freshly dug up. He also did not initially notice an innocuous-looking beer can laying on the side of the drive.

The beer can was the object Phil had in the crosshairs of his scope. It was no empty piece of trash; it was, in fact, filled with primer that would ignite a fuse to a far bigger explosion. Phil and Wyatt had taken the remaining sticks of dynamite—left over from when they'd destroyed the main road—and packed them under the drive near the gate. Phil was waiting for as many of the enemy troops to walk onto the blast area as possible before he detonated the dynamite.

The leader paused as the beer can flashed in the roving glow of his headlamp. Phil's heart started to beat faster in his chest as he watched the man slowly walking up to the beer can, now that he had decided that it was something suspicious. There were around twenty men positioned directly in the blast area at this point, and others close by who would certainly be seri-ously wounded or killed. If the leader picked up the can, he would disconnect the fuse, rendering the trap useless. Phil had to act; it was now or never.

He breathed in deeply and held the breath in his

lungs, eyes focused on the can in his crosshairs. The leader started to bend down to pick up the can, and Phil squeezed the trigger. The shot was on target. There was a bright flash as the primer ignited, and the leader stumbled back in fright but didn't have time to do anything else. The drive exploded beneath him like a volcanic eruption, with a thunderous boom that shook the ground even beneath Phil and Wyatt's feet and sent plumes of earth and torn up bodies a hundred feet into the air.

The men standing in the blast area didn't even know what hit them; they were dead the instant the dynamite exploded. Others, outside the blast area, were hurled dozens of feet through the air and had limbs blown off. The ear-splitting sound of the explosion resounded in a series of echoes that bounced like a pinball around the nearby mountains and valleys.

For a few moments after the sound of the blast faded away, Phil and Wyatt were stunned into silence. Phil could hardly believe he'd just done what he'd just done; well over twenty men had essentially been vaporized by one little squeeze of his finger, and a dozen more had had their arms and legs blown off. It was almost too horrific to even begin to process in his mind, but he knew that as gruesome as it was, it was a matter of life or death; these men had come here to kill, rape, and pillage, and they had known that their intended victims would surely attempt to fight back.

"Pick off the survivors!" Wyatt said, snapping Phil out of this trance of thought.

From far behind them, on the other side of the ranch, came the sound of gunfire, and the men knew the battle had started there as well. This spurred further urgency into their veins, and Phil was quickly able to get over the shock of what he'd just seen and done. He swung his rifle scope up, seeking out targets who had escaped the blast without injury. At least twenty men were uninjured, but they were staggering around in shock, holding their ears; anyone close to the blast had likely had his eardrums blown out and would now be deaf.

Phil and Wyatt started picking them off, dispatching the men with well-placed headshots.

As soon as the surviving invaders saw their comrades' heads snapping back and their skulls exploding, what little fight was left in them departed. After Phil and Wyatt had shot five or six of them, the remaining survivors threw down their guns and fled, screaming into the woods.

After that, Phil turned his scope on the wounded men who'd had their arms or legs blown off. Even though they were evil men, it was cruel to leave them to suffer like this.

"Give 'em a quick death, at least," he said to Wyatt, lining up the head of a screaming, legless man in his scope. "They're human beings, and they deserve some mercy."

"They don't deserve nothin'," Wyatt growled, "but I guess you're right."

They started putting the wounded out of their

misery, but soon the gunfire coming from their rear intensified, and then Phil's walkie talkie crackled.

"Phil, Wyatt!" It was Jonathan, who was in charge of holding the south section. His voice was hoarse and desperate, and the sounds of automatic gunfire and screams were loud and close in the background.

"I'm here, Jonathan!" Phil responded.

"There are too many of 'em!" Jonathan yelled over the barrage of gunfire. "We're about to be overrun. We can't hold this section!"

"Okay, okay," Phil said, his heart hammering. "Retreat to the second position, retreat to the second position! Do you copy Jonathan, do you copy?"

There was no response...only a dead hiss from Jonathan's walkie talkie.

"That's not good," Wyatt said grimly.

"Jonathan, are you there?" Phil asked. "Jonathan, come in! Are you there?"

Still, there was no response but silence.

"Come on, leave these assholes," Wyatt said, getting up from behind his boulder. "We better move."

"Yeah, the others need backup. Let's go."

Phil slung his AR-15 over his shoulder and climbed onto the dirt bike, but just as he was about to kick it to life, the walkie talkie crackled to life.

"Jonathan!" Phil said, scrambling to unclip the walkie talkie from his belt.

It was not Jonathan's voice that came through the tinny speaker, though.

"Hello, cowboy..." Jackson said.

36

"Turn off the walkie talkie, Phil," Wyatt said. "Don't let that psychopath get inside your head."

"What's the matter, cowboy?" Jackson taunted. "Cat got your tongue? Speaking of tongues, I think I'll cut your skinny friend's out and fry it up…or maybe I'll just cut his whole head off and mount it with the others I'll have on sticks by the time the sun rises. I'll make sure you live just long enough to see your wife's head and your boy's head stuck on sticks, mother-fucker, before I—"

Phil turned off the walkie talkie.

"Don't let him get to you," Wyatt said. "We'll blow that son of a bitch's brains out long before he has the chance to put anyone's head on a stick."

"He's killed one of my people," Phil growled, his jaw clenched with rage, "but I'll be damned if I'm gonna let him kill anyone else. Let's go!"

They kicked the bikes to life and sped along the drive. As they rode, they saw flares being shot into the sky, but they were not only the orange flares created by Phil; there were standard pink flares too, being fired by Jackson's men, to light up the battlefield.

As Phil and Wyatt came over the rise, where they were able to see the farmhouse, the barn, and some of the meadows, a terrifying sight greeted them. At least a hundred men were charging across the fields, firing guns and whooping. The whole scene was lit up by the eerie, almost surreal ebb-and-flow glow of the flares drifting overhead and looked like something out of a nightmare. Phil's small pockets of defenders were firing furiously from behind their positions of cover, and David and the women were sniping with rifles from the farmhouse, but even though many of the attackers were dropping dead, the sheer superiority of their numbers was overwhelming, and it seemed that nothing could stop their advance.

Jonathan's position by the stables had long since been overrun, Phil could see, and some of the attackers had dug in by the stables and were using the buildings and hay bales outside them as cover to fire on the farmhouse.

Phil skidded to a halt and grabbed the walkie talkie. Jackson would hear his orders, but he didn't care; he had to save the women and children, and his remaining defenders.

"Everyone, fall back!" Phil yelled into the walkie talkie. "I repeat, fall back to the last defensive position now!" He then glanced over at the distant pen where the cattle were. The sounds of the battle had surely got the beasts worked up into a frenzied panic, and if they were to be of any use in this battle, he needed to unleash them now. It pained him to know that many of them would be killed because they were such a valuable resource on his ranch, but this was a matter of life and death. "Doc Robertson!" Phil yelled into the walkie talkie, "do your thing! I repeat, Doc Robertson, do it now!"

For a few seconds, there was no response, and with a sense of panic rising up within him, Phil wondered if the old veterinarian was still alive. Then, however, under the strange glow of the flares, Phil could just make out a small figure hauling open the gate to the cattle pen. Doc Robertson was still alive, and he flung fireworks into the midst of the herd to set off the animals into the stampede, which was now inevitable.

Phil watched with grim fascination as the huge animals, stirred up by the gunfire and now the exploding fireworks into a frenzied panic, burst out of the pen in a thunderous stampede, racing across the fields in a mad rush—the very fields that a large mass of invaders were running across.

Even above the din of gunfire, the invaders heard the rumble of the hooves and felt the thunder of the stampeding cattle beneath their feet. The panicking beasts swept across the fields in a tightly packed wave, a living, writhing tsunami surging forward. Many of the invaders dropped their guns and turned to run, but a lot of them were simply too close to do anything but turn and shoot desperately into the charging mass of cattle before, like sandcastles on a beach, they were swallowed up and smashed to a bloody pulp beneath the pounding hooves of the stampeding herd.

"Come on!" Wyatt urged. "The stampede is taking plenty of 'em out, but there are a lot more of the bastards who are still fighting!"

He and Phil raced down to the farmhouse, where David and Alice were trying to help the women out through the back door. In the front of the farmhouse, behind sandbags on the porch, Eddie, Fred, and a couple of other defenders were pinned down by heavy fire from the stables and were doing their best to squeeze off bursts of fire at groups of attackers, who kept darting from position cover to position of cover, steadily getting closer.

From behind a tree close to the farmhouse, one of the attackers darted out to fling a Molotov cocktail at the farmhouse. Fred shot the man through his chest, but before he fell, he hurled the projectile, which hit the porch and exploded in a massive fireball.

"Dammit!" Phil yelled. "The house is on fire!"

Because of the intense barrage of bullets, the attackers were pouring into the house from the stables, and the rapidly spreading fire that was starting to engulf the entire porch, Eddie and his little group of defenders were now totally trapped. If they tried to move, they would get cut down by the men in the stables, but if they stayed where they were for much longer, they would be burned alive.

"Wyatt, time to get out the big guns!" Phil yelled. "We have to take those guys in the stables out, and there's only one way to do that! Hurry, get to the hangar!"

They raced in a wide arc on the dirt bikes, cutting across the field between them and the farmhouse, jumping over mounds and crashing through ruts and ditches while bullets flew around them. When they got behind the farmhouse, where Alice and David had gotten the women out of the house, both men jumped off the bikes, letting them fall to the ground with the motors still running; they wouldn't need them again.

"Davey and Alice, lead them to the barn!" Phil commanded. "We'll cover you while you move. You do the same for us!"

"Got it, Dad!" David yelled.

Phil and Wyatt knelt behind a pile of sandbags and started firing with their AR-15s while David, Alice, and the women sprinted across the open ground to the closest pile of sandbags. Phil's mind was racing along at a million miles a minute, and it was almost as if some sort of automatic part of his mind was in control, and he was just observing as he coolly swung the sights of his rifle from one target to the next, firing until each enemy dropped dead.

"All clear!" David yelled from the sandbags. He and Alice started laying down cover fire, and Phil and Wyatt raced across the open ground and dived behind the sandbags, with bullets whizzing around them and kicking up puffs of dust at their feet.

"Hang in there, Eddie and Fred!" Phil shouted into his walkie talkie. "We'll get you out of there in a minute, just hang in there!"

"Hurry, Phil!" Fred yelled back. "These flames are getting closer, and the sons of bitches have us totally pinned down!"

There were two more piles of sandbags between their position and the barn, and the group moved rapidly between them in the same way. Within a minute, they were in the barn.

"You guys, take your positions!" Phil yelled to David, Alice, and the women. "You keep firing until you run out of bullets! Don't let anyone get within a hundred feet of this barn!"

"Where are you going?" Alice screamed, watching as Phil and Wyatt abruptly turned and ran straight back out of the barn. "Don't leave us here!"

"I'll be back!" Phil yelled. "Just keep shooting!"

A minute later, amidst all the noise of gunfire and shooting, David and the women heard the sound of a large motor roaring to life. Then, a couple of seconds later came the sound of screeching tires…and after that, they saw the armored Humvee come hurtling around the side of the barn, with Wyatt at the wheel and Phil wielding an M-60 machine gun from the passenger seat.

"Just like driving a tank," Wyatt said, grinning as he floored the Humvee's accelerator, "except a lot faster!"

"Swing wide!" Phil yelled, pointing to a handful of enemy fighters who had broken cover and were running to get to the farmhouse. "Those guys there, take 'em out! If they get into the farmhouse, Eddie and Fred are dead!"

"Hold on tight," Wyatt growled, aiming the speeding Humvee right at the group of invaders.

They heard the huge vehicle speeding toward them and dropped to their knees, firing at the windshield and engine block, not realizing that the entire vehicle was completely bulletproof. By the time they did realize this, it was too late, and the Humvee plowed through them, scattering them like bowling pins. Broken bodies were flung through the air and crushed under the Humvee's heavy wheels, and the windshield was sprayed with blood. Wyatt and Phil lurched in their seats from the impact of hitting the men but were otherwise fine.

"Get me a good shot at the stables!" Phil yelled.

The attackers in the stables, who were keeping Fred and Eddie pinned down on the burning porch, were all in the loft, firing down out of the windows. Phil started firing the machine gun at the charging men, spraying scything arcs of bullets and cutting down any invaders who were unlucky enough to be caught on open ground.

The men in the stables knew the Humvee was coming for them, and they turned their fire away from Fred and Eddie, focusing it on the approaching vehicle instead. Inside the Humvee, the drumming and thumping of bullets smashing into the vehicle made it sound as if they were caught in the open in a hailstorm.

"How bulletproof is this thing?" Wyatt yelled over the din. "We're taking some serious fire here!"

"It's bulletproof enough," Phil growled back over the hammering thunder of his M-60, as he continued to sweep a spray of bullets over the battlefield. "It'll hold, trust me! Now let's take out those assholes in the stables!"

"They're dead," Wyatt growled, skidding to a halt with a ninety-degree handbrake turn in front of the stables.

Phil didn't waste a single second; he swung the machine gun up and started riddling the entire roof area of the stables with bullets. From inside came the sound of men screaming in panic, and a few dead bodies slumped and slipped out of the windows; those who hadn't been fast enough to take cover when Phil had started his attack.

From behind the cover of one of the vintage tractors nearby, Jackson roared with fury as he saw his men being decimated. Phil and his defenders had fought back with far more ferocity and tenacity than he ever could have imagined...but he had come prepared for an eventuality like this.

"All right, cowboy," he growled, watching as Phil turned the upper portion of the stables building into something resembling a block of swiss cheese, "you wanna play with big guns? I've got a real nice surprise, just for you."

Jackson stuck his fingers in his mouth and whistled to one of his men, a man armored up in SWAT gear, who was carrying a bunch of Jackson's favorite weapons. The man was hiding behind a large tree, where gunfire from the barn was keeping him pinned down.

"I need some cover, Jackson!" he roared.

"Cowardly little bitch!" Jackson snarled back, but he nonetheless picked up his AK-47, popped out from behind the tractor, and started spitting bullets at the barn, causing some of the defenders there to duck behind cover, giving his man enough of a gap to sprint across the open ground between the tree and the tractor.

Once the man reached him, Jackson dropped his

AK. This was because the man, panting and gasping from the effort of sprinting in full SWAT gear, handed him a far more potent weapon: an RPG. He loaded it up, then got down onto his knees with the RPG on his shoulder, taking aim at the Humvee.

Inside the Humvee, Phil stopped firing; he'd used up the whole ammo belt. As he scrambled to reload the machine gun, he caught a glimpse of a worrying silhouette out of the corner of his eye. He jerked his head around and saw that it was no apparition, no conjuration of his troubled mind; there really was a man aiming an RPG at the vehicle.

"Out, out, get out!" he screamed at Wyatt.

"What the—"

"RPG, get the hell out of the Humvee!"

Both men flung open the doors and dove out of the Humvee just as Jackson fired the RPG. The rocket streaked through the air and slammed into the front of the Humvee in a massive explosion, the force of which hurled Wyatt and Phil through the air. The Humvee's armor was strong, but not strong enough to resist an RPG, and the bonnet and motor—the area that took a direct hit—were destroyed, incapacitating the vehicle.

The explosion left Wyatt and Phil stunned and feeling concussed, and their ears rang with a shrill, monotonous whine, but neither of them sustained any serious injuries. Phil's machine-gunning of the stables had killed all the attackers in the roof there, so, sheltered from Jackson and his men by the burning hulk of the Humvee, they had a clear path of cover to get back to the rear of the farmhouse, half of which was now on fire.

"Come on, get up!" Phil yelled, struggling to his feet through the disorientation he felt. He grabbed Wyatt's collar and tried to pull him up. If Jackson and his men charged now, they would easily be able to take out Phil and Wyatt, who were caught out in the open.

"That son of a bitch," Wyatt groaned. He'd taken more of an impact from the RPG blast than Phil had, and he felt like he'd been hit by a wrecking ball. A deep pain throbbed through his entire right torso, and he suspected he'd broken a few ribs. Despite his pain, he understood the danger he was in and forced himself to get to his feet.

Phil wrapped his arm around Wyatt and gave him some support, and they hurried across the gap between the Humvee and the house, while Fred and Eddie used their last few bullets to provide cover fire for them and temporarily pin Jackson down.

"Through the house!" Phil yelled at Eddie and Fred. "Go through the house, meet us out back! The stables have been cleared out. You can move!"

"We're out of ammo!" Eddie yelled.

"It doesn't matter, just go, go now!" Phil yelled back.

He and Wyatt got around the rear of the house, where they were protected from gunfire, and a few seconds later, Fred and Eddie burst out of the back door, coughing and gasping, their faces blackened from smoke.

"The whole place is going up in flames!" Fred gasped.

It was devastating to see his home being consumed by fire, but Phil knew he simply had to ignore it; they had to get to the barn to make a last stand and give everyone a chance to escape before Jackson and his remaining goons overran them.

"Leave it!" Phil said. "Come on, to the barn! Wyatt, give Eddie your AR!"

Wyatt was too badly injured to fire a rifle now, and he handed Eddie his AR-15. "It's got one full clip left," he groaned. "Use it well, Eddie."

"You two go first," Phil instructed. "Move between sandbags and get to the barn. We'll give you cover fire until you get to the first set of sandbags, then you do the same for us while we move, got it?"

"Got it, Phil," Eddie said. "Come on, Fred, let's move!"

The two of them raced across the open ground to the first set of sandbags, while Phil laid down some cover fire. He had to pick his shots carefully because he only had two clips left for his AR-15. Once the two of them reached the sandbags, they exchanged fire with Jackson and his troops, some of whom had raced across the open ground and taken cover by the burning porch. Phil focused his attention on these men and managed to take out two of them with accurate shots to their torsos.

After a hair-raising set of sprints between sandbag piles, with bullets whizzing all around them and thudding into the sandbags, Phil, Wyatt, Eddie, and Fred got to the barn. This was it; this was where the last of the defenders were holed up.

"Dad!" David yelled from the roof of the barn, where he was firing at the invaders from behind a pile of sandbags. "We're running real low on ammo here!"

"How many of them are left out there?" Phil asked.

"I can't really tell!" David yelled back. "But at least a dozen, I think! And...oh shit!"

"What's wrong?!" Phil yelled.

"The big guy, he's loading up his RPG again!"

"Take him out!"

"I can't!" David yelled. "I can't get a clear shot at him! Oh no, I think he's gonna shoot it at the barn!"

"Get out of the roof, everyone!" Phil yelled. "Jump! Get out now!"

David, Alice, and a few other women who'd been shooting from the roof section jumped down into the piles of hay below, and just as David and the last of the defenders in the roof jumped, a tremendous explosion blew the entire roof section to pieces in a billowing fireball of flying debris.

Phil knew now that the battle was lost; they'd fought hard, and their strategy and expert marksmanship had almost overcome the enemy, but in the end, Jackson's superior numbers had simply overwhelmed them. If his people were to survive the rest of the night, they had to leave now. From outside came the sound of roars of triumph at the sight of the top of the barn being blown apart. Jackson's men had been filled with a fresh burst of courage and confidence, and they would surely charge the barn now in their final assault.

"Everyone, go!" Phil roared, his voice hard with authority. "It's over! Get out of here!"

"Lead the way, Phil!" Eddie said. "I'll take up the rear and hold 'em off as best I can!"

"No," Phil said grimly. "I'm not going anywhere."

"Phil, I know you said you were going to fight until the end," Alice said, her teary eyes pleading, "but it's one thing to say it to inspire people, but it's another thing altogether to—"

"I'm staying, no matter what," Phil said to her. The hard, stubborn look he fired into her eyes told her that he wouldn't be budging from this position.

She knew that look well and understood that this was something he had made his mind up about and would not be shifted from.

"Wyatt, lead the way," he added, shooting Wyatt a somber glance.

Wyatt, having grown up with Phil, also knew this look well, and knew that there would be no arguing with him on this. "I'll see you at sunrise tomorrow on the island," Wyatt said, giving Phil one last respectful nod before turning around and hobbling down the stairs into the cellar, where the tunnel was.

"What are the rest of you waiting for?" Phil yelled, tears rimming his eyes. "Follow Wyatt, go on, get out of here! That's an order!"

"Goodbye, Dad," David said, tears running down his cheeks.

"Come on, kid," Fred said, putting an arm around David's shoulder and gently leading him away. "You'll see your dad tomorrow." Fred, however, also had tears in his eyes, and there was no conviction in his words.

"I'm staying too," Alice sobbed, weeping. "I'm not leaving you here to die alone, Phillip McCabe!"

"I'll be fine, Alice," Phil said, his voice cracking. "But you need to go. Now."

He made eye contact with Eddie, and the big man knew what Phil wanted him to do. Eddie walked over to Alice and picked her up, slinging her over his shoulders like a sack of potatoes. She screamed and struggled, but the huge man was far too powerful for her to fight, so after a few seconds of struggling, she gave in, and her body went limp, and she sobbed and wept as Eddie carried her down the stairs.

"I love you, Alice!" Phil called out after them. "Always remember that, baby. I love you so very, very much!"

Eddie and Alice disappeared down the stairs, and then Phil was alone. He didn't have too much time to sit and reflect on this, though, because a Molotov cocktail smashed through one of the windows and exploded in a whooshing fireball a few yards from Phil. He just avoided being splattered with burning gasoline, but some of the flaming liquid landed on a hay bale, which quickly went up in flames. It only took a few seconds for the fire to jump to more hay bales, and soon the wooden walls of the barn were on fire too.

Phil looked around him, rapidly assessing the situation and trying to figure out a plan. The main doors of the barn were blocked shut from the inside, and Jackson and his remaining men would have to ram through them with a large vehicle, which they didn't have. Of course, they might be waiting for the barn to burn down with him inside it, but he didn't think Jackson was the kind of man who was patient enough to just wait out a slow victory like that. No, Jackson was a vengeful man who wanted to look into his enemy's eyes before he died, and Phil was sure he would be coming into the barn to deal with him personally. The only way to do that was through the back door, where everyone had come in from the farmhouse. That, or climbing up the hay bales outside to drop through the roof. Given that Jackson and his men had just blown the roof off, and the structures up there had doubtless been weakened—not to mention the threat of the flames creeping up the walls—Phil was almost certain that his men would come through the rear door.

"Well, Jackson, I've got a few little surprises in store for you and your buddies," Phil growled, a fresh sense of determination flowing through his veins. He hastily checked his ammunition. He had a few rounds left in his AR, and just one clip in his .45. It wasn't much, but it was enough, he hoped. After that, if it came down to hand-to-hand combat, he had a bowie knife strapped to his left calf, and there were a few axes in the barn too.

One of the defenders had also left behind a double-barreled shotgun. Phil had some duct tape and fishing line in his utility belt, and he hurriedly duct-taped the shotgun to some agricultural machinery near the back door, with the muzzles aimed in the direction of the door, and covered it up with a rag, then quickly tied the fishing gut to the triggers and ran it behind the pile of sandbags where he'd make his final stand.

Another Molotov cocktail came flying through one of the windows at the far end of the barn, and exploded into a huge fireball, spreading more flames through the already-burning barn. A strange instinct screamed silently in Phil's mind for him to get down, and just as he dived to the floor behind the sandbags, a deep drumming resounded through the barn as someone outside it started pumping machine gun fire through it. Jackson had taken the M-60 out of the damaged Humvee, loaded up another belt of ammo, and was spraying the whole barn with bullets.

Phil lay flat on the ground, listening to the sound of bullets thumping into the sandbags and whizzing through the air over his head. He waited for a few seconds after the M-60 had stopped and then yelled out, "I'm still in here, Jackson! If you want to take me out, you're gonna have to come in and get me!"

ROBERT WALKER

"My pleasure, cowboy!" Jackson roared from outside the barn.

Phil laid his .45 on top of the sandbags, ready to fire, and then took aim at the door with his AR-15. Two men charged in through the door, guns blazing, but Phil cut them down with his last few AR rounds. He tossed the empty rifle aside and snatched up the .45, but just then, there was a massive explosion that covered him in a cloud of debris and left his ears ringing; Jackson had just fired the RPG into the main barn doors, blowing them wide open.

Phil barely had time to even think before five men came charging through the main doors, while two more came through the rear door. Phil fired the .45 from his right hand, gripping the fishing line in his left, and managed to kill two of the attackers with headshots, and then yanked the fishing line as the first of the men came in through the rear door. The shotgun blast took half the first attacker's head off, and then when the next one came in after him, Phil pulled on the second fishing line, firing the other barrel, which took the man square in the chest.

Bullets thumped into the sandbags from the remaining attackers, but Phil returned fire, taking the three of them out when they tried to rush his sandbags. His heart was hammering, and adrenalin was surging through his veins. A strange silence settled over the barn, aside from the roaring of the spreading flames. Had he done it? Was this it?

Then, through the billowing smoke strode a tall,

powerful figure, gripping an AK-47 in one hand and a saber in the other. "You still in here, cowboy?" Jackson asked, grinning.

Phil stood up and pointed his .45 at Jackson. "It's just you and me now, asshole," he growled. "So come on, let's finish this."

Jackson raised his AK, and Phil squeezed the trigger of his .45, but there was no bang; he was out of bullets. Jackson's AK clicked impotently, too; he was also out of ammo. He dropped the empty rifle and switched to the cavalry saber to his right hand, while Phil tossed his .45 aside and drew his bowie knife, holding it in his right hand, and took an ax off the nearby wall, which he held in his left hand.

"I'm gonna enjoy this," Jackson snarled, grinning savagely as he twirled the saber around in his hand.

Without another word, the men charged at each other. Phil swung his ax at Jackson's head, but the big man was surprisingly agile, and he ducked rapidly under the attack, spun on his heel, and whipped the saber around in a backhand slash. Phil screamed as the razor-sharp steel sheared through his wrist, and stumbled backward, staring in disbelief and shock at the blood-spurting stump where his left hand used to be.

"That's one hand gone," Jackson growled. "And I'm gonna take the other off next, cowboy…piece by piece, you're mine…" He advanced on Phil, chuckling darkly, ready to end the fight and claim victory.

The lake was eerily calm and quiet, and the silence was even more of a physical presence in light of the fact that everyone in the two rowing boats had just come from a battlefield, and the sounds of gunfire and explosions had left their ears ringing with a shrill whine.

Down here, miles from the ranch, there were no lights of fires and muzzles flares, and no sound but the gentle, rhythmic dipping of oars into the black water. It took fifteen minutes of rowing for the fugitives to reach the small island in the center of the lake. Here, they'd be safe from pursuit, if Jackson and his men even decided they were going to come after them, anyway.

They reached the shore, and Eddie and Fred helped everyone out of the boats. While the others went to set up tents in the trees, Wyatt, Alice, and David stood on the shore, staring in the direction of the ranch. The sky above the ranch was orange; the whole place seemed to be on fire now. Alice was still weeping softly, and David had tears in his eyes too.

"Do you think Dad is…" David murmured.

"He'll be okay," Wyatt said stoically. He tried to bolster his words with faith, but he wasn't sure that he would ever see Phil alive again.

"It's all gone," Alice sobbed. "Everything we worked so hard for…all gone. And my husband is…he's…"

Wyatt put his arms around her and hugged her.

"He's gonna be okay," he said to Alice. "He's gonna be okay." But for the first time in many years, there were tears in Wyatt's eyes too.

The three of them eventually made camp on the other side of the island, where they couldn't see the orange glow on the skyline and thus be reminded of the tragedy that had befallen them. Even so, it was difficult for them to not think about the destruction of the ranch and the fact that their friend, husband, and father was likely dead by now.

None of them had a very restful night, and sleep came to the three of them only in short, fitful intervals. Alice, in particular, didn't sleep a wink, and instead spent most of the night tossing and turning in her sleeping bag. Sometimes she would get up and walk down to the water's edge and simply weep.

They were all up well before dawn. Everyone's minds were on one thing: would Phil appear on the distant shore at sunrise, like he'd promised? Or would he fail to show up, never to be seen again?

Alice decided to distract herself and try to keep herself busy by making food. As the darkening sky was growing grey with the coming dawn, she made a fire, opened up a few cans of food, and started making breakfast for everyone.

Soon enough, everyone was up, and the small band of survivors gathered together on the shore to eat breakfast while the sun rose.

"Where do we go after this if Phil…you know… doesn't…" Fred asked.

"We head west," Wyatt answered. "If the invaders have taken the ranch, things won't be safe in this area for many miles. We keep going west until we've crossed the mountains. Maybe with the range between them and us as a buffer, we'll be safe for a while. Maybe."

Everyone ate in glum silence after this. The prospect of having to trek for many days, weeks even, and cross harsh mountain terrain was daunting, as was the prospect of trying to find somewhere to start from scratch again in these difficult times.

In the east, the red sun was already cresting the mountains. Sunrise had come, but there was still no sign of Phil. With every passing minute, Alice and David's hearts sank deeper, and a heavy, intense feeling of despair felt as if it was slowly suffocating each of them. Everyone finished their food and went about packing up the camp in silence, preparing to move on.

The sun was getting higher in the sky now, and it had become clear that Phil was not going to be arriving. After everyone had packed everything up, they gathered together by the water's edge.

"I'm sorry, Alice," Fred said, "but I don't think we should stay here any longer."

"I agree," Eddie said, his face crumpled with sadness. "I was praying all night that I'd see Phil across the water when the sun rose…but it's getting on into the morning now. It's been hours since sunrise, and… well, I don't think he's coming. It's dangerous for us to stay here too long; they're gonna track us and figure out we've come this way. We have to move."

Alice, sobbing, could only nod in response. She knew they were right, but even so, it was difficult to accept the death of her husband.

"Come on, Alice," Wyatt said gently. "I'll help you into the boat."

Everyone packed the rowing boats in silence, and once they'd been cast off from the shore, everyone starting rowing in somber silence too. After they'd got a couple of yards away from the island shore, however, this silence was broken by the distant pop and hiss of a flare being fired.

Above both boats, a distinctive orange flare streaked through the sky. Everyone stopped rowing and turned around to look behind them in surprise… and there, standing on the far shore with a flare gun in his right hand, his clothes torn, his body bloodied and black with smoke, was Phil.

EPILOGUE

*W*yatt, breathing hard, wiped the sweat from his brow with his left sleeve and leaned his weight on the heavy felling ax.

"Sorry, I'd help chop these trees down if I could," Phil said, "but you know that my mechanical hand isn't quite strong enough for that." Using his engineering expertise and some scrap wood, leather, and steel, Phil had designed a basic mechanical hand that he wore over the stump on his left wrist. It was handy enough to eat with or to hold the reins when he rode a horse but was not suitable for anything requiring heavy lifting or exertion.

"Don't worry about it, Phil," Wyatt said. "It's a good workout, and I'm enjoying it."

"Good work, brother," Phil said. "We don't need too much more timber to finish the barn anyway. You don't need anyone else to help down here, do you?"

"Eddie and I will be fine," Wyatt said. "And I asked

David to help out here when he's done fixing the chicken coop. We'll see you around dinner time."

"See you guys then." Phil mounted his horse and trotted back to the farmhouse. While two of the horses had been killed in the battle, Phil was thankful that his favorite stallion had survived.

"How's the tree felling going?" Alice asked when Phil walked into the house.

"Wyatt and Eddie are doing well. I think we'll have enough timber to finish the barn by the end of the week."

"And then everything will almost be back to how it was," Alice said with a smile. "It's hard to believe that we've done so much in three months. It almost feels like the battle didn't happen, like it was just a nightmare."

Thinking about the battle made Phil's stump ache, and he got a phantom pain in the left hand that was no longer there. He still couldn't believe he'd won the duel against Jackson. If the burning beam from the barn roof hadn't fallen on his opponent, knocking him over and stunning him long enough for Phil to slam his bowie knife into his throat, he didn't think he'd be here now. It was pure luck, of course, but Phil liked to think that the soul of the ranch had dropped the beam at that exact moment.

"It was a nightmare all right," Phil said, "but it's one we won't ever have to live through again. When Wyatt and David went on that reconnaissance mission to the two towns last week and found 'em totally deserted and empty of all people except the dead, I felt a lot more reassured. Now that Jackson and all his men are dead, nobody else knows about this place. We're here on our own, secret and safe, and that's how it's gonna stay from now on. The battle wrecked a lot of our crops, but we've got more than enough canned food to get through the winter just fine, and by next spring, I'm pretty damn sure everything will have recovered."

"Come here, Phil," Alice said, smiling.

She and Phil hugged for a long time in silence, quietly joyful in the knowledge that they, their family and their friends were finally safe and sound, and would be for a very, very long time to come.

THE END

Made in the USA
Monee, IL
29 August 2020

40426196R00167